HOME
GAMES

HOME GAMES

BENJAMIN MARKOVITS

HARPER

An Imprint of HarperCollinsPublishers

Library of Congress Control Number: 2019947143
ISBN 978-0-06-274230-8

Typography by Catherine San Juan
19 20 21 22 23   PC/LSCH   10 9 8 7 6 5 4 3 2 1
❖
First Edition

To Gwen and Henry and all their cousins,
who listened patiently to the first draft of this story
over one long Christmas holiday in Austin,
while waiting for the food to arrive.

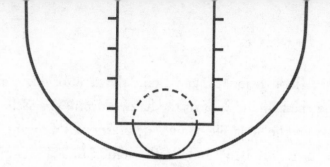

ONE

AFTER SCHOOL, the first thing I do when I get home is take off my jacket and tie and put on my home clothes—a pair of sweatpants and a T-shirt.

"Just like your dad," Mom says, standing in the doorway. "Want a snack?"

"Sure."

Mom pops two Eggo waffles in the toaster. I grab them when they're ready and eat in front of the TV. Then I do my homework. If I hurry up, I can see Jake before dinner. He lives on the seventh floor of our apartment building, three floors below us, and I take the elevator down and ring the bell and wait in the hallway until Mrs. Schultz answers the door. She knows me pretty well. I mean, she just says, "Hi, Ben," and kind of stands aside, like a matador, so I can charge past.

Jake's in his bedroom. It has a big window with all his trophies on the windowsill. Baseball trophies, basketball trophies. And behind them, and down below, you can see the people on the sidewalk and the taxis on the road, like toy people and taxis. Jake's walls are covered in posters— he has a big Carmelo Anthony poster over his bed. Jake's a huge Knicks fan. That's one of the things he likes to talk about.

Today he's in a bad mood because he got a 63 on his spelling test. He's still wearing his school uniform. For boys it's blue shorts or pants and a white shirt and a blue tie and a blue jacket that says Latymer on it, with a kind of oak tree or something stitched into the name. If you want, you can wear a bow tie instead of a regular one, but only a few kids do that, and everybody thinks they're—I mean, either they're joking or they're weird.

Jake somehow manages to wear his uniform like it's home clothes, like he's just slouching around in them on a Saturday morning. His trousers hang down and drag against his shoes; his tie is always crooked.

"What'd you get wrong?" I ask, trying to be helpful. Spelling is one of the things I'm pretty good at, and I look at the paper on his desk.

"Everything."

It was a contraction test—he put all the apostrophes between the words instead of where the missing letter should be. But he gets up and pulls the test away from me. He doesn't want to talk about it, because when he gets a bad grade he's not allowed to play on his Nintendo Wii.

"You know what my dad's going to say?"

"What?" I ask.

"He always says the same thing. *Is this what I pay all that money for?*"

Latymer's a private school—it costs $45,000 a year. Actually, Jake's parents don't pay all that; they can't afford it, so he gets financial aid. But we don't really talk about that. My dad makes a lot of money, but he doesn't like to spend it—"throwing it around," he calls it. So Jake has more stuff than I do, which is weird, because he acts like he has to feel sorry for me when really . . . but it doesn't matter.

"I can't believe our parents *pay* for us to go to school."

Jake says, "I mean, just give me the money. We wouldn't have to do any homework, we wouldn't have to sit there all day."

"What are you going to do with forty-five thousand dollars?" I ask.

"Think of all the pizza that could buy."

"You can't spend forty-five thousand dollars on pizza."

"What do you think's the most expensive pizza you could make?"

We can spend hours talking about this kind of stuff.

Jake says, "Caviar pizza."

"That's disgusting. The most expensive food you can get is truffles," I say.

Sometimes I cook with my mom. She buys me cookbooks and baking books for Christmas and my birthday because I like to read the recipes, even if I'm never going to make them and even if I wouldn't like them anyway.

"Truffles are chocolate," he says.

"That's a different kind. This is the kind that grows underground—they're like mushrooms. You have to get specially trained pigs to dig for them."

"You're making this stuff up," he says.

"It's true. You can spend thousands of dollars on truffles. You can eat gold, too," I say.

Jake stares at me. "You cannot eat gold."

"You totally can. I had it in a restaurant once—pasta with gold leaf."

"What's it taste like?"

"I couldn't really taste it; it just looked cool."

So instead of going to school for a year, we could make a pizza with caviar, which is fish eggs, and truffles, which pigs have to dig for, and gold leaf on top.

"That is one disgusting-sounding pizza," Jake says. "I think I'd rather go to school."

He seems cheered up. "Let's play basketball," he says.

Jake's dad put a backboard and hoop over the kitchen door, so we can play with a foam ball. Our games get pretty rough. Jake is bigger than me; he's stronger, too. I know this for a fact, because he likes to make me arm wrestle against him, and afterward he always says stuff like *That was pretty close*, to be nice.

So we go into the kitchen and start horsing around. It always puts him in a good mood to beat me at some game. He pushes me out of the way and dunks on the hoop, which rattles against the kitchen door. "You're not even trying," he says. "You have to stand up for yourself."

This is his idea of a joke, because it's the kind of thing my dad always says.

They've got a big wooden table in the middle of the kitchen that takes up most of the room. Mrs. Schultz is sitting there, drinking coffee and trying to read a magazine. But she says, "You guys are too noisy," and leaves. "I'll be in my room. Jake, your father and I are going out tonight."

This kind of thing happens only in Jake's house. In

my house if we're too noisy we have to shut up. But anyway, Jake's mom leaves her coffee mug on the table and when Jake blocks my shot he kind of pushes me, too. I don't know, I guess he must have knocked me into the table because the mug falls on the floor with a crash and breaks. There is still some coffee in it.

Their kitchen has black-and-white tiles, and now there's a puddle of cold coffee all over them. I know the coffee is cold because I try to pick up some of the pieces of the mug, and it's just . . . it's just a mess. The mug has a photograph on it, a picture of a pine tree with a mountain behind it, and the words *Yosemite National Park* written around the side. That's where Jake went on vacation last summer. There are some big bits of broken mug, like the handle, and some kind of chalky powder in between them, which has turned to mush.

"Do you think she's gonna be mad?" I ask Jake.

"Nah, she won't be mad," Jake says. "She won't even know."

"What do you mean?"

Jake is the kind of red-haired kid with a lot of freckles. All the moms think he's cute so he always gets away with stuff—I mean, ever since we were little. He has one of those faces where it looks like he's smiling, even if he doesn't mean to. But he's smiling now.

"Well, we're not going to tell her," Jake says. He looks

at me and shrugs. "I don't want to get you into trouble."

Jake grabs a dustpan and brush from the broom cupboard in the kitchen. He gives them to me and I get down on my knees and try to sweep up the pieces. They keep getting stuck on the rubber lip of the dustpan.

"Sometimes my mom glues broken plates or bowls back together," I say. "Maybe your mom can still fix it up. If we wash off all the pieces."

"Nah. Just dump it in the garbage," he says. "She'll never know." So that's what I do.

Jake takes a mop from the cupboard and tries to mop up the coffee, but that only spreads it around. Eventually he finds a roll of Bounty paper towels on the kitchen counter, and we both get down on the floor and start wiping up the mess by hand. We must use almost a whole roll. Our hands are full of soggy bits of paper towel. But we stuff them in the garbage, too. I even dry off the dustpan and brush, because otherwise it seems pretty obvious that somebody has made a mess. We put everything back in the cupboard. Nobody has seen us; nobody came in. The kitchen looks like it did before.

My heart is still beating too fast, and I say to Jake, "I feel like we're lying about something."

But he laughs. "We're not lying, we're just not telling anybody. Don't worry. My mom wouldn't care anyway."

"But if she wouldn't care, why don't we tell her?"

"Forget about it," he says. "I'm in enough trouble already." He means the spelling test.

I want to say, But that doesn't make sense—you're contradicting yourself. But I let it go. Until I get home, when I tell my mom. It's supposed to be, like, a funny story, like, look what Jake made me do. She's putting supper on the table—we usually eat together before my dad gets back from work. At least, that's what we've started to do recently.

She looks at me with a kind of twist in her mouth. She doesn't seem mad, but she doesn't seem happy about it either. "Don't worry about it, Ben," she says, because she can see my face. "These things happen. I can talk to Mrs. Schultz about it tomorrow. She'll understand. It's not a big deal. It's just—it's usually better—just to tell people this kind of thing right away."

"I wanted to, but Jake wouldn't let me."

"Jake isn't the boss of you," Mom says.

Later that night, when I'm getting ready for bed, my dad checks in on me. He usually works late, but if he gets home in time, he comes in and kisses me good night. But this time he stands in the doorway in his suit and tie and looks at me for a minute. "Hey, Dad," I say.

"All right, kid. I think you've got a little explaining to do. Come on."

I guess Mom must have told him, because even though it's almost eleven o'clock and I'm already in my pajamas, he marches me into the hallway. Mom is standing there, looking upset. "What's the point?" she says to him. "I mean, if I can't even tell you a dumb thing like that without . . ." But he ignores her and she follows us out to the elevator while we wait for the doors to open.

"What are you doing to him?" she says. "What are you trying to prove? His sense of guilt is already overdeveloped."

"What does that mean?" My dad keeps pushing the elevator button. It sometimes takes a while for it to come.

"It means he never does anything wrong. He's scared to. Even his teachers say . . ."

"What do his teachers say?" my dad asks.

I look back and forth between them. They're talking about me like I'm not even there.

"They wouldn't mind if he acted up once in a while. Mrs. Klaussen told me that herself. The kids treat him like a Goody Two-shoes."

"There's nothing wrong with being good," my dad says, and the elevator arrives—the doors open, and Mom watches us from the hallway as we get in.

Dad and I ride down to Jake's apartment in silence.

He rings the doorbell, kind of angrily. Jake's mother

answers it. She's wearing a long dress and has on bright red lipstick, but her hair is a mess. She keeps brushing it back with her hand.

"I think Ben has something to tell you," my dad says, in a different voice. I mean, he doesn't sound angry anymore. At least not with her.

I like Mrs. Schultz. She always lets you have as much ketchup as you want when you eat tater tots at her house. And a second bowl of ice cream. She's one of those moms who looks younger than the teachers, like she's Jake's big sister or something. I don't want her to think I . . . I don't want to disappoint her.

"I'm sorry, Mrs. Schultz. I think I broke one of your mugs when Jake and I were playing basketball."

"You *think* you broke it?" my dad says.

I look down and take a breath. "I broke it."

"Oh." But Mrs. Schultz only seems confused. "We have too many mugs anyway," she says to my dad. To me she says, "Don't worry about it, Ben. Really—it's not a big deal. But thank you for your apology."

She closes the door, and when we're waiting for the elevator to take us back to our apartment, my dad asks me, "How do you play basketball in a kitchen?"

I think he's trying to be nice. Maybe he feels bad about embarrassing me, I don't know. We're not really used to being alone together, and I have that feeling you get when you run into a teacher on your own for some reason in the school hallway, and they have to think of something to say to you, and you have to think of something to say to them.

"Jake's dad put up a hoop on the back of the door. They don't really care what we do in there. I mean, they just let us play."

I'm still mad at him, but he just nods.

Our building is this old-fashioned building and even the elevator is, like, a hundred years old. Sometimes it takes forever to come—there are these lights over the doors on each floor, which show where it is, so basically you can watch it crawling along, and if it gets stuck somewhere, while people go in and out, you can watch that, too. I stand there looking up at these lights because I don't want to look at my dad.

My dad says, "Maybe this was a mistake. Maybe I got it wrong."

I don't say anything, and he goes on: "Because I'm not around very much, when I get home, if I feel like . . . there are things going on that really it's my job to kind of deal with, as your father, and I have this very narrow window of time in which to deal with them, sometimes I . . ."

Then the elevator opens and we get in. It's empty—I was hoping somebody might be in it, so we wouldn't have to talk. "Do you understand what I'm trying to tell you?"

he asks. "In my job, it happens all the time. Things go wrong that you don't want anyone to know about. But there are people you can trust and people you *can't* trust—that's the basic dividing line. And, believe me, you want to be on the right side of that line." He's getting worked up again. "Ben, look at me," he says suddenly. "Look at me when I'm talking to you."

I turn and look at him, right in the eyes. I don't even blink.

He's wearing his dark gray suit, which he always wears to work. It has thin white stripes and makes him look even taller than he actually is. I'm not very tall. In school pictures, the photographer always lines me up at the front, with the big kids behind me. Sometimes I think my dad . . . sometimes I think he's disappointed that I'm not going to be as tall as him.

He sighs. "I'm not explaining myself very well."

The elevator opens again, and we walk silently into our apartment.

As I lie in bed (I always leave the door open a little, to let the hall light in), I can hear my parents arguing about me.

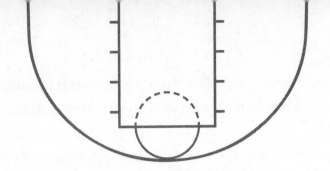

TWO

MY PARENTS ARGUE all the time. Not argue exactly, but bicker—that's my mom's word for it. "Let's not *bicker* in front of Ben," she always says. The problem is, my dad has to travel a lot for work, and my mom misses him. "What do you expect me to do?" he says. "It's my job. What do you think pays for all this?"

He means not only my school but our big apartment on the tenth floor, which has a view of Central Park from the living room window. He means the restaurants and movies we go to and our summer vacations on the beach. Maria, the cleaning lady who comes twice a week, and my mom's pretty clothes and handbags and stuff like that.

"It must be nice to be such an important person," she tells him.

Sometimes I think, if I say the right thing, everybody will get along. Like once, when I was seven and they were arguing about money, I said, "You can sell me. How much am I worth?"

And they stopped arguing and looked at each other. There were tears in Mom's eyes—sometimes she'll cry at anything, but she's hard to predict. Sometimes she doesn't react at all. Dad said, "Ten bucks. I'll give you ten bucks for him." And Mom said, "Fifteen. Look at those cheeks. Fifteen dollars." And Dad said, "Twenty." And they went on like that for a while, saying stuff like "Look at those nice brown eyes, look at his hair."

"He needs a haircut. That'll cost something."

But when I say stuff like that now, it doesn't work anymore.

Dad decides to walk me to school in the morning—maybe he wants to make up for last night. It's only a few blocks. I can see Central Park when I come out of the lobby, which is the big famous park in the middle of New York, with trees everywhere, and funny artificial hills and curvy paths, and even a zoo and a castle. Then we go left to 91st Street, and left again. Everybody seems angry in the morning or in a hurry: drivers honk their horns; you can see school buses stuck in traffic; and I'm happy we don't have to get in a car, especially when the weather is like this—breezy and sunny.

"Are you going away on business?" I ask my dad. This is sometimes why he walks me in the morning—when I won't see him for a few days.

"I'm sorry, Son," he says. "Yes, I'll be sleeping on the plane."

I can see Jake and his mom up ahead, waiting for the light to change, and we cross over together. When we reach the sidewalk again, Jake taps me on the shoulder.

"Race you to the corner," he says. Jake has a lot of excess energy to burn off. At least, that's what my mother says.

He always wins, but I don't mind letting him win. I mean, not *letting* him but racing anyway. At the next corner, I turn around and see my dad talking to Mrs. Schultz. He walks with his hands behind his back, and he's leaning over, too, as if he's listening carefully. He's just being polite—that's what he's always like with the other mothers.

But I don't think he likes Jake much. Or maybe he doesn't like . . . me when I'm hanging out with Jake. When we finally get to the school gates, he sort of holds me back a minute.

"Why aren't you trying?" he asks.

"What do you mean?"

"When you race against Jake, you let him win."

"Jake's the fastest kid in our class," I say, in, like, a hushed way, so Jake can't hear us; but he's talking to Addie and Zach, his other friends, so he's probably not even listening. And Mrs. Schultz is talking to their moms.

"I don't care about that," Dad says, in his normal voice. "You're still not even trying."

"I am, Dad. Jake's just faster than me."

"That's got nothing to do with it," Dad says. "I don't mind watching you lose if I think it's the best you can do."

"It's just a dumb race," I say. "I mean, who cares?"

"That's not the point."

The kids are starting to file into class. I have to leave. "When are you coming home?" I ask my dad.

"I'm not sure yet. It depends how things go."

"Where are you flying this time?"

"London," he says, and puts his arm around me but doesn't really hug me, and after a few seconds I break away. There's a river of kids going through the big double doors and I kind of join the flow. When I turn around at the top of the entrance steps to look for him, he's already gone.

*

Mom picks me up after school—Jake and a couple of his friends are allowed to walk home by themselves. They have their phones out and are going to get something to eat. I watch them walk off together.

"When are you going to let me go to the coffee shop with Jake?" I ask her. "I'm twelve years old. It's just around the corner. Everybody does it."

"I don't like not knowing where you are," she says.

"Well, then, buy me a phone. I'll text you when I get there. I'll text you the whole time—I can leave it on."

"I'm not going to buy you a phone. What do you need a phone for? You're twelve years old."

"This doesn't make any sense," I say. "You're going around in circles."

"I'm just not ready to let you . . . I mean, New York is a big scary city. I don't want you to grow up too fast."

"You don't want me to grow up at all," I say.

The next day, Mom walks me to school. She likes doing it—she says it gets her out of the house, but I think it also makes her feel a little bad. Before she met my dad, she was a teacher, but I've never seen her go to work.

Jake is already in the playground when we get there. Mom starts talking to some of the other mothers, and Jake is talking to Zach and Addie. It's Friday, and they're going to the movies after school. That's all they want to talk about—what they're going to see. They can't agree on a movie; the truth is, I haven't heard of any of them. I just kind of hang around and go, "That sounds great, that sounds really cool." Feeling like a . . . I don't know— feeling like I'm pretending and it's totally obvious but somehow I can't stop, and saying stupid stuff like that is also me, it's who I am. The kid who doesn't know what anybody is talking about but tries to join in anyway.

After school, when Mom picks me up, she sees me standing in the playground by myself. She says, "What are you doing, why don't you join the others? There's Jake."

"I don't want to talk to Jake."

"Did you have a fight with Jake?"

I shrug. "No. I just don't want to talk to him."

"What's going on, Ben?" she says, and eventually I tell her.

"They're all going to the movies, and since I'm not allowed to go, there's no point hanging out with them."

"Please," Mom says. "We've been through all that before. I'm not in the mood right now to have another fight about it."

"I'm not having a fight, but you asked me. So I told you."

Since we're trying not to argue we don't really say

anything on the way home. It's another nice Friday afternoon—there's only one week of school left. Sometimes I think the problem is Mom misses having a job. She has a hard time accepting that I don't really need that much looking after anymore.

I mean, I'm twelve years old, but she still treats me like her brown-eyed baby boy (that's what she calls me sometimes). I'm the last kid in my class not to have a phone. Mom has this kind of hippie thing against them, that's what she calls it. "I'm old-school," she says. She thinks technology is, like, the end of civilization. That's another thing she fights with Dad about—he's always staring at his iPhone.

On the elevator up to our apartment, she catches my eye in the mirror. She can look at me without really looking. We don't have to face each other. "I get lonely when you're in school all day," she says. "Dad's in London again. You see your friends all day. I like to see you."

"I like to see you, too," I say.

"So what do you want to do tonight? It's Friday night, your choice."

"I want to go to a movie."

And she gives me a hug. "Me, too. It's a date."

There's an AMC cinema on 84th Street, just a few blocks from our apartment. "Let's put the week behind us," she says. She lets me choose the movie, so I pick

Ant-Man, which is what Jake and Zach and Addie are going to see. Even though it's PG-13, and I won't turn thirteen until next year. I look around for them at the theater, but I can't see them, and Mom says they wouldn't be allowed in anyway without an adult.

"I bet they could get in," I say. "Jake looks like a teenager."

"It's got nothing to do with what you look like. They need to check ID. It's the law. Kids say they're going to do a lot of things; it doesn't mean they always do them." But then she says, "I don't want to fight with you about it. You'll all be teenagers soon enough."

I don't think she likes the movie much. "It's more your kind of thing," she says to me afterward. It was sunny when we went inside, but it's dark when we come out—the whole world seems a little different.

Even though it's almost ten o'clock, there are still people walking around and sitting outside at some of the restaurants that put tables on the sidewalk. It's pretty warm, even at night. Since I don't have to go to school in the morning, Mom lets me stay out late.

Mom tries to take my hand as we walk home. She hasn't done that in a while. I'm really too old to hold her hand, and I don't want anyone to see us—I mean, anyone from school—so I let go. The traffic on Broadway keeps starting and stopping. I always like to count the yellow cabs. In math we're studying ratios and percentages, and I try to work out the ratio of cabs to total cars at every stoplight. Three cabs, five ordinary cars makes three over eight.

"You know that your father is away on business," she says.

"Yeah, I know. He's in London."

We wait at a cross street for the light to change. Mom keeps talking.

"Right. So, his company has an office there. And they . . . they want him to move out there permanently—he called me last night, which is probably why I've been a little crabby. They want him to take it over."

"Does that mean we're moving to London?" I ask.

She pauses before saying, "Do you *want* to move to London?" Sometimes she does a thing with her voice, where it sounds like she's excited but she really isn't. So I'm trying to think what I'm supposed to say. What does Mom want to hear, and what would Dad want me to say if he were here, too?

"I don't know," I say, looking away. "I mean, I liked it when I visited, but we don't really know anybody there."

We went to London one summer when I was six or seven years old, and I still kind of remember it. There were big red buses and Mom made a big deal about riding on the top deck. Everything tasted funny. They put vinegar on their fries. People always say that it rains in London all the time, but it didn't rain once while I was there. It's just that the sun didn't shine much either—it was mostly gray. It was the middle of summer and I had to wear a sweater. The best thing I saw was a shop that sold umbrellas and canes and stuff like that—some of them had swords inside. That seemed really cool when I was six.

"Well, if you don't want to move to London, you should tell him."

"He never listens to me."

"He doesn't listen to me either." Mom puts her hand on my arm. "But maybe if we both . . . We need to put up a united front," she says.

"What does that mean?"

"We need to stick together. If he talks to you about it, if he asks you what you think, just tell him the truth. Tell him what you told me."

The next day, I go to Jake's apartment and we spend all afternoon playing NBA 2K. Jake beats me pretty much every time. I tell him about London, and my dad's job, and what my mom wants me to say. Jake likes my dad, or at least he wants to *be* like him. When he's older he wants to make a lot of money, he wants to be tall and rich, so he thinks my dad has it all figured out.

One of the things I like about Jake is that nothing surprises him. I think that's because he has an older sister. Jennifer is already in college, she's a sophomore at Brown, and whenever she comes home "she tells it to me like it really is," Jake says. "A lot of parents are going through this kind of thing. This is when it happens."

"What do you mean? When *what* happens?"

"Jennifer says, it's when the kids grow up. That's when the parents start wondering if they even *like* each other anymore."

"My parents like each other." But even as I say it, I don't know if it's true. "I mean, I don't feel like we're very grown-up. All we do is play video games."

"My dad plays this all the time," Jake says. "He kicks my butt."

But it feels good talking to Jake. It's like, with him, everything that happens, whatever you're going through, has a pretty normal explanation.

"You know why your mom won't let you have a phone?" he says. "Jennifer thinks it's because she doesn't have a job—she's overinvolved. That's why she doesn't want you to grow up, because then she wouldn't have anything to do."

"She has a lot to do," I say, trying to stick up for her. "She's always busy."

"What does she do?"

Jake's mom is an accountant; she works for a company that publishes different magazines—there are a lot of weird magazines, like *Antiques Monthly* and *Bird & Bait*, lying around at his house. The truth is, I don't really know what my mom does. I don't think about it much. When I'm at school, I'm at school, and when I'm home, she hangs out with me.

"I think she goes to classes sometimes," I say. "She picks me up from school, she makes dinner."

"That's what I mean," Jake says. "She's overinvolved. That's why she won't let you get a phone. It's like, when we're at your house, she notices everything we do."

"Phones are really the end of civilization," I tell him. "Nobody ever talks anymore, they just play with their phones."

"Talking is boring," he says, so we play some more NBA 2K, and he beats me again.

About a week later, my dad comes home. Usually on his first night back, we eat at Carmine's, this loud, old-fashioned Italian restaurant a few blocks from our apartment. All the dishes are so big that everybody shares. The walls are full of black-and-white photographs of old famous people, like movie stars and boxers and politicians. I always ask my dad to tell me who they are: Joe Louis, Frank Sinatra, Mayor Koch. My dad isn't easy to talk to, but he likes to tell me stories—he knows a lot of information. Anyway, Carmine's is my favorite restaurant. Sometimes we go there on my birthday, too: the waiters bring out a big cake and everybody sings.

But this time, when my dad comes home and before we go to Carmine's, Mom says, "I'm going to leave you two alone for a minute. *He* can explain this one," and she grabs her handbag, puts on her summer coat, and walks out.

"Jenny," my dad says, following her. The trouble with our apartment is that if you want to walk out of the house, you still have to wait by the elevator—you can't just slam the door and disappear. So my dad and mom end up having this argument in the hallway while she waits for the elevator. I can hear their voices, even from our apartment—my mom does most of the talking. Sometimes my dad says something and then she starts again. I just stand in the living room, trying not to listen, and eventually my dad comes back in.

"What are you supposed to explain?" I ask.

It's about five o'clock in the afternoon; his suitcase is still in the hallway. It feels like everything is happening pretty fast; nobody is doing the stuff they normally do, where you're just in a groove and everything is kind of expected and fine. I don't know what's going to happen.

"I've got to go away again next week," he says. "I've

really just come home to pack up a few things."

"You're moving to London." I try to say it so it's just like the answer to a question, like a fact. I don't want to sound like Mom, *nagging him*, he calls it. Mom hates that word.

I can tell he's looking at me, but I don't want to look at him. "Let me just get a glass of water," he says. "I'm dehydrated from the flight." He goes into the kitchen, and I hear a faucet running, and after a minute he comes out again and sits on the couch.

"Come here, Shorty," he says and pats the cushion next to him.

My dad always calls me Shorty. I used to like the nickname when I was little but not anymore. Maybe that's why I don't move—I just stand there.

"I've got to go," he says at last. "The company I work for has an office in London, and they've asked me . . ."

"What do you mean, *got to*?"

For some reason I know this is one of those times when I can get away with being rude. My dad makes the face he makes when he . . . when he approves of something you say.

"You're right," he says. "I've *decided* to go. I'd like us all to go, but your mother . . . has other ideas. Anyway. That's not your problem. This is a conversation we can have when everybody calms down. We don't have to decide anything right now. Everybody's tired, everybody's hungry. Let me just get cleaned up and we'll go out to eat."

My dad disappears into his bedroom and I call out, "I'm just going to see if Jake's around," but I don't think he can hear me. I don't really want him to hear me. If he can come and go whenever he likes, then so can I.

I take the elevator down and ring the bell. Jake answers the door in his pajamas. Basically, after spending the day in bed—he's got a cold. School finished a couple of days ago, and the first thing that happens to him is he gets sick. He says, "Jennifer's here," when he sees me, and rolls his eyes. "With four friends." I can hear noises in the kitchen. Anyway, Jake looks pretty miserable, too. He just wants to watch TV.

So that's what we do, but the girls keep coming in and bugging us. They pretend to think we're really cute. Jake's pajama top has a picture of Darth Vader on it. "I love him when he's dopey," Jennifer says—she's got freckles, too, and red hair, and those kinds of braces that aren't really braces but you can just see a few lines of clear plastic or rubber or whatever they're made of. Jake is really pissed off with everybody. He isn't just pretending. Sometimes he gets like that. Most of the time, he's in a good mood, everything's great, he's kind of running the show, but once in a while it's like . . . he's run out of gas.

"Go bother somebody else," he tells his sister.

"But we like bothering you."

The Karate Kid is on TV.

"This is such a bad movie," one of the friends says.

"The original is much better."

"The original was pretty stupid, too."

Jake finally says, "I'm trying to watch," and eventually they clear out. "Close the door," he tells me, so I get up and close the door. The den is really his dad's office, but it's got a sofa and a TV.

"I think it's really gonna happen," I say, sitting back down. "My dad's moving to London." This is when it hits me for the first time.

"Are you gonna cry?" Jake says.

"*No.*"

"Are they getting divorced?" he asks.

I look at him, but he's looking at the TV. "I don't know . . . My dad just came back from London, and then my mom walked out. They had a big fight by the elevator. I think he wants us all to move there, but she doesn't want to."

We watch the movie for a bit. Two boys are fighting on a mat in front of thousands of people. One of them kicks the other one down; he's hurt and the crowd starts chanting, but slowly he gets back up, standing on one leg. "I love this part," Jake says. The hurt kid does a kind of flip and kicks the other one down. People go crazy. "Do you think he has a girlfriend?" Jake asks.

"Who? What are you talking about?"

"Your dad."

For a second, I can't figure out what he means. "You know, like, in London," Jake says. I don't answer but he's not trying to be unfriendly. He says, "Your dad is still the kind of guy . . . women like guys like that." He's always been embarrassed by his own dad, who works at a pharmaceutical company in New Jersey. Mr. Schultz is not fat exactly, but his shirt is always hanging out of his pants, and he wears the kind of shoes you can walk a lot in. He has a long commute, but whenever I see him come home, he seems in a good mood. Jake wants to be a lawyer. Whenever my dad's around, Jake's always very polite. I thought he was just scared, but maybe it's something else—like he wants to impress him.

"I don't know." And all of a sudden I feel bad about telling Jake any of this. It feels like I'm already taking sides. I don't mean my mom's side or my dad's but like I'm outside the family, talking about them. "I've got to go," I say. "We're going to dinner."

When I come out of the elevator, my dad is waiting for me in the hall. "Where the heck have you been?" he says. "I've been looking for you."

"I told you I went to Jake's."

"No, you didn't. Do you want to go to Carmine's or not? We don't have to go. I've got plenty of things to do at home."

This is his "important person" voice, which Mom hates—where he sounds like he's talking to one of his secretaries and everything has to happen in a hurry.

"Is Mom back yet? Is she going to come?"

He looks me in the eyes now. He kind of slows down.

"I think your mom wants to leave us alone tonight."

"Okay, we can go," I say.

We don't talk much at the restaurant; it's always pretty loud anyway, and we both just kind of look at other people. My dad has his phone out.

"Mom says phones are bad for you," I tell him.

"Yeah, well," he says, but puts it away when the food arrives—a big platter of spaghetti and meatballs, which we're going to share. The waiter brings a couple of clean plates and wipes them with the cloth in his hand. He asks me if I want another Coke because I finished the first one already. I look at my dad, who nods. He's drinking red wine.

I think both of us feel better after eating something; he doesn't seem in such a bad mood. He says, "All work and no play make Jack a dull boy." He's talking about himself—like he's the dull boy. "You know what's hard sometimes about being a kid is that when you're growing up . . . your childhood coincides with the part of your father's life where he's trying to make a career for himself. I mean, this is it for me—this is where all the hard work pays off."

He has another sip of wine, and laughs.

"You know how they pay you for hard work? They give you more hard work. But listen, Ben," he says. "None of this is your problem. I plan to see a lot of you before I take off. I've got two or three clear days. Just a few things to sort out but mostly clear days. What do you want to do? Anything at all. You name it."

"I've never been to Coney Island," I tell him.

And my dad laughs again. "I had no idea you were going to say that." Then he leans back in his chair and looks away. "There must be a lot of things I don't know about going on in that head of yours," he says.

THREE

"WE HAVE TO GO on the Thunderbolt," I say to Mom when she comes in to wake me a few mornings later. "Jake says it's the best ride in Coney Island."

Mom sits on my bed. "Well, you can tell your dad," she says, and when I look at her, she goes on: "I'm not coming along. This is boys' time. I want you two to spend some time together." After a moment, she adds: "That's what he wants, too."

I sit up a little. "Do you want me to—"

"What?" she says.

"I mean, talk to him about . . . London. Do you want me to tell him that I don't want him to go?"

She smiles. "He knows that, sweetie. But you can tell him if you want."

After breakfast, Dad and I set off. "Let's take the subway," he says. "That's part of the whole fun. When I was a kid, I used to ride the subway all the time."

He's wearing blue pants and loafers and a collared shirt, but no jacket or tie. His sleeves are rolled up, so I can see his forearms, which are strong and hairy. Some of the other men on the street, walking toward the station, wear business suits; my dad looks like a different kind of person now.

We take the B train downtown—it makes a huge screeching noise, pulling up to the platform. Everything seems louder underground. I guess it must be rush hour. There are a lot of people trying to push their way on, but my dad finds me an empty seat and stands next to it, holding on to one of the bars. He sways with the train as we roll through the tunnels; it's a long ride. I read my book and my dad manages to read his newspaper one-handed; he keeps folding it over very carefully.

At one point he taps me on the shoulder with it and says, "Hey, look. We're about to go over the water."

BENJAMIN MARKOVITS

We come out of a tunnel and I squint as sunlight pours into the subway car. The train rumbles over a bridge, and my heart jumps like when you go down too quickly in an elevator. I can see boats on the river below—it's funny how flat the water looks. There's a park on the other side, in Brooklyn, and some kids playing on a swing, and then we're rolling over city streets again. Suddenly I feel very happy to be here. I love my dad and we have all day together. Maybe I can persuade him not to go to London.

At Sheepshead Bay in Brooklyn, we get out and switch to the Q train. After that it's just a few stops. Then we walk from the station—it's windy but sunny, too, and you can smell the ocean in the breeze blowing up the avenues. Even with all the traffic, I hear the amusement park before I see it: electric beeping sounds and music playing over a loudspeaker. My dad puts his hand on my hair, and I sort of push against him, to show I don't mind.

We ride the Thunderbolt, which is really just a roller coaster. First you go straight at the sky, right at the sun. The Atlantic Ocean is behind you, and Brooklyn, and streets and cars and houses, and the boardwalk and the beach are somewhere below you, but most of the time I have my eyes closed, trying not to throw up. After that, we spend about five minutes just calming down, then we play Skee-Ball. My dad plays, too, and scores high enough to win a prize. He seems pretty pleased about that and lets me pick out the prize. There isn't anything I want, it's mostly kiddy stuff, but finally I pick a bright bead necklace to give Mom.

"Okay," he says slowly. "If that's really what you want."

"You can give it to her," I tell him. "You won it." But he doesn't say anything.

Afterward, we eat hot dogs with mustard and ketchup and sauerkraut by the beach, and drink soda and look at the water. You can see our shadows on the sand. Because the sun's going down, my dad's shadow makes him look even taller than he really is—we both look stretched out, like we're kind of stretching into nothing. He tries to talk to me about London.

"There are people at my company," he says, "whose job it is just to make sure that when somebody moves to a new office, everything is taken care of. That's their *job*— to make sure that everything's okay. And that goes for the whole family—the apartment, the school. Everything. There's a whole school in London just for American kids."

He shows me pictures on his phone. It has a basketball court and a swimming pool—it's just like a normal school, except it's in London. "It'll be like you never left New York," he says. "Except in London, we'll probably live in a house. We'll have a garden. You can walk out of your own front door." He shows me pictures of the houses, too. They're painted white and look like a wedding cake—the kind you see in movies. He scrolls to another picture.

"There's a street by the school with white lines going across it. They call them zebra crossings, you know, like the stripes. It means the cars have to stop for you. This is the most famous zebra crossing in the world because the Beatles used to make their music at a studio on the same street, right by the school. One of their album covers shows them walking across it." He flicks through to another photo; it's the album cover with four guys on it. They're all wearing different colored suits. For some reason a car is parked on the sidewalk. "People come from all over the world to take pictures of this zebra crossing," my dad says.

"People are weird. Anyway, nobody listens to the Beatles anymore, Dad."

"What? The Beatles wrote five of the greatest songs of all time. 'Hey, Jude.' 'Dear Prudence.' 'All You Need Is Love.' 'Let It Be—'"

"I haven't heard of any of those songs," I say.

"That's because you're young."

"It's because you won't let me have a phone."

"Talk to your mother—that's her department. But you don't need a phone to listen to music," he says. And then he starts to sing, *"Dear Prudence, won't you come out to play . . ."* His whole face looks different when he sings, even his body looks different—he kind of stretches his neck and closes his eyes. He doesn't look like my dad. It's like the only way I know he's my dad is that he's trying to annoy me.

"Why doesn't Mom want to go to London?" I ask him.

He stops singing. "You'll have to ask her that," he says. There's some mustard on my face, and he wipes it off with his napkin.

"Dad," I say. "I'm twelve years old."

"Well, put the food in your mouth then. It's that hole in your face."

He's not angry or anything. This is just how he talks. I think it makes him happy to talk like this to me, like I'm still his little kid. My hot dog box is lying on the bench, and it's sticky with ketchup—he picks that up with the napkin and carries it to the trash can.

"What's going to happen to . . ." I start to say, when he comes back.

"What?" He looks at me. "What's going to happen to what?"

But I don't answer, and eventually he says, "Nothing's going to happen, Ben. Right now, nothing's going to change. It'll just be like normal, except instead of living here and traveling all the time, I'm going to live there. But I'll come back as often as I can."

"Is that what Mom wants?"

"I don't know what your mother wants." He does this thing with his fingers, where he rubs them against his thumbs, like, to see if his hands are greasy. "To be fair, I don't think any of this is what she wants," he says. "But you can help me work on her. You can help me talk to her. That's your job. You can say you want to move to London, too."

I think of Jake, and our apartment, and Central Park. "But I don't really want to move to London," I say. "I want you to stay here."

"Is that what *you* want or is that what Mom told you to say?" he asks.

"She didn't tell me to say anything." But that's not totally true, and maybe I sound like I'm lying, because he looks at me like he doesn't believe me, or like he's trying to figure something out.

"Sometimes I think you guys are happier without me," he says.

"I'm not." After a minute I say, "I don't think Mom is either."

"Well." He stands up, and I can tell the conversation is over. "This isn't for you to worry about, okay. This is something your mother and I need to work out for ourselves."

*

We take a cab back to Manhattan. My dad needs to make some business phone calls and doesn't want to go underground on the subway. I spend the whole time staring out the window. The highway goes alongside a river, and I can see the shore on the other side covered in trees. I don't mind that he's on the phone. We're sort of talked out.

I'm still hungry when we get home and ask if I can have a snack. Mom isn't there, but Maria, our cleaner, is cleaning the bathroom and comes out with a mop in her hand to say hello. Dad retreats into his bedroom to finish packing. I have to follow him and ask him again.

"You've had a lot of junk food already today," he says flatly.

His mood has changed; he seems stressed out. Maybe he's mad because I didn't say I wanted to move to London. But I don't know what I want. I don't want to choose. Maybe I said the wrong things, and if I'd said something different . . . something different would be happening. But maybe it has nothing to do with me. His bed is piled with clothes and the floor is covered in open suitcases; it looks a mess.

"But I'm hungry," I say. I know I sound whiny. I *feel* whiny, too, like nothing's going my way.

"Have a piece of fruit."

"I don't want a piece of fruit."

"Have an apple," he says. In the end we agree that if I have an apple first, I can eat something else, but then I ask him to cut up the apple and Dad gets mad again.

"You're twelve years old," he says. "You can use your teeth."

He closes his bedroom door, not hard but not quietly either, and for a minute I stare at the closed door. I almost say something but don't. I walk to the kitchen and take an apple from the fruit bowl. Then I flop down on the couch and turn on the TV and start flipping channels.

When Maria has finished the bathroom, she says to me, "I'm going to do your room now, okay?" And she gets the vacuum cleaner from the closet in the hallway, so I turn the sound on louder. Maria comes out and starts vacuuming around the living room, too, moving chairs and lifting carpets. It's annoying; there's a baseball game on and I can't hear the commentators.

"Your father is busy?" she asks me.

"What?" I pretend like I can't hear her. And she turns off the vacuum cleaner and stands there, with her hands on her apron.

"Your father is busy?"

"I guess."

Maria has sort of a square wrinkled face and short black hair. She's a nice woman, but the truth is I always feel a little embarrassed around her. I don't like having other people in the house.

"Okay," she says eventually. "If you're watching TV, I can do the kitchen first."

By the time Dad comes out, about a half hour later, I've turned down the volume again and feel better. The Mets are leading the Astros 5 to 1.

"Throw your core away," he says, looking at the apple core, which I've left on the sofa arm.

"Maria can throw it away. She's cleaning up anyway."

"That's not what we pay her for, to clean up after you."

"What do we pay her for, then?" I ask.

Dad looks at me, in a way that makes me blush later that night, when I lie in bed and can't sleep. "*You* don't pay her for anything," he says.

So I push myself off the sofa and pick up the wet core and carry it into the kitchen.

And the next morning, Dad flies to London. He leaves so early that I'm still in bed, but I hear him moving his luggage to the door. When he comes in my room to say goodbye, I pretend to be asleep.

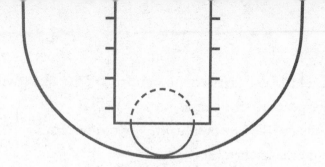

FOUR

MOM AND I ARE SITTING in the kitchen, having breakfast. It's been a few weeks since Dad left, but it's not like he was usually around that much anyway. I mean, we're used to him being gone, even though this time feels a little different.

"There's something I want to talk to you about," she says.

Sunshine is streaming in, and I'm eating waffles with maple syrup. It's a really hot July morning, and I'm not wearing a shirt. Mom tried turning on the air-conditioning, but that didn't do anything to cool things off, it just made a lot of noise. So she opened all the windows. I can hear traffic on the street, a long way below. Motorcycles revving, a big truck going past.

"You remember Granma's house in Texas, right?" Mom says. "I think we might go there for a while."

"For a summer vacation?" I pour a little more syrup on my waffles. That's the kind of thing Mom used to call me out on, but lately she's been letting things slide.

Most of my friends go away on exciting summer vacations, to places like Paris and Hawaii. They come back to school in September with souvenirs, key rings or stuff made out of leather or wood, and they tell funny stories about what happened at their hotels, which make me jealous. If I can't laugh, I always just say, "Oh really?"

We don't usually go any farther than Cape Cod. There's a tiny airport in a field, and the flight from New York takes about an hour. After that a taxi drives us to the house my dad always rents. It's the same place he used to go as a kid. You can see the ocean from the garden, and my mom likes to lie on the beach, pretending to read a book. Working on her tan, she calls it. Since Dad is in London, I figured maybe we wouldn't go this year. That's one of the things I've been wondering about.

"Well, it will be summer when we go to Granma's. But I think we might want to stick around for a while. Maybe move there. Go on, drink your juice," she says, because

I'm just staring at her. For some reason there are tears in her eyes. "Your granma misses you," she says.

"I don't even really know her," I say, setting down my glass.

"Well, this is your chance." My mom clears her throat and tries to sound cheerful. "It's not easy for me on my own, with your father . . . away. This way I can go back to work. Granma can help out and you guys can get to know each other." I don't say anything, and she adds, "It would mean a lot to me."

"You're talking to me like I'm a little kid. If you want to work, go work. I'm not stopping you. Jake already goes to the diner by himself. I can walk to school. I can walk home and stay here until you come back. If you're worried about where I am, you can get me a phone. You can call me whenever you want."

"You sound like your father," Mom says. The way she says it is the way she used to talk to him.

"What do you mean?"

"That's what he always said. Go back to work, if that's what you want. It's like nobody's paying attention to what I actually do. Okay, that's fine, that's my job. But who's going to do your laundry, who's going to pack your lunch, who's going to make sure you do your homework and turn off the lights and wake you up in the morning. . . ."

"Maria does the laundry."

"Maria only comes twice a week."

"So she can come more."

Mom takes a deep breath. "Okay, I don't want to talk about this anymore."

"You always complain to me that *I* don't want to talk about anything, and then when I try to talk about it, you tell me to stop."

"This isn't talking, this is just—you have no idea what actually goes on here. That's fine. You're a kid."

"That's because you treat me like a kid."

"I just . . . I can't have this conversation," she says, and gets up. "I think we both need to cool down."

"I'm not angry," I tell her, but it's not true, because as soon as she walks out of the kitchen, I feel too mad to eat—the waffles are cold anyway, and everything's sticky. For some reason, I hear Jake's voice in my head. He's teasing me: "Are you going to cry?" No, I'm not going to cry, I feel like shouting, but nobody's there.

The rest of the day is like any other summer day. I watch TV until Mom tells me to turn it off. I go see if Jake's around—we play video games. Jake asks his mom if we can go out to the coffee shop, but she says I have to check with *my* mother first.

"Forget it," I say. "She never lets me go."

"Come on, just ask her," Jake tells me.

So I go back to my apartment and in fact she says okay. She's in her bedroom with a bunch of clothes on the bed, but she goes out to the hallway and gets her purse. She gives me a twenty-dollar bill.

"Thanks," I mumble.

I turn to go, but Mom says, "It's hard for me, too, you know. I'm doing my best, but I don't always get everything right. I know you have to grow up, but it's like—I have to grow up, too. I have to let you."

"Thanks, Mom," I say, a little louder this time.

She stares at me for a minute. "Look at me. Just to the coffee shop—eat what you want but then come right back. Wait for the lights to cross the street, but you know all that."

"Do you want me to take your phone, so I can call?"

"Jake has a phone, doesn't he?"

"*Yes*."

She laughs at me a little, because I sound grumpy again. "We can talk about that later, too," she says. She means, getting a phone.

I really can't believe it—I can hardly wait for the elevator to take me back down to Jake's apartment. "She said yes!" But he acts like it's no big deal.

"Bye, Mom," he calls out. "We're going!" We stand in the hallway, waiting for the elevator again. The

twenty-dollar bill is in my pocket, and my hand is holding it so tightly that it's started to sweat.

New York suddenly looks different when we walk out
through the apartment complex courtyard and under the
arch. I'm not used to being out without a grown-up. I
mean, you don't even realize, when you're out with your
mom, that she's making all these little decisions. About
when to cross the street and which way to go. The build-
ings seem taller; the sidewalk is full of people; it's like even
the traffic is worse. I have to pay attention to everything,
but Jake doesn't seem to notice or care. For a second I
think the doorman is going to stop us—like he's a police-
man or something, or a teacher and we're running away.
But we're really just going around the corner to the end of
the block, and then crossing the street, and then walking
another block—under a bunch of scaffolding. Jake has
this rule that you always have to hold your breath when
you walk under scaffolding, but this one's so long we start
running all the way until we get to the Five-Star Diner.

It's three in the afternoon and the place is pretty
empty. We get a corner table, so we can watch the traffic
going two ways—down Amsterdam Avenue and along
86th Street, too. Jake orders a glazed donut and a Coke,
so that's what I get, too.

"My dad wants me to move to London with him." For

some reason, when I say it, it feels like I'm bragging.

"What do you mean?"

"He says there's this great school there, and we could have a whole house, just around the corner from the Beatles' studio. Or something like that. It was weird. It was like he was trying to sell it to me."

"Addie says that when his parents got divorced, he could get whatever he wanted from them. He just had to ask. Nintendo Wii. Tickets to a Rangers game. He even got a dog. They let his sister get her nose pierced. It was like—there were no rules, you just had to ask."

So we start talking about what I should ask for. It's kind of fun. Because Jake says, "It's not just *what* you ask for, it's *how* you ask for it. There's a trick . . . you can't just say, I want this. You have to say, Dad says that in England everybody has a dog, or something like that. . . ."

"I don't really want to go to England."

"But, no, you're missing the point. That's just what you have to say. You don't have to mean it."

"You know what my mom told me this morning? She says we're moving to Texas. Or she asked me if that's what I wanted, but it was, like, this is not really a question, this is just something you're telling me."

"Why does she want to go to Texas? London's a lot cooler."

"That's where she's from. She says she wants me to get

to know my grandmother. I'm like, I've met her, she's like this old lady with one hand—it's all kind of swollen up, it's like this zombie hand." But as soon as I say it, I feel bad. "I mean she's fine, she's not crazy or anything like that. She doesn't smell like pee or anything."

Jake's looking at me like I'm crazy. "What are you even talking about?" he says. "You know, everybody in school thinks you never talk, but you talk all the time. That's what I try to tell them. I can't get you to shut up."

"I just talk to you," I say. But I feel embarrassed, maybe because he seems embarrassed, too. We sit in silence for a while and Jake starts playing on his phone.

Then we go home. The whole thing lasts about forty-five minutes and afterward, for some reason, when he gets out on the seventh floor I don't know if he wants me to come back with him—he kind of walks out when the doors open, and I say, "Okay," and he says, "Okay, see you I guess," and then the doors close and I go up three more floors to my apartment. It's always that way with Jake. Sometimes I think he's my best friend and sometimes I think he just hangs out with me when he's bored because we live in the same building and I'm the only one around.

That night, before turning my light out, Mom comes and sits on my bed for a minute. "Dad said there's this great school in London just for Americans," I start to tell her.

"He said he wants us to move out there. There's somebody in his office whose whole job is to find us a house and . . . just kind of make sure we have everything we need."

"I don't want anyone to find us a house," she says. "We have a house."

"It's not a house, it's an apartment. Anyway, if we have a house, why do you want to go to Texas?"

"What do *you* want to do?" she asks me. I'm lying on my belly and she's giving me a back rub.

"It doesn't really matter what I want, does it?" I say.

"It matters."

"Not really. I can tell you've already made up your mind."

Mom takes a breath. "Ben, it's my job to make the decisions, but I care about what you want, too."

"I don't want anything to happen. I don't want anything to change."

"Well, that's not really up to me. There are some things I *can't* do." And she gets up from the bed. I roll over and look at her, and she bends down to give me a good night kiss. "You'll have to talk to your father about that," she says.

A few days later the movers arrive. I'm busy playing Minecraft on Mom's iPad. She's usually pretty strict about screen time, but right now she doesn't seem to be paying total attention to everything I do. . . . There's a buzz on the entry phone, and then about a minute later the doorbell rings and three big men in brown uniforms are standing outside.

"Is your mom around?" one of them says, and then she comes up behind me and lets them in. They lug a lot of stuff into the apartment—plastic bags and rolls of tape and flat cardboard boxes. There's always somebody holding the freight elevator. And I can smell them in the house, because it's another hot day outside and they've been sweating.

Their uniforms have their names written over the front pockets or kind of sewed on. A short, fat guy named Tomas says, "Hey, give me a hand here." He has a foreign accent—at first I didn't know he was talking to me. "Yeah, you. You know how to fold a cardboard box?"

"No."

So he shows me, and then he carries a few flat boxes into my bedroom and gives me a roll of tape. "Why don't you get started in here?" he says.

Mom brings out a pitcher of ice water and lots of glasses. She sets them down on the table in the hall. I hear her say to Tomas, "He was supposed to go to his friend's house. I didn't want him to have to watch."

"It's better if he helps," Tomas says. I like Tomas, but

I don't like the way Mom talks to him. That's something my dad used to complain about. She talks to everybody like she knows them. But if I close my bedroom door, I don't have to listen. So that's what I do.

It's easy to make the boxes, and kind of cool. They start out flat, like a picture on a page, and then turn into something real, something three-dimensional, that you can put stuff into. But I don't know what to put in. Everything I have ever been given is on the shelves or in the chest at the foot of my bed. Mom is bad at throwing things away. Even baby things, like the stuffed elephant I used to sleep with every night but haven't slept with in ages. For some reason, I call him the Bursar. He just stands there on a shelf, holding up a few books. His legs have gone floppy; he has to balance on his trunk.

After a while, somebody knocks on the door, and Mom comes in. I'm back to sitting on my bed, playing Minecraft. The boxes are still empty.

"Do you need a little help deciding?" she says.

"I don't even know what I'm doing here. The guy just said, 'Get started.'"

For some reason, this sets her off. "What do you think we're doing, we're packing up." A piece of tape has stuck to her dress; her hair has come loose; she's got a pencil behind her ear. "Anything you don't want to take on the plane needs to go in a box."

I look around my room—it's a mess, but it's also, like, my whole life.

And after a minute, Mom says, "Maybe it's easier to start with what you need. I mean, what you want to take with you now. I'll give you a suitcase. Don't take too much, just what you can't live without for the next few months."

"I don't really need anything. Apart from clothes."

"Don't worry about that. I'll pack your clothes."

You can hear the guys making noise in the rest of the apartment, talking and moving boxes around. For them it's just a job, they're having a good time.

"Mom?" I ask her. "What are they going to do with the rest of our stuff?"

"What do you mean?"

"Like sofas and beds."

"It's all going into storage. You know that this apartment doesn't belong to us, we just rent it. I've discussed all this with your father. London's expensive, too—he says there's no point in keeping two apartments. In Austin, we can live with your grandmother, but when we get a place of our own . . . they can ship everything to us. All our old things. It'll be like coming home."

"What am I going to sleep on tonight?"

She looks at me, puzzled. "Your bed," she says.

"I thought they were taking it away."

And she smiles at me, like I'm a little kid. "Oh, honey,

not tonight." Her voice has gone all soft. "After we leave—today they're just doing all the prep work."

"I still don't understand why we're moving to Texas."

"Ben, I thought we talked about that already." Her voice has gone hard again. "I want you to get to know your grandmother, and she can help out, and I can go back to work."

"It just seems like . . . the whole reason we're . . . I thought the reason you didn't want to go to London with Dad is because . . . this is our home. But then we're going away anyway."

"Do you want to go to London with Dad?"

She looks at me and there's only one thing I can say. "No."

"Because you know that moving to London is not really . . . Dad is going to be working all the time. We're not gonna see him anyway. So the only reason to move to London is not really a reason at all."

"So why didn't you tell him to stay here?"

"I tried to say everything I could. . . . I probably said too much. Your father loves you very much. But he also loves his work, he loves being an important person . . . and sometimes, when you're a dad, and you come home after work . . . you don't feel like such an important person anymore. There's nobody you can tell what to do, there's nobody you can . . . I mean, you can try." And she laughs a little, but she doesn't sound happy. "He can't really give you and me performance incentives."

"Are you getting a divorce?" I ask.

She sits down next to me on the bed. "I don't know what we're getting. But I figure, there's no point hanging around here, waiting for him to come back. Might as well go home."

"This is home."

"Oh, honey," she says again, and starts stroking my hair. "It isn't for me anymore."

Jake was at soccer camp in the morning, but after lunch I take the elevator downstairs to see if he's back. Mrs. Schultz answers the door.

"Can Jake hang out?" I ask.

But Jake has come out already to see what's going on. He's still wearing his soccer uniform—blue nylon shirt and shorts, with high blue socks and cleats.

"I have to pack up my room," I tell him. "Maybe you want to look at some of my stuff. I can only take a few things to Austin."

"Go on, Jake," Mrs. Schultz says. "It's nice to have company when you're packing."

So Jake follows me back to my apartment; his cleats click against the tiles. I know what he's thinking about. For my last birthday, Dad gave me a Syma quadcopter drone with a camera, which we like to take to Central Park—it's loud enough to make everybody stare at the sky. Jake always wants to hold the controls.

We spend most of the afternoon messing around with this drone, even though my room is really too small. It's hard to control, and it keeps crashing against the ceiling and wiping out. Jake thinks this is funny, but I worry the blades might break. (The box says in capital letters NOT FOR INDOOR USE. The first time I showed it to Jake, I said, "What kind of idiot would fly a drone inside?" But then we started doing it anyway.) We haven't gotten much packing done when Mom comes in to say there's food on the table.

"Can Jake stay for supper?"

"I'm sure he can, but let him just run down and check with his mom."

I say to Jake, "Everything I don't take with me is going into storage. So maybe there's something you want. Except this," I add, holding the drone controls in my hand and trying not to smile.

Jake starts to go over everything carefully. It makes me feel funny to see him looking like that at all my stuff. He puts his hand in the chest of toys and starts digging around. A lot of this stuff is stuff I haven't played with in years—I can't even remember half of it, but some of it I do remember, and it makes me feel like, I don't know, it makes me feel old. Like I've already outgrown a lot of things that used to make me happy.

But Mom says, "The food's getting cold. You can do that after." So Jake runs down to check with his mom.

At supper, all Jake wants to talk about are my baby toys. He's making fun of me for keeping all these old toys. But he's also joking about what he should take. Part of what I don't like is that I can tell when my mom is . . . I don't know, listening or judging. Sometimes she doesn't like Jake as much as I do; she doesn't think he's nice to me. Or she doesn't like the way I act around him.

Tomas is still there and the other two men. I can see them carrying boxes into the hallway. Their truck is parked in the courtyard, but the freight elevator is slow and it takes them five or ten minutes to go down and come up again and get another load. Every time they come back they're sweating even more than before, and Mom says, "I think there's some beers in the fridge. You've earned them," but Tomas shakes his head.

"Water is fine," he says, and one of the other guys says something to him in a language I don't understand. They both laugh.

"We'll come back tomorrow to finish up," he says.

Meanwhile, I get this stupid idea that Jake is going to ask for the Bursar. Just as a joke, just because . . . he thinks I don't care. Or maybe to make fun of me. For some reason, that's all I can think about, and I can't finish my spaghetti. It's going to be too embarrassing for me to say that I don't want him to take my stuffed animal. I don't think I'll be able to do that, if he asks. I'm going to have to say okay. Either way he'll laugh at me.

Afterward, Mom lets us finish up a tub of chocolate chip ice cream. "No use letting it sit in the freezer." Then we go back to my room and Jake starts looking through my things again. He's gone kind of quiet.

"I guess I don't need anything," he says. There are toys all over the floor and on my bed, piles of books and a whole tangle of jump ropes and yo-yos and stuff like fishing nets for the beach. "Mom says my room is already too messy."

"Well, if you want something, you can have it."

"That's okay, I guess," Jake says. I keep thinking he's going to make fun of me for something, but he doesn't; he can't even look me in the eye. It's like . . . when he gets a bad grade in school, that's what he does: he sort of turns his face away from the teacher. A few seconds later, in break time, he might be just the same, laughing or whatever, but it's like I can see the muscles in his face, making him laugh when he doesn't want to.

Mom walks into the room and says, "Okay, Jake, I'm gonna have to kick you out. We've got a lot to do tomorrow."

Suddenly I say, "You can have the drone if you want, I guess. I don't really play with it anymore, except when you come over."

He looks at me for a second. Then he says, "That's all right. That's like your best thing. You should take it to Texas."

"Take it," I say. "You're better at it than I am anyway."

He stands there, next to my mom. For some reason he looks very small. He's still in his soccer gear, in his cleats and shiny shorts, like a kid who never wants to take off his uniform. I've known him since he was four years old, when his parents moved to our apartment building, and my mom met them in the elevator. She came home and told me, all excited, about a boy who just moved in a few floors down. He's exactly your age, she said. And after that we started going to the park together—Mom and Mrs. Schultz started hanging out, too. I don't really remember what it was like beforehand—it's like he's always been around. Finally he says, like he's talking to a grown-up, "That's all right. I mean, no, thank you." But he's looking at me.

When he goes home again, without taking anything, I pick up the drone and Mr. Bursar and put them in one of the boxes. If Jake doesn't want them, neither do I.

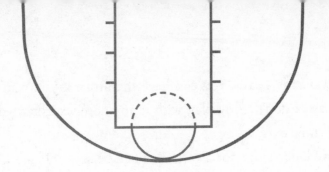

FIVE

TODAY'S THE DAY of the flight. I never sleep well if I have to wake up early. Last night I lay in bed and listened to my mom moving around the apartment. She still had a lot to do. But before she went to bed, she came into my room. I have a digital radio, which shows the time in bright red numbers. It said 11:53. I guess she thought I was asleep. I could see her looking at me.

"Mom," I said, and she jumped.

"Oh, goodness, you gave me a shock." Then she came over and sat down next to me, so the mattress shifted and I rolled against her. "Can't you sleep?"

"I'm too . . . I guess, I'm too worked up." This is what Dad always calls it. Don't get yourself worked up over nothing, he says. You're getting worked up. He says it to Mom as well.

"Me, too," she said. "It doesn't matter if you sleep or not. You can just lie there. You can always sleep on the plane." She put her hand on my hair. "Ben, you're a tough kid." Her hand is always bigger than I expect it to be. I could smell her perfume.

I didn't think I'd ever get to sleep, but the next thing I know Mom is still sitting there except it's sunny. Very white sunlight, kind of cold looking. "Time to get up," she says.

Mom has laid my clothes out on the floor, just jeans and a T-shirt, spread out next to each other like a flat boy that's lying on the ground. She used to do that for me when I was little, and she still does it sometimes if we have to leave the house early. I get dressed and help her carry the boxes and suitcases outside. We have to wait in the hallway for the elevator. Everybody seems to be in bed, except for the doorman, who sees us from across the courtyard and comes over to lend a hand.

"Morning, Mrs. Michaels," he says. "Can I get you a cab?"

"Please." So he walks out in the street to flag one down. Then he helps me load the suitcases into the trunk.

"Young man," he says. "Now you look after your mother, you hear me?"

I smile, but I don't say anything. There's a fountain in the middle of the courtyard, which I used to splash around in when I was a baby. You can see the apartment building behind it, some air conditioners in the windows, but that's not really the part of the building that I live in. I *lived* in. There are some plants growing around it, too. It all looks—kind of old-fashioned, like pictures of the way New York used to be. When people rode around in horse-drawn carriages. That's the last thing I see when the cab pulls away.

Usually I love airplane flights. I like the trays of food and the fact that I get to watch as much TV as I want. Dad always takes the aisle seat, so he can stretch his legs. Mom sits in the middle, so I can look out the window. But today it's just the two of us, and when we walk down the aisle to our row number, there's already a woman sitting by the window.

"Where do you want to sit, middle or aisle?" Mom asks.

I shrug. "I don't care."

She gives me a long look. "I guess you're just tired," she says, but I don't feel tired—I just don't feel like talking. Which is probably why Mom introduces herself to that woman. Her face is very suntanned, skinny, and wrinkled; she wears a lot of makeup.

"I'm Jenny," Mom says, and the woman says, "Everyone calls me Bells."

There's a public announcement: the captain is talking, telling us about the flight time and the weather in Austin; and after it ends, nobody says anything for a minute, and I think, Maybe it's okay—they won't get into a conversation, I can just sit here with my mom, but then the woman says, "You folks from Texas?"

"I am," Mom tells her, and lowers her voice. "He isn't. I've been living in New York for fifteen years. You get to a point in your life where you just . . . want to go home."

I have a book open in my lap, but that doesn't stop me from listening.

"You haven't lost your accent," Bells says.

"I guess that's one thing I *haven't* lost." Mom smiles, in a way I don't like. She only does it for women.

The plane rolls into position at the head of the runaway, and then it starts revving its engines—going faster and faster, and getting louder and louder. When it finally lifts into the air, the cabin goes suddenly quiet. Mom gives me a piece of chewing gum, and I put it in my mouth. My ears feel cloggy. The FASTEN SEAT BELT sign blinks off, and I press the button on my armrest and push the chair back.

Bells says, "You wouldn't believe it, but I've just become a grandmother." She's the kind of person who can start a conversation just by saying stuff; she doesn't need an invitation. Why shouldn't I believe it? She looks old. "That's something that nothing really prepares you for," Bells goes on. Her accent sounds like my mom's—she's from Texas, too. They seem to have a lot to say to each other.

"Is he all right?" Bells asks after a while. "He seems kind of quiet. He hasn't turned a page of that book in about ten minutes."

"He's all right," Mom says. "He's just got a lot on his plate. I'm sorry." She's crying a little, and turns her head away from the lady, toward me. I can see her face all scrunched up—she doesn't want me to see her either, so she sniffs and puts on a smile and turns back. "I guess we both do. It just constantly amazes me . . . how kids can just . . . put up with what you dump on them. Without complaining. Don't get me wrong, if I tell him to put his cereal bowl in the dishwasher, this can be, like . . . a half-hour argument. But then real stuff happens, and they're like, Okay. He's my little champion guy."

"I bet I know what. Maybe he wants the window seat. Am I right?" Bells says that last bit to me, leaning over and touching me on the knee. I think she thinks I'm like seven years old or something, maybe because I'm not very tall. Maybe because that's still how Mom treats me, especially when she feels emotional.

"I'm all right."

"Well, you may be all right, but there's no point in *that* when you can be a whole lot better. Come on." And she picks up her purse from between her feet. "Let's you and me swap. I need to use the little girls' room anyway."

So Mom and I have to get out of our seats and stand in the aisle so she can squeeze through. "You can sit by the window," Mom says. "She won't care."

"I wish you wouldn't talk to people like that," I tell her.

"What do you mean, *people like that*?"

"I mean, about me."

"There," the woman says, when she comes back from the restroom. I'm sitting in her seat. "That's better, isn't it?"

"Yes, thank you."

What else can I say? I mean, people just do what they want to do anyway—it's not up to me. They fly to London, they fly to Texas. They tell you to apologize or change seats. They talk about you in front of your face. They play with your toys or make you clean up their messes or act like something is your fault when it's not. At least now I don't have to pretend to read. For a few hours I don't have to pretend at all, not even to be happy; I can stare out the window at the clouds.

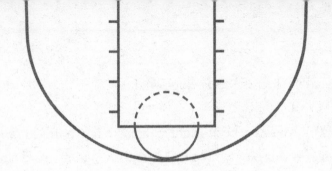

SIX

I'VE NEVER BEEN to Texas in the summer. Usually we go at Christmas or New Year's, when it's nice and sunny but not too hot. But this time, when we walk out of the airport, it's like walking into a bathroom where someone has left the shower on. In about half a minute, my shirt's soaked through with sweat—that's how humid it is. I can hardly look at the road, to watch out for Granma's car, because the sunshine coming off it is too bright.

"There she is," my mom says, as an old white Volvo pulls up next to us.

Granma rolls down her window—I can tell it's the

kind where you have to turn a handle. "We need a storm soon," she says to my mom. "This is too much." And then she looks at me and smiles. "Hey, sweetie. It's nice you're here."

Mom and I load our suitcases into the trunk, then I get in back. The air-conditioning is broken, and the leather seats are so hot I can barely sit on them. I take a sweatshirt out of my backpack and sit on that. Granma keeps the windows wide open, and the air roars through them as she merges onto the highway, overtaking people. The airport is really in the middle of nowhere—there's a big hotel with a big parking lot around it and other than that . . . nothing. Just a lot of highways and empty land. In New York, it's like every square foot of land has something going on. Either a neighborhood or a park or an office building or store. But here even the roads seem empty. Even the skies seem bigger. I look at my mom in the front seat. She has her eyes closed; her hair's blowing back against her ears. And she looks. . . happy.

About a half hour later, we pull up to the house; it looks almost wild. Bushes have grown over the front window; and a big pecan tree, full of leaves, has put most of the front yard in shade. The grass hasn't been cut in a while. Some of it's gone yellow, but it's long enough you can see the seeds, too; it looks like green wheat. "I meant to get Mario to come," Granma says. "I wanted to make everything nice, but he's coming next week. It doesn't matter. What matters is you're here."

"Thanks for picking us up," Mom says.

The house needs painting, too. The walls are supposed to be white, but a lot of the boards are peeling, and you can see gray wood underneath the paint. I get out of the car and stretch my legs again; there's a kind of dust in the air, which sticks to the sweat on my skin. I feel dirty, from the airplane, too. But I don't really mind. It's so hot that all you can think about is getting cool. Or not even that—you don't even think, you just try to move as little as possible, because every time you move, you feel the heat; and what it feels like is this, like a voice in your head saying, I'm here, I'm really here. New York feels like a long time ago.

It takes Granma a while to get the key in the lock. Mom piles the suitcases on the front porch; I help her carry them from the trunk of the Volvo. Granma is still fussing with the door. "I'm so clumsy," she says. But the key finally turns and we go in. It's a little bit cooler inside but not much.

I follow Mom as we wheel the suitcases into the bedroom at the end of the hall. "Just to get them out of the way," she says. Granma has a small house. It's all on one floor—there are only two bedrooms, so when we stayed in Texas over Christmas, Mom and Dad had to sleep on the living room sofa. Everybody fought to get into the bathroom; nobody seemed in a good mood. "But this time around, things will be different," Mom had promised me on the airplane flight. She meant because Dad isn't here. We're going to sleep in the same room, with two beds in opposite corners. At least until we find our own place to stay . . .

"Is this okay, Ben?" she says, quietly, so Granma doesn't hear. "I mean, you don't mind sharing, do you?"

I can tell that Mom is trying to give me a chance to talk, to say what I'm really thinking, because it's not just me and her anymore, it's Granma as well. It's Granma's house. I guess it's Mom's house, too, because she grew up in it, but it's not really mine. I'm like a guest.

"I don't mind."

"It'll be fun," she says, in that voice she sometimes uses when she wants to show that everything's going to be fine.

My bed has little dark wood posts on all the corners, and Granma has laid a quilt over the sheet, which is stitched together from lots of rags or pieces of old clothes. Mom sees me looking at it. "You probably won't need it—it stays pretty hot at night." There's a fan on the ceiling, which makes a creaking noise. It has a lamp in the middle, which you turn on with a metal chain, and the chain keeps swinging around in the breeze. I put my backpack on the bed and Granma comes in.

"I bet you both could use something to drink."

Mom says, "The first thing I need is the bathroom."

"Who said I'm talking to you?" Granma smiles and turns to me. "What do you want? I've got iced tea, I've got Dr Pepper."

I look at my mom. "Go ahead," she says.

"Dr Pepper, please."

"There's no need to stand on ceremony," Granma tells me as she leaves for the kitchen.

Mom is on her way to the bathroom. "There's nothing wrong with saying please," she calls out.

Then I'm alone.

For a minute I just sit there on the bed, which makes little noises when I move; you can feel the springs in the mattress. The bedroom window overlooks the backyard. But there's a porch or something outside, and the roof goes over it, so that the sun doesn't shine into the room directly. It's shady and not cool exactly, but the shade is kind of . . . thick somehow, warm but not hot, the fan is creaking overhead, I'm sitting on this old bedspread in this strange house, and the grass in the yard is so bright in the sunshine that it almost hurts my eyes.

In New York that morning, when we left the house, it was cool enough that I shivered when the fountain in the courtyard caught the breeze. But when you're tired, you feel cold. I'm still tired, but at least I'm the opposite of cold. Eventually I get up and follow Granma down the hall and into the kitchen. She says, "I was just going to bring it to you," and takes a bottle of Dr Pepper out of the fridge. "Do you want a glass?" she asks.

"I'm all right." But she takes out a glass anyway and fills it with crushed ice.

With Mom in the bathroom, it's just the two of us. She has a really old face, so it's kind of hard to tell what she used to look like, because it's so wrinkled. But she moves pretty well, and apart from her swollen hand, she looks all right. A few years ago she had cancer. I don't really remember it, except that Mom went away for a while, and Dad's sister, Aunt Becky, came to live with us in New York—just to take me to school and pick me up, things like that. Granma had an operation and then chemotherapy, but when I saw her again at Christmas, she looked okay, just like, a lot older, and her hair looked thin, and her hand was swollen. The hair grew back, but her hand still looks funny. Mom said it had something to do with the lymph nodes, something wasn't draining properly. . . . I don't like to think about it, but suddenly I feel bad about saying what I did to Jake.

When she opens the bottle of Dr Pepper, she holds it in her swollen hand, but screws the cap off with her other hand. Then she pours it into the ice-filled glass, until it almost bubbles over. "There we go."

Mom comes in, and Granma says to me, "Do you want a scoop of ice cream on that?"

I look at my mother. "Knock yourself out," she says. "Granma's house, Granma's rules."

And that's what it's like for the rest of the day. It's like a holiday, and it doesn't matter what I do, so I watch a lot of TV. Mom is busy unpacking and I hear her talking to Granma, who is busy cooking and talking back. I think I fall asleep late in the afternoon, because it's so hot—that's one of the things they argue about, when to turn the air-conditioning on. Granma says you just get used to it, and anyway, she just has these little AC units in the window, which drip and smell funny and don't really do anything anyway. And Mom says, "Well, that's one thing we can take care of while I'm here. We can put in some real air-conditioning." So they argue about that, too, and when I wake up again, the TV is still on. I'm lying on a weird, not-very-comfortable couch—it's got wooden legs, and velvet cushions that are kind of worn through, and a sort of scratchy woolen blanket on top of it, which some-one must have put over me. The sun is going down, and the air is yellow, like eggs are yellow, sort of oozy, and Mom is crying in the kitchen. Granma sees me—she sees that I've woken up, the kitchen and the living room just have an arch between them—and she makes a face at me, like, Don't worry. I got this covered.

At supper, Granma opens a bottle of wine. We eat in the kitchen. Granma made chicken casserole, and I get another glass of Dr Pepper (even though I don't really like it; it's too sweet) and another scoop of ice cream afterward—for dessert, a big bowl of Blue Bell's cookies and cream. "What do you want to do tomorrow?" Granma asks me.

I eat another spoonful of ice cream. There's nothing I really want to do. I don't mean to be rude, but it's like—I don't know anybody anyway. "I'm fine. I mean, whatever."

"Do you want to go swimming?"

"That sounds nice."

"We could play mini-golf."

"That sounds great, too," I say.

"There's a Peter Pan mini-golf course on the way to Barton Springs. We could do both."

"Okay, sure, Granma. I mean, thank you."

Mom says, "Stop sounding so darned polite, Ben, and say what you actually think."

"I'm saying what I think," I tell her. "We could do all those things. They sound cool."

Apparently Barton Springs is this big rocky pool that's sort of carved out of part of a river. I've heard about it but never been there. There's also a secondhand book store called Half Price Books and a famous record shop called Waterloo Records and an ice cream place that we can walk to called Amy's Ice Creams, where you can ask them to "crush in" anything you like, like Oreo cookies or pecans or Butterfinger candy bars or whatever, into whatever flavor you ask for. This is Mom's idea—she took me once before, over Christmas a few years ago. I say "sure" and she sort of rolls her eyes at me, and Granma says, "Give him a break."

After dinner, I offer to help clear the table. "You've had a long day," Granma says. "You can start helping out around here tomorrow. Or never, so far as I'm concerned."

So I go back to the couch and sit and watch TV, which is great, because it means I don't have to talk. There's a baseball game on, but I don't really care what it is. I just zone out. The next thing I know the TV is off and Mom is sitting next to me on the couch. She's got her hand on my forehead, like she's trying to see if I have a temperature, and the truth is, I feel pretty weird—like, wide-awake and tired at the same time, and just kind of not there. "Come on, Ben. Beddy-bye." She hasn't said that to me in a while.

It feels weird going to bed with Mom in the room. When I was little I used to climb under the covers with her and Dad on Sunday mornings, which is something they argued about, because Dad didn't want it to become a habit . . . but that was years ago anyway.

When Mom goes to the bathroom, I quickly put on my pajamas. She comes back wearing her nightgown, which is faded yellow and has flowers like blue daisies all over it. "It's all yours," she says.

The bathroom has little green tiles, a lot of which are cracked or missing. It smells of lemon air freshener. The mirror is old-fashioned, with patterns cut into it, and the medicine shelf is full of prescription bottles—Granma's medicines. I brush my teeth and wash my face, which wakes me up. Mom is already in bed when I come back in.

"Do you want to read for a bit?"

"Sure, okay."

"Are you going to say okay to everything?"

"Just for the next few years." I smile.

"Well, at least we can laugh," she says, and turns on her bedside lamp.

My lamp casts a little circle of light on my covers, and it makes the rest of the room seem almost black. There's a bright ring around the edge of what I can see. Mom is outside the edge.

"Which is the bed you used to sleep in? I mean, when you were a kid," I ask. I don't want her to fall asleep just yet—I don't want to be left alone.

"This one. The bed I'm in."

"So what was *my* bed for?"

"Sleepovers," she says.

"Does it feel weird, sleeping in your old bed?"

"I've slept in it before," Mom says.

"But I mean, with me here."

She doesn't answer for a bit, and I think she's fallen asleep. Then she says, "When I was a kid, I really wanted a sister. It annoyed me that Mom and Dad got to sleep together but I was on my own. Like I was the odd one out. It's nice that you're here now—I don't have to be lonely anymore." Then she says, "No more talking. I'm tired."

"Okay, good night."

"Good night, Ben."

I try to read again, and after a few minutes Mom's breathing slows down and I can tell she's asleep. After another few minutes I turn off my light, too.

But even with the lights off I don't feel sleepy. All the sounds are strange. The fan is still on, creaking, and the window is open, and I can hear crickets outside, and even in the night it's still hot. Granma has the TV on low, but in the dark, it's like you can hear everything. She's watching the news. . . . It's not a big house, and the walls are thin, and for some reason I get this feeling like I'm just this computer or receiver or something, receiving all this information, like sounds and smells (the quilt on my bed is a little musty—it smells like towels that have been left in the cupboard too long); and it's very hard for me to turn that feeling off. I don't know if I'm happy or not but it's like everything is very close, closer than normal, and sort of bigger than normal, too, like if someone put their hand or something right up against your face and held it there. It takes me a long time to fall asleep.

We spend the next day just doing stuff. Mom has a lot of stuff she has to do, like buy a car. So I help her do that, sitting next to her on the couch, and looking at carmax.com. There's this whole world of people out there trying to sell you their car; it's a little overwhelming. At least, that's what Mom says. But it's also kind of fun, imagining, like, maybe that will be *our* car. Maybe we'll be like the people who drive around in a yellow convertible Chevy Camaro. (Mom says, "We are *not* those people.") Granma brings us iced tea from the kitchen; the fan is spinning above, making noise; and Mom is clicking and saying, "What do you think?" and in my head it's like I'm talking to Jake and asking him, What do *you* think? He has strong opinions about stuff like this. In New York we never had a car.

While Granma sets the table for lunch, Mom starts making phone calls about schools. "Don't even think about it," she says to me. "This is, like, a whole summer away. This is, like, pretend." But it's not pretend: it's going to happen. In five or six weeks, I'm going to go to a brand-new school where I don't know anybody.

Granma says, "Let's eat," but my mom is still on the phone, waiting on hold and sometimes talking to somebody. I try not to listen in, and eventually Granma gets annoyed. "You can do that later," she says. "We're all getting hungry here."

Then when we sit down they have a kind of quiet argument. "There are just a lot of things I have to get done," Mom says, and Granma tells her, "You don't have to do them with Ben hanging around. He's the priority right now."

"Don't you think I know that?" And so on. I just eat my bologna sandwich and pick at the carrot and cucumber sticks Granma put in a bowl on the table.

After lunch, we have more errands to run. Mom has to get her Texas driver's license renewed. "It'll be an outing," she tells me. "It'll be fun. Come on—let's get out of the house. We can't sit around here all day. We'll go for a treat."

So we borrow Granma's Volvo and drive to some office building with a big parking lot around it. It's really incredibly cold in the waiting room, but finally they call our number, and some guy at a desk takes Mom's photo with a little camera; she puts on a big frozen smile and signs some papers. Afterward we go to Half Price Books (I think that's the treat), which is around the corner, but for some reason you still have to get in the car. It feels like everywhere we go in Austin, we end up by the side of some busy road or highway. For a few seconds, when we walk outside, I warm up again, but every time we go inside I start shivering.

Half Price Books is more of a warehouse than a bookstore—the ceiling is made of big square panels. Some of them are missing, and others have been turned into overhead lights. You can hear the hum of the air-conditioning everywhere.

Mom wants to buy a present for Granma, to say thank you for having us. They have a lot of big art books, including a book of photographs about New York. I show it to her, to be funny, and she flips through the pages for a second but gives it back. "That's not really what I had in mind," she says. But she looks at me, too, like, Are you okay? After that, I just wander around—it's a good place to play hide and seek, and I amuse myself trailing after Mom without her knowing it. Eventually I get bored and let her see me. "Oh, there you are," she says, like she's been looking for me, which she hasn't. "Find anything good?" but I shake my head.

There's a comic book section near the checkout, and Mom says, when we're waiting in line, "You like comic books."

A bunch of kids are standing around, laughing and reading one of the stories. They have long shorts and key chains coming out of their pockets and look about fifteen years old.

"What do you mean, I like comic books?" I have to talk quietly, so nobody can hear us, but I hate doing that, because then everybody knows I'm having this embarrassing conversation with my mother.

"You're always asking for comic books."

Sometimes parents get this idea of you, because of something you said like three years ago, which for some reason they keep bringing up. "Jake likes comic books. I think you're thinking of Jake."

"I know the difference between you and Jake."

"Apparently not."

"Tell me you didn't bug Dad for about three weeks to let you buy some issue of *Dead Man Walking* or something like that."

"*The Walking Dead*. And did Dad let me?"

"No. It was like fifty dollars. Maybe they have it here. Go look."

"I know what you're doing," I say, feeling suddenly angry.

"What? What am I doing?"

"You think I'm going to talk to those kids and make *friends*. I'm not going to talk to those kids."

"Calm down, Ben. All I said was, why don't you check out the comic books. I offered to *buy* you something."

But the same thing happens at the swimming pool. About five minutes walk from Granma's house there's a neighborhood pool in the middle of a park, and when we get back from Half Price Books, sweating like pigs in the old Volvo, Mom says, "I could really use a dip." So we put on our swimming things and Mom pulls a dress over her head and we walk down the middle of the road to the park.

The neighborhood around Granma's house is really quiet: all the cars are parked in driveways, and there are these big trees on the sidewalk that arch over the road, so it's not too hot. It's about five o'clock and it's like you can feel the sun over the trees trying to get in.

It's crazy, two days ago I was in New York City, walking down Broadway, and now I'm here.

There are kids at the pool, splashing around, or lying on the grass by the side—even though the grass has ants in it. Some of the boys wear T-shirts even in the water. But I don't see kids on their own. Everybody has somebody to talk to. And I realize that for two days I haven't talked to anybody who isn't Mom or Granma. It's amazing how much noise kids make. You really notice it when you're not part of it. And all the noise sounds different, because of the water, kind of louder and farther away at the same time. Mom jumps in the pool and swims a couple of lengths but then she comes out again and lies on a towel with her sunglasses on.

"I just like feeling myself get dry," she says.

"How long are we going to stay here?" I ask.

"We just got here, Ben. Go swim or something. Find some kids to play with. There are a lot of kids here your age." I think her eyes are closed, though it's hard to tell, under the sunglasses; she sounds sleepy.

"Mom, that's not how it works."

"How does it work?" But she's not really paying attention.

"It just doesn't work—you have to know somebody. Nobody wants to hang out with some weird kid they don't know."

"You're not *that* weird. Give me five minutes," she says, still with her eyes closed. "For about the past two months I've been dreaming of these five minutes."

So I leave her alone and swim a few lengths, even though I'm not a good swimmer. And when I come out again Mom looks like she really *is* asleep. She's just kind of baking in the sun and for some reason I feel sorry for her, or happy for her, or something. So I let her sleep and go for a walk around the park. There's a basketball court and a little kids' playground, with a sandbox and slides, and a small creek or river next to the court, where the water isn't even going anywhere, it's just kind of slimy and covered in reeds. Some grown-ups are playing basketball and talking a lot; it's hard to tell if they're angry or having fun, and I watch them for a while and think about my dad. And then when I come back to the pool, Mom sits up and sort of shakes herself, and says, "All right, Ben. We can go."

The next day Mom buys a car, a secondhand Toyota Corolla. Granma drives us to East Austin, and the guy who sells it to us is a grad student. He looks about twenty-five and has a goatee and an earbud, which seems to be playing something, even when he's talking to us. He just got a job in Boston—he's one of those people who tells you stuff about himself even if you haven't asked.

"I was going to drive it over," he says, "but the truth is, it's not that good a car. It's fine, but for the first time in my life I'm going to be making, like, grown-up money, and so I thought, Buy yourself a grown-up car."

Mom just smiles at him, the way I sometimes see her smile at guys, so maybe they think she's being friendly but really she thinks, You're a jerk. Afterward I have to choose whether to go back in Granma's Volvo or with

Mom, and I'd rather go with Granma but I don't. At least the air-conditioning works in the Toyota, but it makes a clanking noise and the vents drip on your leg if you're sitting in the front seat. The whole car smells like dirty laundry. Mom lets me sit in the front seat. I can tell already that she loves this car.

"I haven't had a car in fifteen years," she says. "We can go anywhere."

It's funny, because in New York she used to argue with Dad about money—she liked expensive things. When she fixed up the kitchen in our apartment she ordered these countertops from Italy, and my dad was like, "I can't actually believe how much this stuff costs." But he let her do it because it was her project and he thought she didn't have enough to do—which doesn't mean they didn't fight about it. One thing I realized is that if you don't say anything, your parents will just argue in front of you because they think you're not really paying attention. But now that we're in Austin she buys this really crappy car from some student and she loves it. I don't get it.

Back at home, Granma says, "You could probably use some wheels as well."

"What do you mean?"

"Let me show you."

And she takes me outside again. It's just starting to get dark, you can see the sun going down behind the trees.

There's a shed by the side of the house that's just full of old bikes. Mom comes out, too, to help me look at them. She gets very nostalgic. "Mostly they're girl bikes, but I had a BMX phase when I was about your age," she says. But they're all in totally unusable condition. The tires are flat, the chains are rusted. They're really dusty, and even Mom says it's pointless; she keeps getting bitten by mosquitoes. My hands are sticky with cobwebs. It's still hot and sweaty outside and when I rub my hand across my forehead, to keep the sweat out, the cobwebs stick in my hair. I feel disgusting. Granma stands in the backyard watching.

"They're perfectly good bikes," she says. "They just need a little fixing up." I guess it makes her sad to realize that this stuff she's been keeping for all these years is just junk; it's not worth anything. Nobody wants it.

I look at Mom, and Mom says, "I think we can afford a new bicycle."

So in the morning, after breakfast, we drive down to this bike shop by a creek or something, next to another busy road, but there's a park opposite. It's one of those shops with a big glass window two stories high. There are hundreds and hundreds of bicycles, all shiny, in different colors and sizes.

Mom says, "Just pick one," but I can't choose. It's, like, what kind of kid am I? Am I the kind of kid who rides this bike or that one? But the truth is, I'm not really any kind of kid, at least, not the bike-riding kind. In New York, I stopped getting bikes for my birthdays when I was, like, seven years old—it was just too much hassle to find a place to put it in the apartment, and wheel it down in the elevator, and cross over at the traffic lights on Central Park West, before I could ride it.

Finally Mom gets fed up and picks a Schwinn Frontier mountain bike for $300. It has a blue frame and big black tires. When we walk out of the shop, I can't tell if I'm happy or annoyed, but Mom says, "It's a bike. Who cares what it looks like. . . . I mean, if this bike isn't covered in dirt inside a week, it's a waste of money. Come on, you should break it in."

And we take it across the road to the park before we go home.

For five minutes I'm just gone—in New York Mom hardly let me walk to the diner, but here, anything goes. It's like even after all those years she was still scared of New York.

There's a concrete path along the creek, covered in pebbles. It curves in and out—it's fun to ride on, it's like riding a wave. Just the noise of being outside is intense, I'm not used to it yet. It's like the heat itself makes a noise, a kind of pulsing noise, as you go in and out of the shade. You have to keep going because it's so hot that if you stop you sort of suffocate, but if you keep pedaling like crazy, the wind cools you down a little, and after five minutes I really have no idea where I am, but it feels great, even if I'm a little worried that Mom is going to be worried, so eventually I turn around and head back. The path is pretty good, but there are cracks in it where you can build up speed and jump, and tree roots growing under it, and sometimes you have to duck under the trees. The leaves are scratchy; the branches or twigs have some kind of green moss growing in all the cracks. There are also a lot of bugs flying around, and by the time I get back to Mom, who doesn't look worried at all but is just sitting on a rock, I'm in a real sweat, and there's salt in my eyes, and dust in my sweat, and my palms are dirty from trying to dry them against my shirt.

"You look happy," she says as I pull up next to her. Then she says, "You don't have to make that face. I didn't mean to spoil it."

*

Right now that's all I really want to do—just ride my bike around the neighborhood. The streets around Granma's house are wide and almost empty; most of the houses have driveways, so there aren't even that many cars parked along the curb. And there are trees along all the sidewalks that spread their branches across the road, so there's plenty of shade.

The asphalt is pretty rough and covered in twigs and pecans, so you can hear your wheels cracking them as you go. On my bike it takes me, like, no time at all to get to the swimming pool, so I can lock it up against the chain-link fence, jump in, just literally kind of stand by the pool for three minutes afterward in the sun, until I'm dry again, and hop back on the bike and head home. Or wherever.

It was my dad who taught me how to ride in New York. My dad is, like, a serious fitness freak and used to go for twenty-mile rides on the weekends, all over New York, along the river, or wherever, which pissed my mom off because she was like, "All week long all you do is go to work, and then the first chance you get, you just head out on your bike. It's like you can't even bear to be around us for more than two or three hours at a time." But he did teach me how to ride in Central Park, first on the Great Lawn, which is this green field in the middle (you can see the Metropolitan Museum on one side, a big wall of glass), and later alongside the reservoir, when I got a little better and stopped falling down.

Sometimes we even went biking together through the park—this was like the one thing we did together where I could tell he was enjoying himself, too. Actually enjoying himself, and not just being patient with me. But he never let me ride on city streets—there was too much traffic.

Even in Central Park he made me stick to the footpaths, like a little kid; he wouldn't let me go on the road. I got bored of my bike, and after a while it didn't fit me anymore, I was too big, and I didn't get another. Until now. But I remember how Dad used to bug me to go riding with him on the weekends, and then gave up asking me, because I kept saying no. I don't know why, maybe I was taking Mom's side, because we'd hang around at home together, making pancakes or something, while he went off by himself.

SEVEN

A FEW NIGHTS LATER, Mom wakes me up, coming in late and getting undressed. (She was sitting on the porch with Granma, drinking wine and talking. I could hear them as I lay in bed. Somebody mentioned Spencer—that's my dad's name. It feels funny to think of him like that, like he's some guy with a name. Mom always calls him "your dad" to me. But I couldn't hear much else; they had the radio on, too.) At first, I don't say anything, but then she switches on a flashlight and starts reading a book under the covers.

"Mom," I say. "Mom."

She looks over at me. I can see her face in the glow. "Go to sleep."

"I *was* sleeping. You woke me up."

"I'm sorry, honey."

She turns off the flashlight, and we lie there for a minute. "How long are we going to stay here?" I ask.

"What do you mean?"

"I mean, when we are going to . . . get a place of our own?"

"I told you already," she says. "This is something we talked about. Right now, I'm looking for a job, and with Granma around, it's just easier."

"You said this was temporary, until we get our own place. That's what you said."

"I don't remember saying that. I probably said a lot of things. You may have noticed, I'm kind of making it up as I go along. Don't you like it here?" she asks.

"It's fine but that's not the point. I feel like . . . there's stuff going on that you're talking to Granma about, but you're not talking to me. I'm almost thirteen years old. You let me bike around by myself. I can go to the stores, I mean. . . . You don't have to treat me like a baby."

"Nobody's treating you—"

"Yes, you are," I say.

"Ben, this isn't just about you. And I like being here. This is a hard time for me, and it's a big help . . . everything's a lot easier for me with Granma around. I don't really understand what's going on. She loves you."

"Of course she loves me, she's my grandmother. She doesn't have a choice."

"That's not how she feels about it," Mom says.

"It's just . . ." I don't know how to explain what I'm thinking without being rude. "It's kind of weird. . . ."

"What's weird? I hate to break it to you, Ben, but what we're going through, a lot of people go through. What's happening to you . . . is not . . ."

"That's not what I mean." But I can't say what I *do* mean, which is that Granma's swollen hand makes me feel weird, and that I don't always like eating her food, because . . . her house doesn't always seem that clean to me. She doesn't have a dishwasher and so we have to wash all the dishes ourselves, and Granma usually does it, and this isn't the kind of thing she cares about very much. Sometimes when I eat breakfast I notice bits of dried cereal on the cereal bowl. That kind of thing. Back in New York, Maria kept everything spotless. But that's not really what matters, that's not what I want to talk about. Finally I say, "I miss you. I miss it . . . when it was just you and me back in New York."

"It's still you and me." I can tell she's upset: she's sitting up in bed, and I can see her pulling her knees against her chest and holding them.

"No it's not, it's you and Granma. You don't even make dinner anymore. I miss your food."

"Forgive me, Ben. You sound a little spoiled right now." Her voice is colder; she's talking the way I sometimes hear her talk with her girlfriends, when she disagrees with them. "Don't you like Granma's cooking?"

"Of course I do. Just forget about it. I'm sorry."

"I've got a lot going on right now, too. I need all the help I can get."

"I know, I'm sorry. I'm just a spoiled kid."

"You're not a spoiled kid, you're my beautiful . . ."

"I know you love me, Mom. Don't worry about me. I'm fine."

I think maybe the conversation is finished, so I roll over in bed, with my back to her; it's easier for me to sleep that way, facing the wall. A few minutes go by, I can hear her breathing. But then she asks, "Do you miss Dad?"

I don't want to hurt her feelings, but I can't tell what she wants me to say. Also, I want to tell the truth. "I don't know."

"It's okay to miss him."

"Of course it's okay."

Now I guess *I* sound a little bit mad, but I don't know how to say anything so it sounds normal. We don't speak for a while; I can't get back to sleep. It feels weird, lying there like that—I don't think Mom's asleep either, and eventually I turn around again. "Do *you* miss Dad?" I ask her, and she gets out of her bed and comes into mine. She creeps under the blanket.

"How could I miss Daddy when I've got you?" she says.

"Do you think he misses us?" I can smell the shampoo in her hair and the wine on her breath.

"I think he misses *you*," Mom says.

"If he misses me so much, why did he go to London?"

"That's got nothing to do with you."

"That's what I mean."

"I mean, he wanted you to come, too—you know that, right? He wanted you to come along. But I wouldn't let you. I said, you're mine, all mine," and she gives me a hug. We lie like this for a few minutes until she kisses me on the head and gets up. I feel embarrassed—it's like I'm too big for her to share a bed with now. Like I was asking her to comfort me, so she did, but that's not really what I was asking. I wanted to know what's really going on, what she thinks about Dad and what Dad thinks about her, and what's going to happen next year—the kind of stuff she was talking about with Granma.

*

One thing I like about Austin is Granma's backyard. In New York, it took us about five minutes just to exit the building, but here I can walk right out of the kitchen and be outside.

There's a big bamboo hedge between Granma's garden and the next-door neighbors'. It's kind of scratchy inside; last year's leaves are still lying on the ground, and the bamboo stalks grow in all kinds of directions, so you have to fight your way through. Eventually I come up against an old fence, which is partly broken but must have been put there before the bamboo got so tall. I can see through the mesh into the neighbors' backyard; a flat dodgeball has been left against their side of the fence, and when I look up, I see a trampoline—one of these big ones. It must have been there awhile, because the grass underneath it has turned to dirt.

I push my way out again and start to explore. There isn't much to look at even though Granma's yard is pretty big. Just an old sycamore tree at the back, with a bit of rope dangling off a branch, like maybe it used to be a swing. There's a garden shed, too, with all kinds of stuff inside, not just bikes and gardening tools but things Granma doesn't need anymore but doesn't want to throw out. Like a floor lamp with a dusty paper shade and an

95

old rusty saw hanging from a nail in the wall. I also find cardboard boxes full of newspapers, a leather armchair with foam coming out of the seat, and a bucket of tennis balls.

If I stand on the leather chair, I can reach the saw. It's still pretty sharp, and I wander outside again and squeeze into the bamboo hedge. If I cut down a few stalks, I can make a den, but it's hard work—they break into these tough little strands, and at the end you always have to kick against the stump to break it off, and then pull it, while a strip of the bamboo peels away. But I make a nice little clearing, just big enough for me and maybe one other person. When I'm sitting inside there, nobody can really see me.

Mom comes out after a while. She has a towel in her hand—she's wearing a swimsuit. Granma follows her, in a baseball cap, to keep the sun out of her eyes. It's starting to get pretty hot, and I can see bits of dust floating in the light between the bamboo leaves.

"Where's Ben?" Mom asks.

Granma takes a folding chair from the back porch and starts setting it up in the grass.

"Maybe he's on his bike somewhere."

"Did he tell you he was going out?"

"I don't remember. He asked to be excused from the breakfast table."

"That's not the same thing. Do you think I should look for him?"

"He's probably in his room or in the bathroom. Don't worry about him. He's fine."

But Mom gets up anyway (she was lying on her towel in the grass) and goes to the shed. Then she lies down again.

"His bike is still there."

"You worry too much, Jenny."

"He's not the happy-go-lucky kid he looks like. He tells me things he doesn't tell you."

"He doesn't look like a happy-go-lucky kid."

"That's why I worry. We had a fight last night."

"What about?"

But Mom doesn't say anything for a while. Then she says, "Nothing much. Just what you'd expect. It wasn't really a fight."

The lawn looks very bright from where I'm sitting, and Mom and Granma are partly hidden by the bamboo leaves. But I can see them, too. Granma pushes herself up out of the lawn chair, and for a second I think she's going into the house, maybe to check on me, but she stops at the back door and bends down. Then she straightens up and starts moving slowly around the patio. I can see a hose in her hands—she's watering her flowerpots, and when Mom says something to her, Granma says, "You have to speak up. I can't hear you."

"I talked to that woman at the middle school today."

"What'd she say?"

"Looks like I have a job."

Granma keeps watering the flowers—she gives every pot a good soak. After a minute, she turns off the hose and walks slowly back to her lawn chair. Mom sits up in the grass.

"Aren't you going to say something?"

"Are you sure you're ready to go back to work?"

"I meant something like, congratulations." Mom laughs.

"I'm happy for you, Jenny. Of course I am. I just worry about Ben."

"He'll be in school anyway."

Mom lies down again; she puts her sunglasses back on. I'm sitting very still now because I feel like if I even move an inch, somebody will hear me. There are a lot of old bamboo leaves on the ground. It's very dry; everything rustles.

"Kids get embarrassed by that kind of thing," Granma says.

"What kind of thing?"

"Going to school where their mom works."

"Well, at least I can keep an eye on him. Anyway," she

adds, after a minute, "I'm only part-time. He'll hardly know I'm there."

There's a noise behind me, and I turn around slowly. Somebody's jumping on the trampoline—it makes a sound like a rattle, but there's also a kind of twangy noise, like picking a guitar. It's a girl with short yellow hair. She's wearing jeans but nothing on her feet, which even from where I'm sitting look dirty. It's kind of hyp-notizing, watching her go up and down—she goes pretty high. But then someone calls out, "Lunchtime!" and for a second I think it's my mom, but it's not. She's still lying in the grass, but she sits up now and says, "Seriously, where's Ben?"

"I don't know," Granma tells her, getting up. She sounds a little worried now, too.

"Ben!" Mom calls out.

Granma goes in the house and comes back out again. "He's not in his room," she says. "He's not in the bath-room."

"Ben!" Mom calls again. For a minute, they both go in the house—I can hear them calling my name, a little fainter now, and sometimes louder. I don't know why I don't say anything, I just don't. Then Mom walks into the garden again, wearing shoes and a button-up shirt over her swimsuit. She goes to the shed to get out a bike, but she's still shouting my name. The girl on the trampoline next door has gone inside, and I step out of the bamboo hedge.

"Jesus, Ben," Mom says. She lets go of the bike, which falls down on the grass. "Where the heck were you? You scared the daylights out of me."

"Just here," I say. There are bamboo leaves in my hair, and my face feels dusty with dirt.

"What were you doing in there?" Mom says, and Granma comes out again. "He's here, he's here," Mom tells her. "He was hiding in the bamboo."

"I wasn't hiding!"

"Then what were you doing?"

"Nothing."

"How long were you there for?" Mom asks.

"I don't know. I was just . . . making a den," and I show her the saw.

"Jesus, Ben," Mom says again, and then sort of hangs her head. "Calm down, everybody's okay." She's talking to herself, and laughs. "Give me that for starters," she tells me, and takes the saw away. "Where'd you find that?"

"In Granma's shed."

"It's fine, Jenny. He's fine," Granma says. She's standing on the back porch, holding the screen door in her hands. "Come on in, it's lunchtime anyway."

But as we walk inside, Mom turns to me again. "How long were you sitting there?" she asks quietly.

"I don't know. A while. All morning." But she doesn't have time to respond before Granma tells me to wash my hands before sitting down to eat.

After that, I start hanging out in the den. Granma lets me take cups and plates out there, and even a little dingy rug from the front porch. I lay it on top of the old dead leaves, for something to sit on. Sometimes I take a book out there. It's a good place to read—the bamboo stalks make tiger stripes of sunshine and shade. Nobody bothers me. That's the funny thing about being on your own. Even though I get bored after a while, I don't really like it when people . . . interrupt me, even though I'm not really doing anything important.

Sometimes the girl with yellow hair comes out to the trampoline, and I wait around to see if she'll come. A whole morning might go by and I don't see her, but then another time she'll jump for hours, just going up and down and not even looking happy or sad, but just jumping.

I miss Jake. When he was around, I didn't notice the way time passes. But now every day seems long.

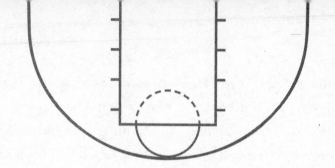

EIGHT

DAD CALLS the night before school starts. It's the third
week in August and still incredibly hot. Even at night you
just want to take your shirt off; even your skin is like too
much to wear, it's so hot. Everybody's in a bad mood, and
even before I get to the phone, Mom is shouting at him.

"You said you'd call yesterday," she says. "I don't care
what's going on at work. I need to know when . . . We
have to prepare ourselves for these conversations. There
are consequences, right? I'm the one who has to pick him
up off the ground afterward. This is like the last thing he
needs right now. Why? Because he's got school tomorrow.

It's his first day. He's anxious enough about that as it is. . . ."

I'm sitting in the kitchen with Granma, and she looks at me, raising her eyebrows. "I guess that's Dad on the phone," I say, and she sort of laughs. Eventually Mom calls me into the hall.

"It's your father," she says, passing me the phone.

"Hey, kid," says the voice in my ear.

"Hey, Dad." All I can see is the front door, and my shoes on the mat, and Granma's sun hat on a hook. It's dark outside, but there's a light on the front porch that shows the driveway. The front door has a kind of window in it; sometimes the sprinkler sends a whip of water against the glass. It's funny to think that somewhere a few thousand miles away, my dad actually exists. He's sitting in a room somewhere, he's about to go to bed.

"I'm sorry about yesterday," he says. "I was stuck in the office. When I told your mother I was hoping to call, I didn't realize you'd spend all day sitting by the phone. . . ."

"Honestly, it's fine. It's not a big deal. I didn't even know you were supposed to call."

"Well, that's not what your mother says." After a pause, he says, "Let's start this over. Are you nervous about school tomorrow?"

"I don't want to go. Is that the same as being nervous?"

He laughs.

"When will I see you again?" I say. There's a silence on the other end. I don't want to break it, but it goes on long enough that I can't help myself. "I know you're busy. You've got a lot of work."

"It's true," he says. "And Texas is a long way—it's farther than New York. But we've got an office in Houston, which gives me an excuse. I'm hoping to come out after Christmas for a couple of days. . . . I've talked to your mother about this, too. I don't think Christmas itself would be a good idea. Your life is confusing enough as it is. But maybe we can take a little trip. I don't know, just you and me. That's the plan, at least—that's what I'm hoping for."

"Okay," I say. What else can I say? It's not up to me.

"Pass me to your mother again," he says, before hanging up. "I want to exchange some civil words. And, Ben?" He waits for me to say something, but I'm just listening—I don't know that I can talk anymore. It's like a kind of staring competition; this time I win. "Good luck at school," he says eventually. "It's never as bad as you think it's going to be."

Mom drives me to school on the first day, but on the way, she says, "Tomorrow, you have to take the bus, like everyone else. I don't want you to be one of those weird kids who comes to work with Mommy."

A week ago, she finally told me herself what was going on. She didn't know I'd overheard her and Granma talking. "I found a job," she'd said. "That's what I've been doing all summer, looking for work. I'll be teaching social studies at your school. Just part-time."

"But you haven't taught in years."

"Teaching is one of those careers where people are always leaving or starting over." She looked at me; for some reason, she seemed emotional. "This is a big deal for me. I haven't worked in fifteen years. I need to hear you say that it's okay, that you don't mind."

"Of course it's okay," I told her.

I guess it's Mom's first day of school today, too. Which is why she's all dressed up—she wears a skirt and a blouse, and I can smell her perfume in the car. She looks like a teacher now, like some woman you don't really know, who talks to you in a friendly way but like a stranger.

For the rest of the twenty-minute ride, we don't say much, until we pull up at the school. It's more like a campus; there's a parking lot and the grounds are huge and covered in fresh-cut grass, like a park. My old school in New York always seemed pretty big to me, but it was nothing like this. The building looks like it was just finished, like it's a Lego model of a building instead of the real thing. It's got white bricks with red around the edges, and there's a big chunky archway you have to walk through to get inside. There are shiny tiles in the hallways, and everything echoes. It feels like there are thousands of kids. That's the other thing: the kids in my New York school were pretty rich, but there was a uniform so we all dressed the same. Here people wear whatever they want, except shorts, which seems dumb, because it's like . . . a hundred degrees out. I hear some kids speaking Spanish in the hallways. Everybody seems to know where they're going.

Mom takes me into the main office to introduce me. There's a woman at the reception desk, talking on the phone, but she smiles at me. Somebody is watering a plant on a filing cabinet. Mom tells me their names, but I can't remember them—it's all a blur. She says, "Where's your homeroom?" and I stare at my schedule, which is printed on a piece of paper. None of it makes sense to me. The rooms are just numbers, but the man with the watering can points me in the right direction, and Mom says, "Good luck, Ben," then changes her mind and gives me a quick hug. After that I'm on my own.

In homeroom, the first thing we do is get our locker numbers. There are long rows of metal cupboards in the hallways, painted blue. Most of the kids have brought combination locks with them; and after the bell rings, they troop along to find their lockers and get set up. But I don't have a lock, and anyway, I don't really see the point. It's just another reason to get lost.

My schedule is weird—classes seem to end at weird times, like 9:27. Then the bell rings and you have to find the next class. Just to get from one place to another you have to dodge all this traffic. I keep checking my schedule, then stuffing it back into my pocket, so the paper gets all crumpled up. Then I forget which pocket I put it in. It's like that all morning. At the beginning of every class we say our names, but I can't remember anybody. Teachers assign seats, but I know I'll forget those, too. At least once you're sitting down, it's, like, okay . . . for the next half hour, I know I'm in the right place.

By lunchtime, I'm totally exhausted. Mom comes and finds me. She's wearing a badge on her blouse now that says MRS. MICHAELS. There are picnic benches outside the cafeteria, in the shade of a big old pecan tree. Granma has packed lunches for both of us, and we walk outside.

I unwrap my peanut butter and jelly sandwich. The pecan tree drops nuts and twigs and leaves onto the concrete, which has little pebbles in it, so bits of nuts and leaves get stuck in between. I keep looking at the ground.

Mom says, "I forgot how cold it gets in the

air-conditioning. Tomorrow I'm definitely going to bring a sweater."

A few kids stop by and say, "Hello, Mrs. Michaels." It's the first time I've heard anyone call her that since we left New York.

"I want you to meet my son, Ben," she tells them. "He's new here. He's in the seventh grade. Keep an eye out for him, will you?"

Everybody has to pretend to be nice because I'm the teacher's son, but really . . . I mean, nobody wants to talk to me.

When they've gone, I ask Mom: "How come people still call you Mrs. Michaels? That's Dad's name."

"It's still my name, too."

"But it doesn't make sense. I thought you wanted a divorce."

Mom brushes crumbs off the picnic table. I can tell she's thinking about what to say. "I don't know what I want. But I've had this name for a long time now. You get used to it."

"I don't get it."

Instead of answering, Mom stands up and smooths out her skirt. She takes a mirror from her purse and checks her makeup. In school, even though she tries to be nice to me, she's kind of different—she's not totally Mom, she's also someone else. I can tell she's nervous, too, or busy, or distracted.

After lunch, kids wander off to their lockers, but it seems like a waste of time to me. Maybe they just want to stand around and talk or something. I don't have anyone to talk to anyway, so I just grab my backpack and go.

But it's getting pretty heavy by this point: we have quite a few books. That's mostly what we seem to be doing today, getting textbooks, and some of them are as big as shoe boxes. Social studies is the worst—the textbook weighs about five pounds, and I can't even fit it into my backpack anymore. I have to carry it in my arms.

There's only one more class to get through—English. I feel like I've run a marathon or something, or stayed too long in the pool, and I'm all kind of shrunk and worn-out. Everything echoes in my head. On the way to the classroom, somebody says, "I guess you know this already, but you can put some of that stuff in your locker."

It's the girl from next door, the girl with the yellow hair. My heart jumps—it's the first time somebody has talked to me all day. I mean, somebody who isn't a teacher. She's shorter than she seemed on the trampoline. I'm used to being one of the smallest kids in class, but I can look her in the eye.

"I didn't bring a lock."

"Well, you're going to hurt your back carrying all that stuff."

"It's not too bad. I don't really mind."

She shrugs. "Suit yourself." But she's still walking with me. "I'm Mabley, by the way. It's kind of a dumb name, but I guess I'm stuck with it." She says "I guess" a lot, but she also seems pretty sure of herself.

"I'm Ben." But I don't mention that we're next-door neighbors.

After school, I wait for Mom in the parking lot by the car. She's a little late coming out, and when she sees me, she says, "You look like I feel."

"What do you mean?"

"Tired," she says, putting down her purse on the hood of the Toyota, and another bag, and her bottle of water, and trying to find her keys. "Go on, say it."

"Say what?"

"Do I have to go back there tomorrow?"

She opens the car and we get in—it's nice to be able to shut the door on everything. She feels like my mom again; it's just the two of us.

"Do I have to go back there tomorrow?" I ask.

"You and me both, kid," she says.

The school bus leaves at seven o'clock the next morning, so Granma wakes me at six. "I don't mind getting up," she says. "It's the only cool hour in the day."

It's funny because Mom is in bed on the other side of the room. She groans and rolls over, like a kid. "I don't want to get up," she says, and Granma gives me a look. Like we're the sensible ones.

We have breakfast together while Mom showers and puts on her "work clothes"—a skirt and tights and polished shoes. After that, she's like a different person. She tries to act normal, but it's a bit like a teacher trying to act normal: you can tell they're pretending or thinking about something else.

Granma sees me carrying textbooks under my arm.

"Didn't they give you a locker?" she asks.

"I didn't have a lock."

"That's something we can fix right now," she says, and goes to what she calls the "everything cupboard" in the hallway—it's where she keeps nails and light bulbs and restaurant match books, stuff like that. "Aha," she says, and holds up an old combination lock, the kind you use on a bicycle chain.

"I bet you don't know the combination," I tell her.

"Are you doubting me, Ben Michaels?" She smiles. "It's here somewhere."

But it's true, she can't find the number—usually she writes them on a yellow Post-it note, and she starts poking through an old coffee can full of scraps of paper.

"It's fine, Granma. I don't really mind carrying my books around."

"Don't be silly," she says, still rummaging through the cupboard. "Kids'll make fun of you otherwise. The lockers are where everybody hangs out—I remember that much."

"Really, Granma." I touch her on the shoulder, to make her turn around. "I don't want a locker. It stresses me out, getting to class on time anyway. This way I can't forget anything."

Finally she stops and gives me the once-over—she looks at me for about half a minute. "At least take this," she says, and hands me an old canvas satchel from the cupboard. It's kind of a cool bag; it's got pockets and flaps on the front, and little slots for pens, and a leather buckle. I put my math book inside.

Mom walks me to the bus stop. The sun is just coming up as we leave the house; there's still a kind of mistiness or grayness in the air, but even while we wait for the bus to come, you can feel the day getting hot.

My stop is at the intersection of a big road with a lot of traffic and a quiet road shaded by tall trees. Kids start showing up, mostly too tired to talk. There's a house on the corner, with a metal fence in front, a sprinkler in the grass, and a newspaper lying on the front path in a wet bag. I wonder who lives there and wander over to look at it. They've got an old refrigerator on the front porch, and a couple of armchairs and a wooden coffee table, like it's an inside room—a kitchen or a living room. If I stare at the house, nobody will talk to me, which is what I want.

Somebody says, "Good morning, Mrs. Michaels," and Mom says, "Morning, Mabley. Do you know my son?"

"We met already," Mabley says. "He likes to carry his books around."

Mom gives me a look.

A few minutes later, she kisses me on top of my head, before walking back to Granma's house. Her job is only part-time so she doesn't have to drive in till third period.

"It's not really fair," she says to me quietly. "You have to work harder than I do."

"I don't mind."

I want her to go so I can get on the bus next to Mabley and maybe sit next to her. If I stand in the right position on the sidewalk, we might end up in line together when the bus arrives. Then we can share one of the bench seats. But it's embarrassing, trying to talk to her when Mom's around.

After she's gone, Mabley says, "You're that kid I see in the bamboo bushes all the time. I can never tell what you're doing in there."

"Nothing much," I say.

"Sometimes I think you're watching me."

"I just like it in there." I can't tell if I'm blushing. "Everybody leaves me alone."

"Okay," Mabley says. Maybe she thinks I'm being rude. When the bus arrives, she gets in after me and sits down a few rows behind me. I stare out the window at the road—it's funny how you can get used to anything. Even another day of school.

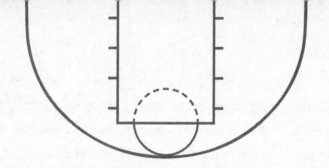

NINE

IT'S RAINING at lunchtime. A kind of hot, heavy rain that goes straight down. Mom told me this morning that she couldn't see me for lunch—she had a meeting—so I stare out the windows of the hall doors for a minute, wondering if I should eat outside anyway—there's a picnic bench under part of the roof. But it looks pretty dreary outside. The rain is coming down hard enough that it splashes off the concrete when it lands.

Inside, the electric lights look different: they look too bright for some reason, like they have to work harder because there isn't any sunshine coming in. In the end, there's nothing I can do but face the cafeteria, hundreds of kids sitting around and eating, talking at the same time. At least I don't have to wait in line, I've got my lunch in Granma's satchel. Mabley sees me just kind of standing there in all the noise, looking for an empty seat. One of the kids at her table gets up to bus his tray, and she calls over to me, "Hey, Ben. You can sit with us."

The tables are these big round plastic tables and have room for about six or seven people; Mabley introduces me. There's a boy named Pete Miller, who I recognize from one of my classes. When he sees me, he says, "It's the bag man."

Mabley frowns at him. "What are you talking about?"

"Look at him," Pete says. "He's got all these bags. Everybody has to watch out when he sits down; they kind of duck under their desks. He's like swinging these bags left and right. He's a menace."

"Peter Miller, you talk a lot of nonsense. Sit down, Ben. Don't listen to him."

"I'm telling you," Pete says. "He's a danger to society. It's like bags are his superhero weapon. They call him Bagman."

"I don't like lockers," I say, feeling stupid.

"Lockers are like kryptonite to Bagman," Pete says.

"Peter Miller, stop it," Mabley tells him, but you can tell they're friends.

"I'm just messing with him," Pete says, and looks at me. "You don't mind, right? What's your name?"

"Ben."

"Ben doesn't mind," he says.

But that's what it's like all lunch. There are other kids at the table, including a boy called Jeff who wears his outdoor jacket inside. He gets pack lunches, too, and his mom always gives him a bag of Goldfish crackers. Sometimes he takes a handful and puts them in the pages of an open textbook. Then he smashes the book shut and pours the cracker dust into his mouth. It's kind of disgusting. Mabley seems to collect these people; they all seem to know each other from the school marching band. Jeff plays the snare drum, and there's a girl named Natasha who puts her tuba on the seat next to her and pretends to give it lunch. Mabley plays tenor sax. But mostly what they talk about is normal stuff, like teachers and tryouts. Pete keeps coming up with new superhero names for me. Like Mr. Two Bags or Backpackman.

"Don't listen to him," Mabley says. "Peter's just a jock. This is how jocks talk to each other—they don't know any better. This is how they try to make friends."

I look over at Pete. He has freckles and the kind of hair that comes out over his forehead and you can't quite tell how it stays in place. For some reason, even though I don't like him, he reminds me of Jake. They are both the kind of kid who thinks that if something seems funny to them that means everybody else is having a good time, too.

After school, I catch the bus home. Some kids walk, but not many; others get rides. It's stopped raining by this point, but the grass is still wet and the sidewalks are still dark. The ground sort of steams up; the sun looks hazy. There are kids everywhere, standing in different groups, talking. All these buses come and go and I look out for Mabley, because I don't know which bus is mine.

When it comes, we sit together on one of the bench seats. "Your friends seem nice," I say, just to say something, and she kind of laughs.

"Don't worry about Peter, he just likes playing the clown. He's a good kid," she says, like she's older than he is. For some reason, I feel jealous of him. I feel jealous of Mabley, too. She acts like she's known him for years, which I guess she has.

The bus ride lasts twenty minutes, and we get off just over the road from where it picks us up. Then we cross the street and walk home together. We pass the house with the refrigerator on the front porch, and I point it out to Mabley. "Wouldn't it be great?" I say. "I want to have refrigerators everywhere. That way you can always get a cold Coke or a bowl of ice cream."

"I want a refrigerator in my bedroom."

"I want a TV in my bedroom."

"My parents have a TV in their bedroom," Mabley says. "They used to let me watch cartoons with them on Saturday morning. But now Dad says I'm too grown-up."

There are twigs and leaves all over the road because of the rainstorm, and I kind of kick them along as I walk. Water is still running along the curbs and making noise as it goes down the drains.

"I share a bedroom with my mom," I say.

"Oh really?" But I think Mabley feels embarrassed, because she doesn't say anything else.

"I don't think she'd let me watch TV in bed," I say. "She won't even let me have a phone."

"Phones are bad for you."

"That's what my mom says."

"They suck out your brains and turn you into a zombie. I've seen it happen."

"You sound just like my mom," I say.

Then we're at Granma's house, and Mabley kind of looks at me, like, See you tomorrow, and walks up her own front steps. Mom's Toyota isn't back yet—it's just Granma's Volvo in the driveway. When I get inside, Granma is messing around in the kitchen and puts a plate of waffles on the table for me. "How was your second day of school?" she says.

"Fine," I say.

*

Mabley is one of those kids who seems to know every-body. She's always friendly, even early in the morning; people like her. And she's good at noticing stuff. If some-body has a new haircut, she notices right away and says something like, "You look nice today, Colleen. You had a haircut. They did a nice job." She says this kind of thing to the boys, too. She doesn't care who she sits next to.

Some days, I think we're becoming friends. She says hi to me in the morning, and we get in line for the bus together and share one of the bench seats on the way to school. But then at other times, she talks to somebody else, kids I don't know. She's really the only one I talk to.

I've started catching the bus by myself. Mom likes to drive in early. "Just to get my head on straight," she says, "before the chaos begins." I always check for Mabley when I walk up the road to the bus stop. There's usually a handful of tired-looking kids standing around with back-packs at their feet. One day she isn't there, and I wander over to look at the house with the refrigerator on the front porch, when somebody grabs me from behind.

"Pinch, punch, first day of the month," she says. It's Mabley.

I stare at her.

"It's the first of September. My great-aunt taught it to me—she was born in Wales. I'm named after her, even though she spells it different."

"I don't understand."

"Here's what you're supposed to do back." She pretends to hit me, then kind of scuffs one of her sneakers against the back of my leg. "A slap and a kick, for being so quick. Unless they say no returns."

"I really have no idea what you're talking about."

She smiles; she's in a funny kind of mood. I mean, she has a lot of energy, she wants to make me laugh, but it's also like she's bored and she just wants something to happen, she wants a reaction. Maybe I disappointed her, because she says in her normal voice, "It's just a silly thing. It basically means good morning."

"Good morning to you, too."

The bus comes, and we file on. Mabley's behind me, but the seat next to me is empty, and she sits down.

"I don't even know my great-aunt," I say, because she isn't talking. "I don't even know if I have one."

"Mine died last year. She lived in San Antonio."

"I'm sorry."

"It's fine. She was crazy. She drove my dad nuts, but she liked me."

For a while we don't say anything—it's only seven thirty in the morning. My brain is still half asleep. Then Mabley says, "How old are you?"

"Twelve. Why?"

"I don't know. You just seem young for seventh grade. Young and innocent."

"My birthday's around Easter . . . so I don't usually get a big party."

"Why not?"

"Because everybody goes away for spring break. We used to go away, too."

"That sucks," she says, and I think the conversation's over, but after a minute she says, "What school did you go to before?"

"It's called Latymer. It's in New York." And suddenly I remember waiting for the elevator in the morning and sometimes meeting Jake on the way to school. It seems like years ago.

"*I* want to go to New York," Mabley says. "I've never been."

"My dad lives in London. They've got a . . . there's a school there, just for Americans. It's right by where the Beatles . . . there's an album where you can see them crossing the street. It's like a famous place to cross the street," and I hear her laugh, and want to keep talking. But I can't think of anything else to say, so I just say, "That's where I want to go."

She says, "Everybody wants to go somewhere."

The bus isn't air-conditioned, and already the leather

seats feel sticky to sit on. We stare out the window for a while and then she asks, "When did your parents get divorced?"

"They're not divorced."

"I'm sorry," she says. "I'm not trying to be . . . it's just that you said once you shared a bedroom with your mom, and I felt bad about not saying anything. I usually try to say something when people tell me stuff."

"I don't know what they are. . . . My dad just moved to London, and my mom didn't want to go. She's from Texas. I guess she wanted to come back home. We're just living with my granma until we get our own place."

"It must be nice to see your granma," Mabley says.

"It's all right."

I can always tell we're getting near the school because the bus goes under a highway. Even with the windows closed you can hear the traffic rumbling overhead.

After the highway, the streets seem to change. There's a lot of building going on, brand-new houses with big windows and metal towers and brightly colored walls. But there are also some older houses, where the paint is peeling, and the porch is filled with stuff like sofas and boxes and just . . . stuff. One house has a big front yard with cars on the grass. There are tires lying around and other car parts. Sometimes you see people messing around in the yard or sitting on the porch, drinking soda.

I don't want the bus to arrive—I just want to keep sitting there with Mabley and looking out the window. Because as soon as we pull up to the school, I'll have to get out and join all the other kids going to school and sit in classes for the rest of the day with everybody else.

Pete Miller's in my math class. We sit next to each other at the back, but even though we have lunch together every day, Pete doesn't really talk to me unless Mabley is around. When the bell rings, it takes me a while to get my bags together, and Pete always walks out with other kids. But I don't really mind. It's fine with me if people leave me alone.

Our teacher is Ms. Kaminski. She's a bony, friendly woman who wears thick glasses and a lot of bracelets and necklaces. Every day, at the beginning of class, she actually gets an apple out of her bag and puts it on her desk, like a teacher in a TV show. She likes trying different kinds of apples, and sometimes you can get her to waste a few minutes at the beginning of class by asking her what kind of apple she has today. They have all kinds of funny names, like Envy or Gala or Pink Lady. She says the study of apples is called pomology. She buys them in Central Market, which is a big supermarket that Granma sometimes goes to.

But today she has a different announcement to make. "There's going to be a citywide Number Sense competition. For those of you who don't know, it's basically like doing your multiplication tables but just with bigger numbers. We need three kids from the school to enter, which means that for the next few weeks, a few minutes before the bell rings every day, we'll be doing practice tests. Think of it as the math tryouts," she says, looking at Pete.

Pete's on the basketball team. Last year, he was the only sixth grader to start, and this year he's probably going to be captain. There was a big article on him in the school newspaper, with a picture of him shooting a basketball, when they announced the teams—the tryouts were last week. Everybody seems to know his name. Even some of the teachers come up to him at lunch to talk about basketball. But I think I can beat him at Number Sense. Math is probably my favorite subject.

I used to practice the times tables with my dad. That's one of the things we did together. On most nights, when I was little, Dad got home from work after I was already asleep. Sometimes he came into my bedroom anyway and woke me up. I could feel him sitting next to me.

"Hey, Shorty," he would say.

"Hey, Dad."

"Sorry to wake you up." He'd put his hand on my

back and give me a tickle under my T-shirt. Sometimes I thought he didn't really know what to talk to me about. We'd sit like that for a few minutes. Then he'd suddenly say, "Six times eight."

"Forty-eight."

"Eleven times twelve."

"One hundred thirty-two."

"Fifteen squared."

"Two twenty-five."

It made him happy if I got the answers right. Afterward, Dad would push himself up on his knees, sounding tired. "That's what I do all day," he liked to say. "Play around with numbers. All right, Son. I think we both need to get some sleep. Good night."

For the rest of the period, even when we're talking about other things, I think about the Number Sense competition. I really want to win. With five minutes left, Ms. Kaminski tells us to put our books away. All we need is a pencil and a piece of paper. "I'm going to read out a few questions in a row, and you have to write down the answers as quickly as you can. *Without making notes*—that's important. I'll be walking up and down the aisles just to make sure that nobody cheats."

My heart has already started beating faster, even though I tell myself, Don't be silly, this is just a practice test. Nobody cares, it doesn't matter. My brain has gone blank, but sometimes that's a good thing—it's like wiping the blackboard clean before you start.

Ms. Kaminski reads out the first question: 23 times 27. And suddenly I feel happy, because I know the trick—my dad taught it to me. If the tens digits are the same, and the unit numbers add up to ten, there's a shortcut you can take. You just add one to the first tens digit, and multiply it by the other, then you multiply the unit digits together, and that's your answer. It sounds complicated, but actually it's pretty simple. My dad showed me why it works, but I can't remember the proof. That doesn't matter because it works anyway, you don't have to know why. Three times two is six, and three times seven is twenty-one, so the answer is six hundred and twenty-one.

After that, it all seems pretty easy. I just have to stay in the zone. It's like my brain is better at this stuff than I am, so long as I get out of the way. At the end of the test, Ms. Kaminski goes over the questions one by one. She expects us to call out the answers, but I don't like showing off. Sometimes I raise my hand, but by that point some other kid has probably beaten me to it. Pete is one of them, he keeps shouting the answers and getting them right, and then I realize that he's been looking at my paper the whole time and calling out whatever I've written down.

This is how I know, because I finally slide a textbook over my answer sheet, and he sort of smiles at me, like, *gotcha*. I mean, like you do when you've been playing a trick on somebody and they finally realize it. And when you don't react, or at least, not the way they want you to, it's like you're the weird one because you don't think it's funny.

The last question of the day is a bonus question: 99 x 91.

"Anybody know this one?" Ms. Kaminski asks.

I like her, but she isn't the kind of teacher who understands the kids very well. She always seems to be nice to the wrong ones. "All right, Pete," she says at last, when nobody answers. "Go ahead."

"I think we should let somebody else have a chance," Pete tells her.

I put my hand up, and Ms. Kaminski finally notices me.

"Yes, Ben?" she says.

"Nine thousand and nine."

"That's right," she says. "I'm impressed. Where'd you learn how to do that?"

"There's a trick," I tell her. "My dad showed me."

Ms. Kaminski is standing in front of her desk, with her hands behind her back. She has a way of standing with her feet together, like a ballerina, totally still. And she uses her voice like she's acting in a play—she says everything very clearly, like it was written down some-where, and she's trying to project her voice to the back of the room.

"Do you want to explain it to the rest of the class?"

My face feels hot; it's all gone quiet, and when I start to talk, a couple of kids call out, "We can't hear you."

"Why don't you stand up?" Ms. Kaminski says.

I push my desk back a little, but everybody's looking at me. "You just . . . it's when . . . it's when you're multi-plying two numbers, and they end in . . . When the units add up to . . . ." It sounds really . . . it sounds embarrassing, like, if you ask me what I'm really thinking, what I'm thinking about is tens digits and units digits, and I know what they're all thinking. They're thinking, What a nerd. Finally the bell rings. Ms. Kaminski tries to make them wait until I've finished, but everybody gets up anyway. It's a relief.

Afterward, she stops me on the way out—she puts a hand on my shoulder and closes the classroom door. "I'm sorry I put you on the spot like that," she says quietly. "You did great. Your dad must be a good teacher."

She looks at me, and I don't say anything. Her face is kind, but I don't want to look back at her. "There's nothing to be ashamed of," she says. "There's nothing wrong with liking math. Go on, get some lunch. You've earned it."

Pete is waiting for me in the hallway.

"What'd you do that for?" he says. When Mabley isn't around, he sounds totally different. His face has gone red, except for the tip of his nose, which looks pinched and white.

"What do you mean?"

"Cover up your answers like that. Like I was copying you."

"You *were* copying me," I tell him.

"Who cares? It's just a stupid math thing." Then he says as he walks off ahead of me, "I thought we were friends."

"But—" I start calling after him, but he doesn't turn around.

When I get to the cafeteria, he's sitting at the table with Mabley and everybody else. He smiles at me, and I think, maybe he isn't mad at me anymore. When I sit down, he says, "Does your dad know any other tricks?"

Mabley says, "What are you talking about?"

"Ben's dad sounds pretty cool. He knows a lot of *tricks*."

I get out my sandwich and start to eat. Pete says, in his teacher's pet voice, "Do you want to explain it to the class?"

"You know I didn't want to do that."

"I still have no idea what anybody's talking about," Mabley says.

"Ben's like a mathlete," Pete says. "He's got a computer

brain. You just have to plug him in sometimes and wait for the answers to come out." Nobody else is paying attention, and eventually they start talking about something else.

I finish lunch early and walk outside on my own. It's a bright sunny afternoon but less hot than a few weeks ago. Already a few leaves have started falling from the trees. There's a bit of wind, which keeps blowing them around. Some kids on skateboards, wearing black clothes and backpacks covered in stickers and badges, mess around by the curb of the parking lot. I watch them playing and talking together.

The bell's going to ring in a few minutes, and I'll have to go back in with all the other kids. You don't have room to think in school; there are too many people—it's like they crowd into your brain as well. But for a few more minutes, standing around in the leaves on my own, it's like my head is quiet.

I can't understand why Mabley hangs out with Pete. She's friendly to everybody, but Pete is only friendly if you count making fun of people as friendly. It bugs me that he has an article about him in the school newspaper, that even the teachers think he's smart and funny. When really he's just mean. But for some reason I'm the only one who can see it. Maybe because he's a bit like Jake, because I had years of putting up with that kind of thing from Jake, but the funny thing is, I miss him, too. Then the bell rings, and I go back in.

After school, Mabley sits next to me on the bus. The heat is on and the windows have started to fog up—you could play tic-tac-toe on the glass. "You walked off early at lunch," she says, touching my shoulder, and I turn to face her.

"Why do you like Pete?"

It seems to me that if you're going to get to know people, if you're going to be friends, you have to be honest, you have to talk about what you're actually thinking about. At least, that's the kind of mood I'm in right now. I've been brooding about it all since lunch.

"Peter?" She looks surprised.

"Yes, why are you his friend?

"What do you mean? I've always known Peter."

That's another thing that annoys me.

"Why do you call him Peter? Everybody else calls him Pete."

She doesn't answer for a while. Then she says, "What's all this about? Why are you mad at me?"

"I'm not mad at you."

"You sound like you are."

I look out of the window for a minute—at people's houses. Somebody's raking up the front yard; there are big black trash bags in the driveway. When I turn back toward Mabley, I try to use a different tone of voice.

"I'm just tired of being . . . Pete always makes fun of me."

"He's just goofing around, it doesn't mean anything. He does that to everybody. It's just his way of . . ."

"You know, he cheats," I tell her suddenly. "Today we had a math test, and he looked at my answers."

We're passing under the highway now. There's a traffic light, and you can hear the traffic echoing under the bridge, and then the light changes, and when we come out again on the other side, it's just another neighborhood, with cars parked in the driveways and leaves lying in the yards.

"You should know something about me," Mabley says carefully. "I don't like talking about people behind their backs."

"I bet Pete says stuff about me."

"Peter never talks about you," she says.

Usually, when we get off the bus, we walk home together—it's only three or four blocks. But this time she stops to talk with somebody else for a minute. She had overheard a conversation, where this kid was getting a dog, and Mabley wanted to know what kind, and I kind of hang around for a few seconds, listening in . . . but nobody turns or says anything to me, and eventually I think, What's the point, and start to walk off alone. After a couple of blocks, I look back to see if Mabley is following me, but the sidewalk is empty, so I kick a few leaves and go home.

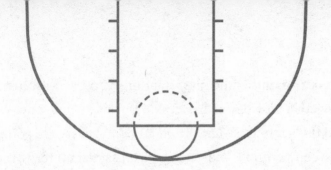

TEN

MS. KAMINSKI HAS PROMISED to announce who's going to be on the Number Sense team. We've spent the past few weeks practicing. Every day, for the last ten minutes of class, Ms. Kaminski calls out math questions and we hand in our answer sheets at the end of the period—she writes down our scores in one of those heavy grade books with ruled lines. Pete's still sitting next to me, but I don't bother covering up my answers. I don't even look at him.

She makes us wait until the end of the period before telling us to put away our books. "Our first competition is next month," she says, standing as usual with her feet together in front of her desk. "But we've got some work to do before that. Kids from all over the city are going to be competing. I know a lot of you signed up for this and want to go. It breaks my heart we can only pick three of you, but that's just how it is. . . . So, I'm just going to say the names, without more ado. Laura Kirkup, Pete Miller, and Ben Michaels. I know all of you are going to want to wish them good luck . . ." and then the bell rings, and that's how quickly the whole thing happens, just like that. Everybody gets up to leave.

For the past few days, I've stopped eating lunch in the cafeteria. I keep hoping Mabley will say something to me about it—we still ride together in the morning. But sometimes we don't even talk at the bus stop. She has a lot of friends; she doesn't seem to care who she sits next to. Sometimes she says to me, "See you at lunch," as we drift off in separate directions in the hallway. But then on the bus ride home she doesn't mention it. She always has a lot of things to talk about at the end of the day, mostly with other kids.

Mom mentions it, though. Some of the teachers take their breaks outside, or they drive somewhere for lunch, and once she sees me eating my salami sandwich by myself on the picnic table under the big pecan tree. It's getting cooler, so I keep my jacket on and eat quickly.

She leaves the other teachers and walks over to me. "Hey, Ben. Everything okay?"

"Hey, Mom. Sure. Why?"

"I mean, you're sitting out here by yourself. It's kind of cold."

It's weird how easy it is not to tell her stuff. "I guess I wanted some fresh air."

"Well," she says, "if you're going to eat lunch outside, you need to wrap up a little warmer when you leave the house."

Later that night, over dinner, Mom asks me: "Do you have any friends?"

Granma has cooked chicken-fried steak with gravy and mashed potatoes. I always seem to be hungry these days. Anyway, it makes Granma happy to watch me eat.

"Leave him alone," she says. "He's doing fine."

"I know he is." Mom is using her teacher voice. "He's doing great. But I just want to know what's going on. I don't see you hanging out much with the other kids in your grade."

We always eat supper in the kitchen, which has a bright yellow table that's big enough for four people. If Granma has something in the oven, she can check on it without getting up from her seat. Tonight she's baking an apple pie for dessert—I can smell it.

"What would you count as a friend?" I ask. For some reason, I feel pretty angry with Mom. I mean, she's the one who made us come to Texas. She's the one Dad walked out on. Maybe it's just because we have to sleep in the same room, because she teaches at my school. I need a little space.

She looks at me, surprised. "What do you mean?"

"You asked me if I had any friends, and I want to know what counts."

"A friend is somebody," she starts to say, and then stops. "I'm not asking you to keep score."

"A friend is somebody," Granma interrupts, "when you don't have to wonder whether they're a friend or not."

I have to think about this for a minute. "There are kids I talk to."

"When I saw you at lunch today," Mom says, "you were eating by yourself."

"I talk to somebody on the bus."

"Well, why don't you have lunch with him?" Mom asks.

I don't want to say it's a *her*. "I didn't feel like it today."

"How often *don't* you feel like it?" Mom's accent has changed since we moved from New York. Or maybe it hasn't changed but it just sounds normal now. In New York it was always like she was pretending. She said "y'all" and stuff like that, just to make a point, I guess, but it was always like—it was like when she wears too much makeup, or something, and I feel like, it's embarrassing. But over here she fits in fine; I'm the weirdo.

"Most days," I tell her. Then, to change the subject: "Granma, can I have some ice cream with my apple pie?"

"Of course," she says, "that's what it's there for." But Mom makes a face.

"What?" Granma makes a face back at her.

Sometimes they act like that, like sisters; or Granma acts like she's really Mom's bratty teenage kid, and Mom is too strict. Like Granma and me are on the same team against her. She takes some ice cream out of the freezer and gets her scoop from the drawer. "I want some ice cream, too."

"I don't want him eating too much junk," Mom says.

"This is good Texas ice cream."

"I just don't want it to be a sign of something. Sometimes people eat too much when they're not dealing with other stuff."

"You read too many magazines. It's a sign that he's growing is what it is," Granma says.

*

In the morning, as we walk to the bus stop, Mom says, "How come you don't bug me about getting a phone anymore?"

"What's the point? You're not going to give me one anyway."

"That never stopped you before."

"Well, that was before." I kick a few leaves along the ground. It's another cool day, cloudy, too. "Do you want me to bug you?"

Mom puts her hand on my arm. "I want you to do something other than say *fine* and *thank you* and *leave me alone*, which is basically all that you say to me. You just climb into this hole whenever I'm around."

"No, I don't." But it's true, which annoys me, too. "First you complain if I ask for a phone, and now you complain if I don't. You're driving me crazy."

"You sound like your father," Mom says.

We walk a little farther in silence. All the houses here have grassy front yards, and sometimes there's a sidewalk, but sometimes there isn't, and we have to walk in the road. Which doesn't matter, because there are hardly any cars; we can kind of spread out. At the end of the block, Mom says, "I want you to *want* a phone. That seems like a normal thing . . . for us to fight about. Like, get off the phone, do your homework, stop talking to your friends."

I can see the corner where the bus stop is, just at the top of the rise.

"Phones suck out your brains anyway," I tell her.

She usually carries one of my book bags if she walks me to the bus. At least until we get near, so the kids don't think, Look at that kid. His mom still carries his bags. She stops now and gives it to me; I sling the satchel over my shoulder. "I'll make a deal with you, Ben," she says. "If you talk to somebody new today, I'll give you a dollar."

"What am I supposed to buy with a dollar?"

"Well," she says, "if you talk to somebody new every day for a week, you'll have five dollars."

"How will you know if I talk to somebody new?" I ask her.

"Because you'll tell me."

"What if I lie?"

She gives me a don't-be-silly look, a teachery kind of look. "You don't lie, Ben. I know that."

"No," I say. "That's true. I don't lie, and I don't talk to people."

And I walk off to the bus stop by myself.

But at lunch that day, I don't want to sit at one of the picnic tables in case Mom comes out and sees me. So I wander around the grounds, looking for a place to eat where nobody can bother me.

The school building is brand-new, but there used to be an old school in the same place. When they tore it down, they had to rebuild everything, including the football field and the picnic area and the chain-link fence that keeps us from going into the street. But if you look closely, you can see leftover parts of the old school, like a water fountain or an old brick wall.

Pennsylvania Avenue is the name of the street, which is funny, because that's the address of the White House. I mean, where the president lives. Maybe that's why they built the school out of white brick. There's a parking lot by the side of it, and then a field, and you can see neighborhood houses over the road. It must be weird living right opposite the school. Some of the houses are small and look like they could use some paint. The roof sags or there are broken steps up to the porch. But others are in pretty good shape.

We're not allowed to leave the school grounds, but I can wander down to the football field—which is on a slope away from the school, so it always gets muddy in the rain. There's no fence on that side, just a big road at the bottom, with some benches and a bus stop and a few trees. It's far enough away that I can feel like I'm not even at school; nobody knows I'm here.

That's where I go today. There's a wooden hut in a

corner of the campus, which I have never been to. I walk across the football field to get there, but it's still cold out; the field is empty. I reach the hut and notice that there's a padlock over the door, but the hinges are loose. If you pull on the door a little, you can look inside. I see an armchair, an electric heater, and a television set sitting on a wooden crate. But nobody's there.

I walk around the hut, which is surrounded by trees. Some of them must have been too big to cut down—they seem to lean their branches on the roof. I find a bike rack under one of them, pretty rusty, with a lonely wheel still locked to one of the crossbars. On the other side of the tree I see a basketball court.

It's just a square of concrete, with a pole stuck in the ground at one end and a dirty backboard and a bent old rim and raggedy net. The court is covered in leaves. One of the tree branches grows so close to the backboard that you can only shoot at it from the side. Maybe that's why I have never heard of anyone playing there. You can hardly see the basket unless you walk right up to it. The whole thing looks like part of the tree.

But there's a bench by the side of the court, and that's where I have lunch.

After that, I start going there every day. As soon as the lunch bell rings, I race to the cafeteria—well, as fast as I can, with my backpack and satchel—and stand in line with all the other kids to buy my carton of chocolate milk. Then I walk out the glass double-doors and lug my stuff over to the basketball court to eat. It's a relief to put everything down on the bench, and take out my sandwiches, and just have twenty minutes to myself, without having to say anything or look at anyone or pretend like I'm paying attention.

ELEVEN

MS. KAMINSKI RUNS a homework club after school, and she expects everybody on the Number Sense team to come to it. There are a lot of kids there—it's really just an after-school thing for kids whose parents don't get home until later—but she tends to put us in a corner by ourselves, so we can practice. We've been doing this for a couple of weeks now, and the tournament is in just a few days. Pete almost never comes, because the basketball season has started, and they've got practice, too. But Laura Kirkup is there every day.

Laura is very quiet; she's one of these girls who kind of

hides behind her hair. Her dad is supposed to be rich—I think he runs some IT company—but you'd never know from Laura. Her clothes are from Gap or Old Navy; she also wears a lot of University of Texas gear, like a Texas Science hoodie. Every time she talks outside of class, it's like a surprise. You can tell she has a lot of private opinions.

Sometimes Ms. Kaminski plays music while we work—she has a CD player on her desk. Mostly she just plays classical music, because it's not "distracting," she says, but once she put on the radio, just to see what was playing, and "Yesterday" came on. I never know any songs, but I know this one, so I said to Laura, "The Beatles," and she said, "Yeah, I know." I said, "My dad is living right around the corner from where they recorded all their songs. In London." And she said, "I like the early stuff more. If you're going to be cheesy, you should just go for it. Like, *I want to hold your hand*. You know . . ." and she sang the lyrics or sort of hummed them under her breath.

I don't really have any good opinions about music, so I didn't say anything and that was the end of the conversation. I think she might be smarter than me—she's very good at long division.

When Pete shows up, he pretends to be incredibly enthusiastic. He compliments Laura a lot, and I can't tell what she thinks of him—if she likes him or not.

Sometimes I think she does, and sometimes I think she can't stand him. She's hard to read.

Afterward, I catch the late bus home, which means I don't ride with Mabley anymore. Dinner is usually on the table, then I do my homework and go to bed. It's a pretty tiring day.

At the beginning of November, we get this mini heat wave, where the leaves have mostly fallen but the skies are bright blue. It's sunny and warm, like a nice spring day in New York. It's lunchtime, and I'm sitting on the bench by the basketball court, when a voice behind me says, "What are you doing out here?"

My heart jumps and I turn around. It's the groundskeeper. I've seen him before from a distance, mowing the grass on his John Deere mower or lining the football field with white paint. But I've never talked to him. He has a clean bald head, which he probably shaves. His beard is going white, and he wears overalls that make it hard to tell if he's fat or skinny.

"Just having lunch," I say. "Is that okay?"

"I'm not going to stop you." He looks like he's going to walk away again, but then he doesn't. "Where are your friends?"

"I just like to eat by myself." I don't know if this sounds rude, so I add, "It gets really loud in the cafeteria."

But he's not really listening. "Kids used to come out here all the time," he says. He's still looking at me like he doesn't know what to do. "I used to keep a ball in the hut for them to mess around with. But they haven't come in a while." After that, he leaves me alone—he goes back to the hut.

He shows up again the next day with a Spalding basketball in his hands—he pretends to pass it to me, suddenly. I reach out to catch it, and he laughs because he's still holding on to the ball in one of his big hands.

"You didn't tell me your name," he says.

"I'm sorry. I'm Ben."

"No reason to be sorry, I didn't tell you mine. It's Sam." He takes a shot and misses, then chases the ball down slowly—he's wearing heavy boots. "I used to come out here, too," he says. He tries again; this time it goes in. "Anyway, if you want to play, you can play," he says and passes me the ball, bouncing it hard off the concrete surface of the court and into my hands.

I expect him to walk away, but he just stands there. "What are you waiting for. Let's see your jump shot," he says.

This makes me nervous. I'm standing about six or seven feet from the basket, and sort of throw the ball at the rim—it hits the front end and bounces off the back-board and slips through the net.

"Not like that," Sam says.

He gets the ball and walks over to me. "Hold it like this," he says, pushing my wrist back and placing the basketball on my palm. His hands are strong, and he's got a tattoo on his forearm of an eagle dragging an anchor by the chain. "Point your elbow at the rim." He shows me by going through the motion himself, bending his elbow and straightening it, while the wrist rolls over, and holding his hand out afterward in that position. "Now you try."

This time, when I shoot, the ball hits the rim and bangs away.

"Better," he says.

For the next few minutes, that's all we do—he watches me shoot and tells me what I'm doing wrong. "No, no, no," he says, even if the shot goes in. "Not like that. Bend your legs. Jump straight up. Follow through." He pushes my elbow into place, pointing it at the rim. It feels weird, like walking tip-toe in a line—trying to stay balanced. He makes me practice one-handed, too. "Your left hand's got no business pushing the ball. It's just a guide dog."

"But I'm not strong enough." Every time I try to shoot it *his* way, the ball falls short.

"Start close," he says. "Do it right."

Sometimes, even when I miss, he tells me, Now we're getting somewhere.

"All right, kid," he says at last. "Practice, that's all it is. Just leave the ball under the bench when you're finished."

And he walks back under the trees to the caretaker's hut.

For a minute, I watch him go, until he disappears around the corner, then I start shooting again. The ball is a little flat, I can hardly bounce it high enough to dribble. And every time I miss, it rolls into the leaves. But that doesn't matter—I chase after the ball and shoot again. For some reason it calms me down just to do the same thing over and over. The last time I played basketball was in Jake's kitchen in New York, with a foam ball, when we broke his mom's mug . . . and afterward my dad marched me downstairs to tell Mrs. Schultz about it.

Eventually the bell rings, far away. I've forgotten about school and it takes me a second or two to realize where I am. Then I roll the ball under the bench and pick up my bags—the backpack first, and then the satchel over my shoulder—and walk across the football field to class.

At lunchtime the next day I go back. All the leaves have been swept, and when I finish my sandwiches and look under the bench, I notice that Sam has pumped the ball up, too. Shooting on that court isn't easy, though. On one side, you can't shoot at all, because of that tree branch.

But even on the other side, a telephone wire has started to sag, and you have to shoot over it.

That doesn't bother me. I was always better than Jake at shooting a basketball, and sometimes I talk to him in my head. I turn everything into a conversation. *There's this tournament next week. I'm on a kind of math team, and this kid called Pete Miller copied my answers to get in. . . .* But then I realize, Jake and Pete would probably get along pretty well. They both like to—not pick fights exactly, but just talk, and get things started, and see what happens. If I hadn't lived in the same apartment building as Jake, we would never have been friends, because I'm not the kind of person he usually likes. He'd know what to say to Mabley, too, if she sat next to him on the bus. Jake can look after himself. All these kids would probably like him better than they like me.

The bell rings, so faintly that I almost think it's my imagination—like I sometimes hear my mom's voice calling me when I'm biking with the wind in my ears. I walk past the hut and knock on Sam's door, to give him the ball back and say thanks. Really, I hope he isn't there, I feel shy around him, but he comes out with a sandwich in his hand. I can hear the TV on; there's some soap opera music in the background.

"Thanks for pumping it up," I say. He's a lot taller than

me, but I try to look him in the eyes.

"How come you have all those bags?" he asks. "Don't you have a locker?"

"They gave me one, but I don't know where it is."

"Well, we can find that out," he says.

"That's all right. I don't really mind. This way I don't forget anything."

He looks at me and shakes his head. "One of those kids, has to do everything his own way. . . ."

"Anyway," I tell him. "Thanks—for pumping it up, and sweeping the court and everything."

"It's my job," he says. I feel like he's watching me as I carry my bags back to class.

On the morning of the tournament, I have to take the bus as usual, but after homeroom all the kids who are going to compete meet in the parking lot, where another bus will take us to some high school gym. It's not just the math nerds, but there are all kinds of nerds hanging around—Latin nerds, social studies nerds, French nerds. There are about twenty kids going. Some of them are two or three kinds of nerd at the same time. That's what Pete says, getting on to the bus. "Man, what a bunch of weirdos, and I'm one of them." Ms. Kaminski is coming along, too. She smiles at him.

"There's nothing wrong with being unusual," she says.

"I didn't say unusual, Ms. Kaminski," Pete says. "I said weird."

He's in one of his moods, where he acts like he likes everybody and everybody is having a good time because he's around. The bus isn't full. Laura moves over to the window seat and says to Pete, "You can sit here," as he walks down the aisle. There are rows of two seats each on either side. Pete looks at her and says, "Gracias," which annoys me, because it's like, for some reason he thinks it's funny, or maybe he's trying to be polite, or pretending to be polite, and that's the joke. I don't know, but somehow it's annoying. Anyway, he doesn't sit down with her but makes a sorry face and heads toward some boys at the back of the bus.

Laura doesn't say anything to me. The seats in the row behind her are free so I sit there, next to the window. Then Mabley comes on the bus, looking around, like everybody does, to see who they want to sit next to.

"I didn't know you were coming," I tell her. "What team are you on?"

"I'm a Latin nerd. *Eamus, Crabrones!*" she says loudly, almost like she's talking to people at the back. But then she explains to me: "*Crabrones* means hornets," and walks past me. A hornet is our school mascot. I look down the aisle to see where she's sitting—with Pete and a few other kids at the back of the bus. Nobody sits next to me, so I spend most of the ride staring out the window or at the seat in front, where I can just about see the top of Laura's hair. She has black hair. It's only a fifteen-minute drive.

LBJ High School looks a bit like our school, a big white building with a lot of green around it. We park in the parking lot, where there are a bunch of yellow buses lined up like number two pencils. Somebody behind me, one of the boys sitting with Pete, says, "Who's going to get off the bus first?"

"There's no way I'm going to get off . . . the bus," Pete replies, and everybody laughs. "Hey, Ben. You going to get off . . . the bus?"

Mr. Hauser, one of the other teachers, stands up and says, "All right, guys. Cut it out. Let's . . . exit in an orderly fashion." It's like he's sort of going along with the joke but at the same time pretending not to. He has a badge hanging around his neck, and wears a brown shirt all buttoned up and tucked into his pants, even though he's a little overweight. His hair is short and you can see colored patches of what looks like dried skin underneath it. He teaches science.

There's a flat roof over the school entrance, with words written along the side: LBJ Purple Pride. And underneath that: Preparing today to conquer tomorrow. This seems like the kind of thing kids make fun of, and since Mabley is sort of near, just a few kids away, I catch up to her and say, "Preparing today to conquer tomorrow," in like a teacher's voice, like I'm being serious, even though it's stupid.

"What?" she says.

She didn't hear me, and so I have to repeat myself, but it's not even worth it. "Purple pride," I say in the same dumb voice, and she kind of sidles off with me, I think she puts her hand on my elbow, as we're walking into the school—you can already feel the air-conditioning coming at you through the double doors.

"You know what they were joking about, right?" she says. "Back on the bus."

"What are you talking about?"

"It's just stupid," she says. "It's not even really mean. It's just a dumb boy thing, but I guess if you don't know what they're talking about . . . Anyway, you probably know anyway."

We're in the hallway now, and Mr. Hauser is saying the stuff teachers usually say, like, "This is a school, and for most of the students, this is an ordinary school day. They're trying to learn. . . ." Some of the boys kind of snicker. "I'm ignoring that," he says, "and what we're going to do now is walk as quietly as we can—and that means *without* talking—to the gym, where . . ."

"Of course I know," I tell Mabley.

"I just didn't want you to think . . . the joke is on you,

because it's just something dumb . . . they say to each other. It's like being included."

But then Ms. Kaminski sees us talking and puts a finger to her lips.

The LBJ gym is like any other school gym but bigger. There are bleachers on either side, with groups of kids from different schools sitting on them, and rows and rows of tables set up on the court itself, which shines under the lights. Everybody's talking; it's not loud exactly, but there are a lot of small noises coming from different places. It's very disorienting, like being in a swimming pool. It's almost like even if you do say something you can't hear yourself because the ceiling is so high it all just sort of drifts away.

All the kids from my school separate into their different nerd groups, so now it's just me and Pete and Laura and Ms. Kaminski. Pete is still in his good mood, he's having a good time. Laura is quietly concentrating; she doesn't talk much either. There are two rounds of Number Sense: one in the morning, and then one after lunch, if we make it through. The team competition and the individual competition happen at the same time. Ms. Kaminski doesn't know yet whether if we make it into the next round as a team we'll automatically be considered for the individual competition, too.

"I'm trying to get clarification," she says.

Sometimes when I look at my teachers now, I see my mom—the way she has to pretend every day and put on makeup and a matching outfit, just to go to school and do her job. That's not the real person. Nobody would really want to say things like "trying to get clarification" if somehow they weren't forced to, but my mom likes her job, too. Sometimes she seems happier at school, talking to the kids or with other teachers, than she does at home with me and Granma. So I don't know. Ms. Kaminski has decided to be the kind of teacher who wears a lot of bright clothes and necklaces and bracelets, even though she's isn't particularly young or pretty, but she's very good at being that person.

For some reason Pete has started saying gracias all over the place but not like the Spanish word—but like, grassy-ass, like he's never actually heard anyone speak Spanish in his life. It's incredibly annoying. So when Ms. Kaminski gives us our pencil packs, with number two pencils and a separate extra-large eraser (she's got them all ready and says we can keep the clear plastic case afterward, with one of those zips you just slide across the opening—it says Hornets Math on the side, and I know she probably paid for them herself), Pete says, "Grassy-ass," forgetting that he's talking to a teacher, but maybe not really, because

Ms. Kaminski doesn't say anything. Then we have to find our seats and the competition begins.

There are brown envelopes on the tables with the questions on them, and we each get a sheet of paper for writing down the answers, but we're not allowed to write down any calculations or notes. So it's like the opposite of a normal math test, where you have to show your work. Number Sense is totally mental.

Most of the questions are pretty easy, but the point is, you have to answer them as fast as you can. Questions like "1/2 of 39 is _____" or "3/5 equals _____%." There are tougher questions, too. "517×25," for example. Or "$69 \times 17 - 45 \times 12$." Basically, the trick is to break down all the questions into different parts, where each of the parts is pretty easy, like 7×60, but then you have to remember your answers to all the other parts, too, and add them together. As soon as I sit down, my palms start to sweat. The test lasts forty-five minutes, but I hardly even notice the time. Then the bell rings and I haven't finished. There are eighty questions and I've answered seventy-three of them.

Afterward, I ask Laura, "How many did you answer?" and she says, "I got to the end, but I skipped four or five along the way."

Pete overhears us. "If you don't know something, you should just guess. I mean, why not."

I say, "How many did you answer?"

"All of them." He smiles at me.

Ms. Kaminski lets us wander around the gym, as long as we don't disturb any of the other tests. Pete knows kids from other schools. Laura brought a book along—she's reading *Children of Dune*, it's as thick as a brick. There are hundreds of kids in the gym, a lot of them sitting at the plastic fold-out tables on the court and writing furiously, with their heads down, concentrating, and the rest just hanging around and talking, so there's like this continuous noise that never really gets louder or softer.

For lunch, I eat my usual sandwiches, sitting with Ms. Kaminski on one of the bleachers. "Your mom must be really proud of you," she says. I mean, it's just something to say, because we're sitting there, and she doesn't know what else to talk about.

"I guess."

"I know she is," Ms. Kaminski says. "She talks about you all the time. She wants to know how you're doing."

I don't say anything—it's not really a question—and anyway, it bugs me that my mom talks to my teachers about me in the staff room. That's not something an average kid should have to deal with. But I can't really say that to Ms. Kaminski, who eventually breaks the silence herself.

"You're doing great, that's what I tell her. Because you are."

She has a nice face. I guess she's older than most of my teachers, but she still wears makeup and has long dangly earrings that are long enough you can actually hear them sometimes. When she talks to you, she lets you know that you've got her full attention, like that's what you want; but the truth is, I don't want it—I don't want her attention at all, so I feel bad and just kind of don't say much, because I don't know what to say.

But then her phone pings, and she scrambles to take it out of her handbag because she's waiting for the results. Laura came third, I came eighth, and Pete came twenty-second. The top ten kids get to compete in the next round to go to sectionals, but we did well enough so we can compete as a team, too. Ms. Kaminski looks very excited. Laura is there; she puts her book down to find out the results but doesn't really respond in any way except to nod, and after a minute she starts reading again. But we can't find Pete—I can't see Mabley, either.

I say, "I'll go look for him."

The afternoon Number Sense test is at one o'clock, which is in twenty minutes.

"Okay," Ms. Kaminski says. "You've got a watch, right? Meet me back here at ten to one," and she wanders off, too, with her head going from side to side. She has to keep adjusting her clothes when she walks.

There are some emergency exit double doors at the back of the gym, but they haven't been properly closed, so I figure the alarm probably won't go off. Anyway, Pete is just outside, having lunch with Mabley. He's lying on his back in the grass and Mabley is sitting cross-legged and picking bits of grass and throwing them at him, which he doesn't seem to notice.

"We're not supposed to be outside."

That's the first thing I tell them, which makes me feel stupid—like a teacher's pet or something.

"Oh my God." Pete pretends to be scared or not even pretends really, but just enough to make me feel dumb. He sits up suddenly.

"Ms. Kaminski is looking for you. The next test is at one o'clock."

"I don't really feel like taking any more tests." He sweeps some of the pieces of grass off his shirt. "I'm not a calculator."

"We got the results back from this morning."

"So how'd you do?" It's like he thinks that's why I told him, so I can brag.

"Not great. Like I told you, I didn't even answer all the questions."

"So how'd you do?" He's looking at me properly now.

"I came eighth."

He's still looking at me, smiling a little. "How'd *I* do?"

"You can ask Ms. Kaminski."

"But I bet you know."

I feel embarrassed in front of Mabley. I feel like—I want her to know that I did better than Pete, but I'm annoyed that Laura did better than me, and I also feel like there's something not nice about the fact that I want to tell Pete how he did, which makes me look bad.

"She told all of us. Laura came third."

"And what about me?" He's still smiling.

"I don't remember."

"Yes, you do," Pete says.

"I don't know. Something like twenty, but I don't know." It's hard not to sound like I'm rubbing it in. There's this thing my voice does, which even I can hear. The best thing is just to keep talking. "The next test is at one o'clock. We have to go. Ms. Kaminski is looking for you."

"I told you, I don't feel like going." He lies down again, like he's bored with the game. "Mabley and I are going to do something. I don't know what we're going to do."

"We're playing hooky," Mabley says. It's the first thing she's said since I got there—but she likes the word. She's the kind of kid who likes to use phrases like that. "Why don't you come with us?"

I can't tell if she wants me to or not. "But we've got to take the test."

"My test is over," she says. "I don't know how I did and I don't care. Sometimes I get too hung up on that stuff. My grandmother once told me, it's important sometimes to break the rules. So that's what we're going to do."

"What are you going to do?"

Pete is laughing, like a kid who can't stop—he's doing the laugh you can just do if you want to laugh. Most kids have a laugh they can force, just to show they're laughing.

"I don't know." Mabley is laughing a little, too. It's infectious. "We'll think of something."

"But we need you, Pete. For the team competition. You need three people to compete."

But he can't stop himself—he's even losing his breath. I look at them both for a moment. It's like we're playing some game, but I don't like the team I'm on. There's nothing I can do about it, though, because that's just how it is, that's who I am, the kid who is going to go back inside to take the test, because his teacher is looking for him.

"You should come with us," Mabley says. She brushes the grass off her lap and stands up. There's a kind of park outside the school, with a few trees, but most of the leaves have fallen. It's a sunny day, though, the sky is blue, and everything feels weird—warm and dead. "Let's go, Peter." She pulls him up, and he looks at me.

"You coming, too?"

For a second I think, maybe he wants me to. There's a parking lot next to the grassy area, and after that, a quiet street with a few houses on the other side. And after that, who knows. Somewhere in the distance you can hear highway sounds, a lot of cars driving smoothly at the same speed.

"What are you going to do?"

And Mabley pulls something out of her pocket. "I've got ten dollars. I'm going to find something you can get for ten dollars." She leans her head a little to the side. "You coming or not?"

"I've got a test."

"Suit yourself," she says.

And they walk off together through the grass toward the parking lot. I watch them go, then suddenly worry that the double doors have locked behind me. For some reason, panic rises up in me, like water spilling over a glass, but when I push against the doors, they open—and I go back inside the gym and close them behind me. It takes me a minute to get used to the change of light. There aren't any windows, just long rows of electric spotlights in the ceiling.

When Ms. Kaminski asks, "Where is he? Did you find Pete?" I shake my head.

"This is serious," she says. "We need to know where he is." But it's almost one o'clock so Laura and I have to find our seats again, because the test is about to begin.

Afterward, on the bus ride back to school, Mabley and Pete sit in front together with all the teachers. I can tell they're in trouble. Mabley doesn't look happy—when I walk past them in the bus, she doesn't even look at me, but she's not looking at Pete either. She's sitting next to the window and staring out. They're not talking to each other, Pete is playing with his phone. By that point I already know that I'm not going to sectionals. Nor is Laura—only the top four get through, and she came fifth. I came seventh. Because only two of us competed, we can't go as a team either. In a funny way, I'm almost glad: it makes things easier with Pete because now I have a reason not to like him.

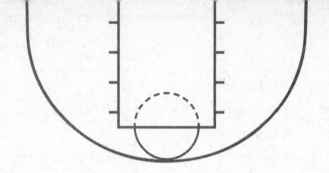

TWELVE

FOR A FEW DAYS AFTERWARD, kids are talking about Pete and what happened at LBJ. There's a rumor going around that he might be suspended from the basketball team. It's a big deal—it's one of those things that kids get angry about, where they get mad at the principal. Some people want to start a petition. I hear them discussing it as I wait in the lunch line for my carton of milk. Mabley doesn't say anything to me—we haven't really hung out since the tournament. I don't know if she blames me, if she thinks I told on them.

Finally, on Friday morning, I manage to sit next to

her on the bus. She makes me nervous now, but I say, "I didn't tell on you. I don't know what you guys did or who . . . found out or whatever, but it wasn't me."

"Tell on me about what?"

"At LBJ. When you guys . . ."

"That was my fault. I wanted to do something stupid, to see what it's like. Now I know. It's no big deal. If you do this kind of thing," she says, "you have to face the consequences."

"What about Pete?"

"What *about* Pete?" she asks.

"Nothing, I don't know."

When Mabley doesn't want to talk about something, there's nothing you can do—she just looks at you like everything's great.

"How's Laura?" she asks, changing the subject.

We're pulling into the parking lot. But parents are dropping off kids in cars—there's always a traffic jam coming into school. Kids on the bus are getting their backpacks ready, but we have to wait, even though the stop is just a few yards away. When the driver turns off the engine, the whole bus shakes and sighs.

"What do you mean?"

"Laura Kirkup. I thought she was your math buddy. I thought you liked her."

"Like her?" I'm not sure what Mabley is talking about.

"She kind of scares me. You never know what she's thinking."

"Who knows what anybody's thinking," Mabley says.

The doors are open now; everybody's streaming off, heading for their lockers before school—but I've got all my books with me and head straight to homeroom.

Laura waits for me after math class—she eats lunch with her own friends, but we walk to the cafeteria together. "I hope they *do* suspend Pete from the basketball team." She's normally a quiet kid; she's normally a bit like me. It's funny to hear her talk like that, like she has all these strong feelings all the time.

"I don't even know what they did," I tell her.

"They just had lunch at KFC. But to get there, you have to cross over the highway. We weren't even supposed to leave the campus. They could have gotten run over. *Real* stupid," she says.

But saying it like that makes me want to stand up for them. "They just wanted to get away from that gym. Don't you think there was something . . . all of us sitting there, taking tests . . ."

"Nobody made them sign up," Laura says. "I'm sorry, I don't feel bad for Pete. Those kids act like nobody else exists." She means Mabley, too. "We could have gone to sectionals," she says.

But nothing happens to Pete in the end. That night, the Hornets win another basketball game—Pete scores twenty-one points. It's almost Thanksgiving, and that's kind of the general spirit, forgive and forget. Pretty soon, nobody cares about the Number Sense competition. We have a short week, and then four days off. Ms. Kaminski brings a pumpkin pie to class on Wednesday. "My daughter made this," she says proudly, so I eat my piece, even though the crust tastes kind of raw.

It doesn't matter; we're all going home. I hear kids making plans for the long weekend. It feels weird—it's still sunny out, they talk about going swimming. In New York, you wonder when it's going to snow, you can see your breath outside, the stores have lights in the windows, they're getting ready for Christmas; but in Austin you only see stores when you drive somewhere. And I don't have anybody to make plans with, so I pretty much stay at home.

Mom lets me sleep in on Thanksgiving, but around eleven o'clock she comes into our bedroom. I'm awake now, reading in bed. She says, "Do you want to help me and Granma make the dinner?"

"Maybe," I say. "I'm just reading my book."

She goes to get something from her closet but then kind of hangs around.

"What are you reading?" she asks eventually.

"*Tom Sawyer*," I tell her. "It's our homework."

I'm hoping she'll leave me alone, but she just stands there, and I finally look up.

"In New York, you used to cook with me all the time." She sits down on the bed next to me; I roll over a little. She's holding the subway map apron she wore in our old apartment.

"Granma does most of the cooking here," I tell her.

"That's because I'm working."

"I wasn't complaining. You're the one who brought it up."

"*I* mind," she says. Her voice is the voice she uses when she wants me to feel bad about something, because I'm disappointing her, or maybe just making her sad. "Come and cook with us. It's Thanksgiving."

"In a minute," I say, and go back to my book. Mom stands up at last, and the bed shifts, and I hear her footsteps on the old wooden boards. She closes the door behind her. The room feels empty again.

For a minute I just lie there with the book on my lap. I'm propped up on the pillows, and there's a shaft of sunlight, coming from the window near Mom's bed, that falls on my lap. It's another sunny day that seems even sunnier because of the yellow leaves. But I'm not reading anymore; my concentration is broken. In New

York, our kitchen window overlooked 85th Street, but if you put your head out, you could just about see Central Park. With the window open, you could hear the traffic on Central Park West. It was the one place in the house Mom never cared about making a mess. Once I asked her why not, and she said, "Because your father leaves me alone in here. This is my territory," and without really thinking about it, I get out of bed.

I'm still in pajamas but that doesn't matter. It's warm in the house, and I put on some slippers and go into the kitchen. For the rest of the day, that's what we do—make messes. We make cranberry sauce and two kinds of stuffing, and Granma bakes a kind of sweet potato pie. It's really more of a soup, with canned pineapples and marshmallows bobbing around in it. The turkey's already in the oven, but every half hour Mom lets me pull it out and with a baster squirt whatever juice is lying at the bottom of the pan over the bird.

It gets really hot in the kitchen, and at one point Granma has to sit down. Her face looks red. She has wispy gray hair and a few whiskers around her mouth as well—it's easy to see them in the heat, because they stand out. I don't like to look at her swollen hand. It feels like it must hurt, even though Granma says it doesn't; she says it's just swollen. Around four o'clock, Mom asks me to set the table and Granma pulls out a kitchen chair, carries it next to the sink, and climbs on it.

"What are you doing?" Mom asks.

But she doesn't answer—she's got a wooden spoon in her mouth, and she's rummaging through one of the cupboards over the counter and steps down again with a tablecloth in her hand. "Use this," she says. It's covered in yellow roses, with thorns and green leaves.

Mom helps me drag out the table in the living room. We lay the cloth over it, and then I get Granma's best china from the mahogany closet next to the window. I've never opened it before—it's full of plates, teacups, jugs, and serving bowls, stuff like that. Old dusty bottles of alcohol stand on the bottom shelf.

"Doesn't it look nice?" Granma says when the table is laid, with the turkey steaming on a big platter.

"Isn't it too much food for three people?"

But Mom gives me a look.

"I've got everybody here that matters," she says.

Afterward, Mom and Granma clean up—I'm allowed to sit on the sofa and watch football games. But when the table is cleared, and the pots and pans are dripping on the kitchen counter (I can see them through the arch), Mom comes in and tells me to scooch over. "Where's the remote?" she says.

"I'm watching the game."

"It's family movie time," she says.

"I'm watching the game," I tell her again.

"Granma doesn't want to watch football."

"I don't mind," Granma says. "The only thing I care about is sitting down."

"Well, you can sit down here," Mom says, making room on the couch. She's found the remote control and starts flipping through channels. "Where are you going?" she asks me, because I've stood up.

"My room."

"What are you going to do there?"

"I'm going to read my book."

"Let him go," Granma says, but Mom calls me back.

"Don't spoil it now, Ben. I thought we were having a good day."

I look at her for a moment. "We *were* having a good day, and I was watching a football game."

"You weren't even really watching. Who was playing, what was the score?"

"The Cowboys, it was . . ."

But the truth is, I can't remember, I was kind of zoning out, and she says, "See, I told you so. Come on, Ben. Sit down—I can see that smile."

"I am *not* smiling."

"Okay, nobody's smiling. Nobody's happy. We're all

miserable. Just sit in your room, why don't you."

"Mom," I say, and Granma says, "That's enough, Jenny."

"I just want to sit and watch something on TV with my son on Thanksgiving. Is that too much to ask?" There are tears in her voice.

"It's fine, it's fine. It's not too much," I tell her.

"I get tired, too. This isn't easy for me either."

"It's fine, it's okay." I walk back to the couch. "See, I'm sitting down. The son is sitting down. The son is watching TV."

"There's nothing good on anyway," Mom says, and throws the remote control on one of the chairs. But I reach over and get it and start flipping through channels—there's a Paul Newman movie on, and Granma says, "Let's leave it right there," and I squeeze up next to my mom and say, "See? Everybody's happy."

So we watch the movie. Paul Newman is this old guy—I saw him in this movie called *The Sting*, and he looks much older now. Everybody's kind of pissed off with him, and he pisses everybody off. He lives in a small town, where it seems to snow a lot; everything looks kind of run-down. There's a lot of swearing. It looks more like New York than Texas, and after half an hour Granma falls asleep. Her mouth is open, and she snores. I poke my mom, and Mom looks at her for a minute.

"She's all right," Mom says.

For some reason, when she's sleeping, you see how small Granma is—just a sack of bones, really, apart from her swollen hand. It's kind of embarrassing; she makes a lot of noise. You can see the hair around her lips move when she breathes.

Mom puts her arm around me. "I'm having a nice Thanksgiving," she says.

When the movie's over, Granma wakes up. Nobody's really hungry and Granma doesn't want to cook again anyway, but I have a bowl of cereal while I watch *SportsCenter* on TV. Granma's already in bed. Mom stands in the kitchen archway and looks at me. "That's what your father always ate when he came home late from work."

She dries up the pots and dishes and puts them away, then goes into the bathroom to get ready for bed. When I come in, her light is already off—I get undressed in the dark and slip under the covers. I've got a little pocket flashlight that Granma gave me, so I can read at night . . . and I turn that on and read under the scratchy wool blanket. But it's kind of annoying, holding the book in one hand and the flashlight in the other, and eventually I give up. But I'm still not very sleepy, and after a while, I say,

"Mom"—quietly, so she can only hear me if she's already awake.

"Yes, Ben?" Her voice seems a long way away.

"Is Granma all right?"

"What do you mean?"

"Because of her hand."

"Don't worry about that, Ben. It's just the way it is now. I don't think it hurts her."

"I don't mean to be rude, but why doesn't she—I mean she's got lots of hair on her chin. . . ."

"Oh, she doesn't care anymore. You get to a point where none of that stuff matters."

"Couldn't she just . . . shave?"

"If you shave them off, they just come back worse." Nobody says anything for a while, and I think that might be the end of the conversation. But then my mom's voice comes out of the dark. "Are you worried about her, Ben? She's in pretty good shape. At her age, you just get tired sometimes. At my age, too," she says, and laughs. "Good night, Ben."

After that, I lie there and listen until I can hear her breathing. The curtains are closed, but somebody left the porch light on, and I can see a crack of light falling on the bedroom floor. For some reason, I start talking to my dad in my head—I just tell him everything that happened today, how I helped out in the kitchen, and Mom got mad at me about the football game and almost cried. Then Granma fell asleep watching the movie. There are a lot of leftovers, I tell him. We didn't have enough people to eat it all.

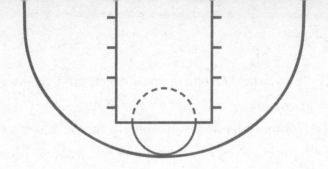

THIRTEEN

A WEEK AFTER THANKSGIVING, Mom says to Granma and me, "Well, at least one of us has made a new friend. I thought I might invite somebody for dinner tomorrow night."

We're watching TV before bed, all three of us sitting on the sofa. When the program goes to a commercial, Mom turns off the sound.

"Are you sure that's a good idea?" Granma says. "I don't know if we're ready for this yet."

"Oh, he's just a friend. And anyway, Ben already knows him. It's Mr. Tomski, your social studies teacher. He likes you," Mom tells me. Then the show comes back on, so we don't have to talk about it, which is fine with me. I've noticed that it takes me a while to react to anything—I don't even always have a reaction. Sometimes it takes me a few days.

Mr. Tomski is one of those teachers who's easy to distract. He's normal height, maybe a little fat, and he always wears a jacket and tie to school, but he never looks well-dressed. His shirt hangs out, and his jacket looks old and dirty. His shoes always have mud on them, probably because he lives on a ranch. Sometimes he wears glasses, but he can never find them when he wants to.

If you want him to stop teaching, you just have to ask him about his ranch. He has a lot of stories: about his animals, and the people he bought the ranch from (Mr. Tomski says they were "real old Texans"), and how much it costs to feed a pig or how much you can sell a pig for at Johnny G's Meat Market. Most of the kids like Mr. Tomski, but they don't have much respect for him. "Just ask him about his ranch," they say. "Then you don't have to learn anything."

He's also the head coach of the basketball team. Kids think this is funny, too. "That dude does not look like he ever played basketball." As soon as somebody starts making fun of a teacher, everyone else joins in. "He looks like a homeless guy." "My dad says he couldn't dunk a donut in a cup of coffee." That's the kind of thing they say.

They also tell stories about his car. Once, after a basketball game, the school bus broke down and Mr. Tomski and some of the parents had to drive the players home. "Don't go in his car," Pete said afterward. "It smells like a farm in there. He's actually got straw in his car. You get covered in hay. I had to take a shower when I got home. It smells like poo." I heard all this waiting in line at the cafeteria.

This is the guy my mom invited for dinner.

In class the next day, I wonder if he's going to say something to me about coming over. I always sit at the back because I don't want anyone to call on me. That's one good thing about Mr. Tomski—he's not one of those teachers who calls on you if you don't raise your hand. But it's just a normal class; he doesn't seem to notice me.

Mabley sits next to me on the bus ride home. Now that the Number Sense competition is over, I don't have to stay after school.

"You want to hear something weird?" I tell her. "Guess who's coming to dinner at my house tonight."

"Who?"

"Mr. Tomski."

For some reason, I feel bad even talking about it, but

I talk about it anyway. It's like I'm using this information to say something funny, because I want Mabley to
be interested in what I say, but the information isn't really
information—it's something actually happening to me.

"It's not that weird," Mabley says. "It's like, medium
weird. It's on the weird scale, but it's not . . . I mean, your
mom is a teacher. They're just like colleagues, right?"

"I don't know. What am I supposed to say to him?"

"Remember to raise your hand before you speak,"
Mabley says. But she's not really making fun of me, she's
just trying to go along with it.

That night, when the doorbell rings, Mom calls out,
"Can you get that, Ben?" She's getting changed in the
bedroom, and Granma's busy in the kitchen. So I open
the door and there he is. He's got a bunch of flowers in his
hand, and he looks about as nervous as I feel.

"Good evening, Ben," he says, and clears his throat. "Is
your mom at home?"

I notice two little pink marks on his nose, where his
glasses must have pinched him—but he isn't wearing
glasses when he comes to our house. It feels funny to have
a teacher on our doorstep.

"She's just . . ." but I don't want to say she's getting
ready, like she's trying to make herself pretty for him.
"She told me to get the door. You can come in."

Mr. Tomski wears the same jacket and tie he always

wears to school. He doesn't know whether to give the flowers to Granma or to wait for my mom. In the end, Granma takes them off his hands and puts them in a vase, which she sets on the table.

"Don't they look sweet," Granma says. I can tell she's making an effort to be nice.

"Hey, Mom," I call out, toward the bedroom. "Mr. Tomski's here."

"Please," he says. "Outside of school, you can call me Tom."

"Is that your name?" Granma asks, laughing. "Tom Tomski?"

Mr. Tomski has a lopsided face, with heavy cheeks and thick eyebrows. He also has a lot of very black hair, but either he didn't comb it or it just got messy anyway, because it sticks out in all directions. When he smiles, it looks like he's sucking on a piece of candy.

"My Christian name is Harlan, but I never liked it much. Everybody just calls me Tom." He talks kind of slow—like he has nowhere to get to and doesn't mind passing the time. Then Mom walks in, wearing a green dress. She gives him a hug and we sit down.

Granma has made meat loaf with tomato sauce, and Mr. Tomski eats his plate clean, twice. But he doesn't "contribute much to the conversation," as Granma likes to say. He lets her and Mom do most of the talking—they kind of fight and tease each other at the same time. "One thing I didn't realize when I moved back home," Mom says, "is just how much I would regress. It's like Ben and me are the kids again. We even share my old bedroom. I used to lie in that bed and think, I wish I had a sister. Or a brother. And now I've got Ben."

And she looks at me with big eyes, where I can see the makeup on her lids. But this is something private she told me—it upsets me that she's telling it to Mr. Tomski. It also feels like she's showing off, and one of the things she's showing off about is how well we get along. I don't know what to say, but it doesn't matter because Granma says, "And I get to be the mean old mom again. I go in and say lights out, kids."

But this isn't even true. "You always go to bed first, Granma. Everybody falls asleep before me. I have to read with a flashlight under the covers."

"It's good to have a kid who loves to read," Mr. Tomski says, just because it's the kind of thing a teacher is supposed to say. "You never read again like you do when you're young."

"Oh, Ben always has a book in his hands," Mom says. "Sometimes I can't get him out of bed."

Eventually, Mr. Tomski sits back and pulls out his tie again—he had tucked it inside his shirt, between two buttons.

"That was a fine meal," he says. "Thank you, Mrs. Koehner."

Granma smiles. "It's nice to have people to cook for."

Granma starts clearing the table and brings out coffee and an apple pie. Mr. Tomski shifts his head a little to the side, because those flowers are blocking his view, and says, "Jenny tells me that your father used to play basketball."

It takes me a second to realize that he's talking to me. "I guess so."

"He played in college, or so she tells me."

"I don't really know," I say.

"Well, maybe you'd like to try out for the team some time. One of our kids is moving to Albuquerque at Christmas. We'll have a vacancy on the roster."

"I'll think about it, Mr. Tomski." I say this in my "polite voice," but what I really mean is "leave me alone."

"I tell you what." He doesn't seem to take the hint. "The new year is a good time to start new things. How about you come out anyway, when we get back from the holidays? We could use a manager; there's always something to do." He moves the flowers a little so he can look at me. "Not a bad way to make some friends," he adds.

"That's a great idea, Tom," my mother says.

She gives me a sharp look, which means, *Behave yourself.* But I'm angry and don't want to behave.

"Did *you* ever play basketball?" I ask him. "I mean, in college."

Mr. Tomski leans back in his chair. "I always had a great love for the game of basketball. More love than talent. I played a little in high school. Mostly I sat on the bench. In college, though, I volunteered to be the team manager. I got to travel around with the players and watch their games. I also did things like wash their uniforms and keep score in practice, that kind of thing."

"That doesn't sound like much fun," I say.

Mr. Tomski takes a sip of coffee. "You know what I always loved about basketball?" he asks me. "It's like a problem to be solved. And part of that problem is people. You have to work out what kind of people you are dealing with, and what they can give you, and what they *can't* give you. It's a little like teaching that way."

One of the things that annoys me about Mr. Tomski is the way he gives you his complete attention. I think he thinks that . . . I don't know, it's like he wants you to know he's taking you seriously, but really it just makes you feel like a little kid. But he talks to everybody this way, even my mom.

"The other thing about basketball," he says to her, "from a coach's point of view, is that people leave you alone. This is a football town. If you're the football coach, you get people breathing down your neck, partly just because of the money involved. It costs about five hundred dollars to outfit one kid to play football. Basketball is basically free. You can do what you want."

At this point it's a little after ten o'clock. Mr. Tomski puts his hands on the table and slowly pushes himself up. "It's been a treat," he says, mostly looking at Granma. "But it's a school night and I need to get my beauty sleep." He turns to me. "Good night, Ben. I've told your mother, she's got a lot to be proud of. You're not one of those kids a teacher has to worry about, though I wouldn't mind hearing from you a little more in class. I have a feeling you've got good things to say."

"I'll try, Mr. Tomski."

He smiles at me. "Tomski's fine for the classroom, but we can work on that, too."

Mom gets up. "I'll walk you out," she says. She follows him to the door and leaves it open as they stand on the front porch. I start helping Granma clear the dessert plates, but she's not really doing anything—she's just standing at the sink. After a minute, she kind of comes to attention. "Leave that, Ben. Why don't you get ready for bed." I can tell that she's listening for the door to close; she's waiting for Mom to come back in.

"Okay," I say, but I don't move either.

Then Mom comes in and says, "I can do this in the morning—I'm not teaching till third period."

"I don't mind," Granma says.

"That was a nice meal you made. Tom said how much he enjoyed himself. . . . He hasn't had much home cooking since his divorce." Then she looks at me; her makeup has started to smudge around her eyes; she seems worn-out. "Ben, it's late, and you've got an early start. If you get ready now, we won't all be fighting for the bathroom."

Even after I'm lying in bed, I can hear Mom and Granma talking in the kitchen. Just their voices, not the words. They must be doing the dishes—I can hear the clink of plates and pots, too, and fall asleep before Mom comes in.

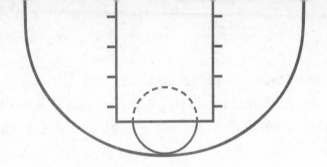

FOURTEEN

ALL THE TEACHERS kind of give up teaching for the last two weeks of school before winter break. Even Mr. Tomski—I was worried he might try to talk to me in class, but he treats me just the same and leaves me alone.

There's going to be a big Christmas band concert, and Mabley and some of her cafeteria friends spend every lunchtime rehearsing. Sometimes I see them in the halls, lugging their instruments around. It doesn't really matter to me—I don't eat lunch with Mabley anymore, but still I feel jealous watching them troop off together, talking about all the stuff you talk about when you're doing the same thing together. She says hi whenever she sees me, but she's friendly to everybody—she says hi to a lot of kids. It's different for me. She's one of the only people I talk to.

It's getting cold now. There are these low December skies that seem to go on forever, but I still go out to the court to eat lunch. Shooting and chasing the ball down warms me up. All morning I look forward to these twenty minutes by myself, and afterward, when I'm sitting in class again, I look out the window and imagine I'm still there.

On the last day of school, Mom offers to drive me home after class. "We can go out for hamburgers," she says. We're walking to the bus stop in the morning. It's still dark outside. You can see lights coming on behind curtains, people getting up for work. It's cold but not New York cold; there's a mist in the trees. Part of me wants to catch the bus home with everybody else. But I say, "That'd be great," because I think that's what she wants to hear.

"It's a date," she says. "We could use a little just-you-and-me time."

The usual crowd of kids is waiting at the corner—I can see them at the end of the block. But Mom stops for a second, with her hand on my sleeve. "There's something else I want to say," she says. "Your dad called last night. He's still hoping to come for a couple of days between Christmas and New Year's. There are people he has to see in the Houston office. But he's not sure."

"Where's he going to sleep?"

"What? I don't know, Ben. He'll find a hotel."

"Because I can sleep on the sofa, if that makes a difference. I don't mind."

"It wouldn't be *you* on the sofa anyway," Mom says. "Anyway," she says again—she seems distracted. "You know what he's like. There are plans and plans. It's a long way from London. It's a long way from Houston, too. But either way you need to be prepared, that's why I mentioned it. Are you all right?"

"I'm fine, Mom. Don't worry about me."

She looks at me, holding me at arm's length—like she's checking my face for symptoms or something. "I'm going to say goodbye here." And then she laughs. "It's a little early in the morning for kids to have to talk to one of their teachers. That goes for the other way round as well."

On the bus, Mabley sits on the seat in front of me—there are four kids squeezed on her bench. Normally, the driver doesn't allow more than three. But today she doesn't care, it's the last day of school. Everybody's talking about Christmas. Mabley's going to San Antonio, where her grandparents live. They have a ranch, with chickens and pigs and a cow and three horses. "Basically," she says, "they just put me to work. I love it." Even when she talks about this place, her voice changes. Her grandmother has a real Scottish accent, even after fifty years in Texas. "She calls me *that child*," Mabley says. "*Is that child ever going to grow? What do you give her to eat? A crust of bread?*"

The sun comes up while we wait in traffic at one of the lights. It's so low in the sky, the driver pulls down the flap over the windshield. It's a weird kind of white light; you can see the sunshine climbing over the raised highway, which casts a wide stripe of shadow over the road. All the cars sparkle.

Mabley leans over the back of her seat to talk to me.

"Are you going somewhere for Christmas?"

"My dad is coming," I say.

She doesn't say anything, but she makes her eyes wide and opens her mouth in wonder. Her face has a lot of expressions she can do. She uses it like that, too, like she doesn't care about how she looks.

"Well, he said he was going to try to," I tell her. "I don't know."

Something's gone wrong with the heating when we get to school. It's turning into a pretty warm day, but nobody can control the temperature. Ms. Kaminski opens all the windows; you can hear the cars going by outside. She has a Santa hat on, and the apple on her desk is a candy apple with a ribbon around it—Pete gave it to her as a present. Some kids leave early to get set up for the concert; there's going to be an assembly in the afternoon. But nobody does any work anyway, and after lunch we all troop over to the main gym. The good thing about assemblies is you just have to sit there—you don't have to do anything, or pay attention, or talk to anybody.

I've never seen Mabley play the saxophone before. She sits in a row on a plastic cafeteria chair with everybody else in the wind section. Her short yellow hair falls across her face, and she has to flick it aside, so she can read the music. The conductor, Mr. Hoskins, is a stocky guy, kind of square, with short gray hair, almost like a crew cut. He's wearing a blue jacket that comes down pretty low on his pants. When he waves the baton around, it's like his feet are stuck in cement in the ground and his whole body is trying to get away.

They're playing the theme tune to some movie—I think it's *Braveheart*. It starts out slow and squeaky and then gets loud and squeaky. The acoustics in the gym are pretty terrible anyway: it's like a bad radio. Also, there are a lot of flutes. It's one of those songs that's meant to make you feel happy and sad at the same time, it's pretty cheesy, but even though I don't want to, that's what I feel. All these kids are playing their best, and it's not very good because they're kids; but when they grow up, they're probably going to stop playing musical instruments any-way, because that's what most people do, and this is really the one time in their lives where they're going to try to be good at stuff like this.

We spend the last class of the day watching a movie and then the bell rings and even before it's stopped ring-ing kids are headed out the door. It's like they've all eaten ten bars of chocolate, everybody's got a sugar rush. I have to get my bags together but at least I can skip the traffic jam by the lockers in the hallway. Mom is a little late, but I wait for her by the Toyota, in the afternoon sunshine. The temperature is something like sixty-five degrees; it feels like a spring day in New York. Kids are streaming out, cars pull into the parking lot or inch their way behind the buses. Teachers come out, too. I see Mr. Tomski with something in his hair, like he keeps trying to get it out, rubbing his head with both hands, but he's also smiling. And then someone stops to talk to him, and it's my mom, and I wait for a few minutes watching them before she heads over to the car.

"There you are," she says, opening the door. "Well, we made it. People say the first six months are the hardest."

"First six months of what?"

"When you move somewhere, when you start over."

"After that, everything's easy."

"Everything's a piece of cake," she says.

*

On Christmas Eve, my dad calls. Granma picks up the phone. She has a short conversation and then I hear her say, "Do you want to talk to the big one or the small one? All right, all right," and she passes me the handset.

I'm sitting in my favorite chair and watching *The Simpsons*. It's the one show my dad used to watch with me in New York. Sometimes I had to ask him to explain the jokes. But whenever it was on, I'd say, "Hey, Dad, Dad, it's *The Simpsons*," because I knew he'd let me watch. The Christmas tree next to the television is already decorated, and Mom comes in and says, "How can you stare at the TV with all those flashing lights?"

"He's talking to his father," Granma tells her.

"Oh."

I hear all this, but I'm also listening to my dad. "I'm not going to be able to make it this time, Ben. I don't know if your mother said something to you. . . . I was hoping to come see you for a few days after Christmas. But it's not going to be possible. I'm sorry," he says. "They're working me pretty hard over here. Do you know what time it is in London?"

"What time is it?" I press the mute button on the remote control.

"Midnight," my dad says, sounding closer. "Midnight on Christmas Eve. And I'm still in the office." He laughs, but after a moment, he adds, "I miss you, Son."

"I miss you, too." Mom has gone back into the kitchen, Granma's in her room; they're leaving me alone. "Dad," I say, "Dad," and he says, "What?"

"What's that school in London called, the one you talked about?"

"What school?" he says.

"The one American kids go to, near where the Beatles used to . . ."

"It's called the American School. Why are you asking?"

For a second I don't answer.

"Why do you want to know, Ben?"

"I don't know. I was just . . . telling some kid at school about it." Then I say, "Dad, I'm not sure I like it here."

"Why not?"

"I don't really know anybody. The kids are all . . . they act like this is their home, and it's not mine. On the last day of school, they were all making plans to see each other. I didn't have anybody to make plans with."

"Give it time, Son," he says. "These things take time."

"I want to live in London with you."

I can hear him on the phone, even though he doesn't say anything—I can hear him breathing. Eventually he says, "I'd like that, too. This is something we can talk about. Right now, they're working me pretty hard. But we can talk about it."

"I miss New York," I say.

"Well, London isn't New York. Okay, kid. I just wanted to say Merry Christmas. Everything's going to work out. It's hard at the beginning, but after a while . . . And if it doesn't work out, you fix it, right? Is your mother around? I should probably say hello."

"Mom!" I call out. "Mom!" But she can't hear me, so I have to get up off the sofa. "Wait a minute, Dad," I say and put down the phone. "Mom!" I shout, walking into the kitchen. For some reason it really annoys me that she can't hear. But the tap is running; she's standing over the sink and turns around. "What?"

"Dad wants to talk to you."

"Oh, he wants to talk to *me* . . . ," she says in a funny kind of voice. She walks into the living room, drying her hands on her apron.

"He says he can't come." I follow her quietly. I want to warn her. "He's not going to be able to make it."

She's already angry when she picks up the phone.

"So you're not coming," she says.

For the next few minutes, I only hear her side of the conversation. "You realize what this does to him," she says. "It'd probably be easier if you didn't make promises you can't keep. It doesn't matter . . . that doesn't matter. It's what he hears. He hears that you want to see him, and then you don't. I'm the one who has to deal with him . . ."

"Mom," I say. "Mom, it's all right. I'm all right."

But it goes on like this for another few minutes, and then she hangs up. "Come here," she says afterward, and opens her arms. There are tears in her eyes. "I'm sorry, Ben. It's better just the two of us, anyway. You and me, kid." I let her hold me, because it's what she wants.

"I'm fine," I say, talking into her apron. "He's just working hard, he explained it."

"It's not your job to make excuses for him," she says.

The next day is Christmas, another sunny day. I go into the garden after breakfast and poke around the bamboo for a while, hoping Mabley comes out. Then I remember, she's in San Antonio. The trampoline is covered in leaves. So I take out my bike from the shed and ride around the neighborhood. A couple of boys are playing football in the street, but I don't know them. The swimming pool is empty in the park. Nobody's really using the playground, except the kiddy bit, with little slides and swings; a couple of dads are leading their toddlers around. The grass is yellow; the basketball court has wet patches on it: it must have rained last night. Eventually I bike home again—the day seems pretty long.

Mom is in our bedroom, where I'm not allowed to go because she's wrapping gifts. Granma's fussing in the kitchen.

"Maybe you'd like to call one of your friends," she says. "One of your friends from New York."

"I don't know Jake's number. I never used to call him, I just knocked on his door."

"I'm sure your mother can find it," Granma says.

The first time I call, nobody answers. It's exciting to hear it ring, and I can see the hallway in his apartment where they keep the phone. Funny to think that just because I pressed some buttons, two thousand miles away in New York, there's this noise . . . just a few floors down from where I used to live. But when the answering machine finally comes on, I feel relieved. I don't leave a message.

A few neighbors stop by to say hello. Granma has been living in the house for over fifty years, and a lot of the people she used to know on her street have died or moved out, but there are new families around with small kids, and sometimes the mothers ring the doorbell. ("Checking up on me," Granma calls it.) Someone brings gingerbread cookies, and I eat one politely. Mom makes coffee; they sit around and gossip. "It must be *so* nice for you to have a full house again." That's the kind of thing they say. I'm glad when they go.

Afterward, we sit down to Christmas dinner—on the dark wood table that usually lives in a corner of the living room. "Where you can see the Christmas tree," Mom says. She puts on a fancy cloth and lights candles. We're all pretty sick of turkey after Thanksgiving, so Granma makes a brisket, which is easier, and everybody likes it more anyway.

"I don't believe in food as punishment," she says.

After dinner, I call Jake again. But the phone keeps ringing and the answering machine clicks on again.

We open our presents. I get two big ones and a lot of small ones. The big present from Granma is an old pocket watch, the kind that you hang on a chain, which my grandpa used to wear. When he was young, he served in the merchant marine. He helped carry supplies to soldiers in the Second World War. Granma likes to tell me stories. He worked in the engine room. A lot of cargo ships were lost, torpedoed by the Germans. The back of the watch has a logo on it that says *Acta Non Verba* and Kings Point 1943.

"Do you know what that means?" Granma asks. "*Acta non verba*?"

"No." I hold the watch to my ear to listen to it ticking.

"Actions, not words."

"Great." Mom rolls her eyes. "That's just what he needs to hear. Because Ben's real problem is that he talks too much, right? He sits there in school every day eating lunch by himself. . . . I have to *pay* him to talk."

"*Acta non verba*," I say, and Granma laughs. "Anyway,

you never *did* pay me."

"That's because you never talked," Mom says.

My second big present is a new fountain pen with a gold nib in a velvet case that shuts with a loud snap. A pack of ink cartridges, too. I also get a diary with a leather cover and a page for each day of the year. "You've got a lot going on, stuff you might want to remember," Granma says. "This way you can write it down."

I give her a hug, then I give Mom a hug. It used to be, when I hugged her, that my arms went around her waist. Now I can feel something under her shirt at the back— her bra strap. My head is at her shoulder, I let go pretty soon. When we're finished unwrapping, I ask, "Can I call Jake again?"

"You can try," Mom says.

This time Jake's mother picks up the phone. "Hi, Mrs. Schultz," I say. "It's Ben . . . Michaels calling. Is Jake around?"

"Hey, Ben." Her voice is super friendly—it's the voice grown-ups use to talk to little kids. "He sure is. I'll go get him."

But when Jake answers, I don't know what to say. I panic. "Hey, Jake" is the best I can come up with.

"Hey, Ben." His voice sounds different from what I remembered. I mean, he sounds like Jake, but it's also like . . . he's this other person, while in my head, when I've been talking to him in my head, it's like, I know exactly what he's going to say.

"What did you get for Christmas?" The phone line isn't great; there's a little delay, so we end up answering at the same time. "I got an old watch and a fountain pen."

"I got a dog," Jake says. "My sister is really pissed off. She bugged my parents for a dog for years, and now she's in college. . . . Mom said, it's because I miss her. Which is just . . . I mean, I said, Hey, Jennifer, look what we got to replace you. It's a bearded collie; it's like one of those dogs with so much hair, it can hardly see. . . . I mean, I just kept laughing. Jennifer was so pissed off."

"That's funny," I say. "That's so funny." But it doesn't sound like I mean it, I don't know why. And he kind of runs out of steam; he doesn't say anything else. He doesn't ask me any questions. Finally, I say, "What did you do today?"

"It snowed last night, so we went to Central Park. We had to take the dog for a walk anyway. Dad made me clean up her poop. Then we had a snowball fight and I hit Dad in the nose. I couldn't tell if he was mad or just pretending to be mad."

"There's no snow here. It's like eighty degrees outside. I've been playing a lot of basketball."

"Who do you play with?" Jake asks. It's the first thing he's asked me, but I don't want to answer because the answer is nobody.

"There's this kid called Pete," I say. It's not really a lie, it's just like I'm answering a different question. "He's like the star of the basketball team. Anyway, we went to this Number Sense competition, and he got annoyed because . . ." But it all gets a little complicated. For some reason I don't want to talk about Mabley, even though she's really the point of the story. Or not the point exactly, but the part I want to talk about, even though I also *don't* want to talk about her. It doesn't make sense. "For a while, it was like, they might suspend him from the team," I say. "But he's too good. Anyway . . . nothing happened in the end. They didn't do anything." It feels like a lame way to finish the story and I don't think Jake is paying attention. He hasn't said anything for a while.

"You probably have to go," I say.

"Yeah, I should probably go."

I hang up, and it's almost a relief to get off the phone.

"How's Jake?" Mom asks. She and Granma were doing dishes in the kitchen, but as soon as I hang up they come in.

"Yeah, he's good."

"It's so nice you got to talk to him. I bet he missed you.

Did you tell him you missed him?"

"Mom . . ."

"What?" she says.

"Of course I didn't tell him that."

"Why not? It's true. I bet he misses you, too."

"He didn't sound like . . ."

"What?" Mom says. She's standing with her hands on her hips. Her hair is a little frizzy from the heat of the kitchen—she looks mad, which isn't how she means to look, but I don't think she can help it when she's in one of her *I'm concerned about you* moods.

"Nothing."

"No, I want to know. He didn't sound like what?"

"Nothing . . . he didn't sound like anything."

"That's not what you were going to say."

"Why do you make me say things I don't want to say?"

Mom looks at me with wet eyes. "I don't make you . . ."

"Yes, you do, all the time. *Ben doesn't talk. Pay Ben to talk.* I'll talk when I want to."

"Okay, Ben. All right."

"I'll talk when I feel like it. I mean, what's the point? What do you want me to say? Do you want me to say that Jake sounded totally fine? Like, he's got a new dog, and he's at home . . . I mean, he sounded fine. What do you want me to say?"

"Nothing. I want you to say what you want to say."

"Well, I don't want to say anything."

"Fine," she says. "Let's nobody say anything."

And Granma gives her a look. Like, leave him alone. Let it blow over. As if I can't see.

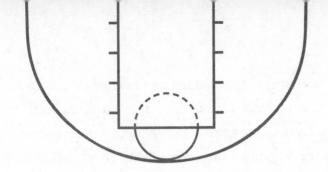

FIFTEEN

FOR THE REST OF THE VACATION, Mom makes me use the diary—it's called "keeping a diary" apparently, like keeping a dog or something, like you have to take it for a walk every day. (Jake gets a dog for Christmas and I get an empty book with lined pages.) But it's my fault. One morning I complain to her, "I'm bored," and she says, "Why don't you write something?" and I say, "What should I write?"

"Granma gave you that diary. She'll be upset if you don't use it."

"But I don't have anything to write about."

Granma's gone shopping and we're sitting at the kitchen table, which is still full of breakfast stuff. It's my job to clear it, which basically means putting everything in the sink, but it only takes about five minutes, and since I don't really have anything else to do, I'm not in any hurry. It's eleven o'clock in the morning.

"Write what happens to you."

"Nothing happens to me. I sit around all day. Sometimes I sit in the yard, sometimes I go for a bike ride. Nothing happens."

"Write what you're thinking about, write what you're feeling."

"I don't really think anything."

"We both know that's not true, Ben." But a few minutes later, she says, "Just write anything. Write down the weather."

So that's what I do. Every morning I check the temperature on Granma's outdoor thermometer, which is shaped like a fish for some reason and is nailed to the wall by the back door. After breakfast, I describe what I had for breakfast, and I check the overnight scores in the sports page and write some of those down, too. But sometimes I add a few lines before going to bed, about what I did that day, before Mom turns my lights off. It's usually a good excuse for staying up a little later. Sometimes I write about where I went on my bike, the different routes, or list what we watched on TV after dinner. It turns out to be pretty easy to fill a page.

Then it's the new year and school starts again.

Mom wakes me up at six thirty in the morning, which hurts again, because I'm used to getting up whenever I want. But I put on my clothes and brush my teeth and eat a bowl of Cheerios and head out the door. It's still dark outside, and it feels like this is real now, this is my life.

Mabley is already at the bus stop, talking to other kids, but she stops talking and comes over to give me a hug. "Did you have a good Christmas? What did you get?" she says, but then the bus arrives and she climbs on with other people. I sit behind her and I can hear their conversation.

Some girl says, "It doesn't feel like Christmas unless you at least see *some* snow." Her grandparents live in Colorado; she went skiing on Echo Mountain.

Mabley says, "For me it doesn't feel like Christmas unless I'm clearing out horse manure from the stable. I guess everybody's different."

Then we drive under the highway, and through the neighborhood streets around the school, and pull into the parking lot. It's just another school day.

In social studies class, Mr. Tomski pulls me aside after

the bell rings. "I look forward to seeing you at basketball practice today."

I stare at him.

"Your mother said you wanted to be the manager," he says. "Just go to the main gym after the last bell. I'll show you what to do—it's all pretty straightforward."

When I don't say anything, he puts his hand on my shoulder. "Give it a try, son. Everything looks worse from the outside. We'll have some fun today."

After lunch, I run into my mother in the hallway—she's talking to one of the other teachers, and laughing, the way she does sometimes with other people, because she wants them to like her.

"Mom," I say, and she turns around, still smiling.

"Hey, Ben"—like she's surprised to see me, and everything's great. "This is my son, Ben," she tells the woman. "He's in seventh grade."

"I've heard a lot about you," the woman says. She's wearing a sweatshirt that's too big for her. It says, Kettner's Cafe, New Braunfels, Texas, on the front, and underneath: "*Sprechen Sie Bratwurst?*"

"Mom, can I talk to you?"

"Sure, Ben." She's still in social mode—like I'm one of her students.

"In private."

"Excuse us a minute," Mom tells the woman, and we go into an empty classroom. It's a biology classroom and there are posters of skeletons all over the walls, diagrams of hearts and lungs, and a big papier-mâché rhinoceros sitting on one of the desks, with a Santa cap on its head.

"That was rude," Mom says, "and I don't like being rude."

"Mr. Tomski told me to come to basketball practice today."

"I thought that's what we decided."

"You decided it! You did! I never said I was going to go."

Mom says quietly, "Keep your voice down, Ben. This is my place of work. The people here are my colleagues and students. You cannot talk to me this way in front of them."

"What about me? I'm your son."

"Then talk to me like my son."

"That's what I'm doing."

"No, you're talking to me like a spoiled, angry . . ."

"I don't want to be the basketball manager," I say.

"Give it a try, Ben. Right now you don't want to be anything."

"I don't want to be here, that's for sure. I don't want . . ."

"What do you want me to do then?" and suddenly my

mom sounds angry, too. "I can't make your father come back, I can't do that. I'm doing what I can. I need your help."

"You can't make me go to basketball practice either."

"No," she says, sitting on the teacher's desk. She isn't shouting anymore—she just sounds tired. "I can't make anybody do anything, obviously."

But then the bell rings, and Mom says, "I have to go teach. You have to go learn. You know what I expect of you . . . what I'm asking you to do. Give it a try, Ben, please." She opens the door again, and all the school sounds come back in; kids in the hallways, everybody talking and in a hurry. Three eighth graders come into the room and look at me, laughing. I pick up my bags and squeeze past them.

After my last class, when the long bell rings, I wait in the hallway until most of the kids have gone, then walk down the empty corridors to the gym. Most of the players are getting changed, but I just sit on one of the bleachers and wait for them to come out of the locker room. Mr. Tomski drags a bag of balls through the office doorway onto the court, but I don't know what he wants me to do with them.

Eventually he calls out, "Maybe you can help me with these."

He's putting orange cones down in a pattern—around the three-point line, at the free throw line, and at a few other places in between. "I'd like you to set these cones up the same way on the other side of the court," he says.

So that's what I do. Pete's probably watching me—setting everything up so he can play. Meanwhile, Mr. Tomski gets the players in a circle and takes them through some stretches. They're all wearing white practice uniforms with HORNETS written across them in orange letters and a picture on the back that looks more like a friendly bee. It's a dumb mascot, but I still feel jealous of those kids, because they belong together, and I don't. It's like, ever since I left New York, I'm on the outside looking in. That's why you need a best friend. With Jake around, I was on the inside.

For the next two hours, I chase balls and move the cones around. Mr. Tomski gives me a clipboard, which has a piece of paper on it with all the boys' names. Whenever they run a drill, Mr. Tomski wants me to put a mark next to the name of the boy who took the shot. An *X* if he misses the shot, and a check if he makes it. I feel sneaky, writing down these marks, because it's just for the coach—the kids don't get to see them. But it also makes me feel like I have some kind of power.

Pete is the best player on the court. He comes first in every race and ends up with the most checks by his name.

Even the net acts different when Pete makes a shot—the ball spins back and almost seems to bounce into his hand. If he *does* miss, he scowls and shakes his head like he's mad at somebody—like somebody *made* him miss. In fact, he even blames me. One of my jobs is to stand under the basket and get rebounds, then pass the ball back out so kids can work on their jump shots. Anyway, Pete doesn't like the way I pass him the ball. He's left-handed, so he wants me to throw the ball to his left hand. But three or four kids are shooting at once, I'm just trying to keep up.

"Come on, Ben!" he says. "I'm waiting."

For some reason this reminds me of Jake. Sometimes, when we were hanging out, I used to wonder why I liked him. I mean, would I like him if I just met him, if he wasn't already my friend? Jake is one of those kids . . . Even in school, he asks for a lot of attention. I don't really like attention. Whenever he got a test back, if he got something wrong, Jake would say, "Oh, come on!" Like, loud enough for the teacher to hear. Not like he was really mad but just kind of pretending to be mad, so the teachers had to say something. And they always fell for it, they always said, "What is it now, Jake?" Pete's kind of the same way. It's like, whenever he misses, he has to let everybody know that something's gone wrong, this isn't supposed to happen. It's like he thinks, How could this happen to *me*?

At the end of practice, I walk around the court with a big sack and put the balls away for the last time. The basketball office is next to the locker room, so I carry all the equipment through and dump it on the floor. The door swings shut behind me. Some of the boys come into the locker room. I can hear them talking.

"I don't even know why he's here," somebody says.

"He's always carrying that clipboard around." It's Pete's voice. "It's kind of creepy. I'm, like, get away from me. You're not the coach."

I wait for a minute, until they go off to the showers, before walking out again.

Mom is supposed to pick me up at the gym. There isn't a school bus at six o'clock, so most kids need a ride. At first, I think she must have forgotten, but then I hear her saying, loud enough so everyone can hear, "Look at you. My basketball boy." She's been talking to Mr. Tomski.

Pete's just coming out of the locker room with wet hair. His face looks pink and hot from the shower. "Hey," he says to me, but quietly, so nobody can hear. "That's a good name for you. Ball Boy." He means like those kids at a tennis match who have to run around and get the balls for everybody else, who don't even play. And then he calls out, "Hey, Mrs. Michaels. Ben did great," and he says to me, so Mom can hear him, "See ya tomorrow, Ben."

"You hear that?" Mom says to me as we walk to the parking lot. "You're already making new friends. Pete Miller's a real popular kid. Even I know that."

When we get in the car, Mom's still talking about it. "I told you that you'd have a good time. Didn't I? And you didn't want to go. Sometimes I'm right, sometimes I know even better than you do, what makes you happy."

I don't say anything. After our fight at lunchtime, I don't want to pick another fight. I don't want to tell her, Mom, I hate it here and I hate the basketball team. I hate everything. I want to go back to New York. Or London, or anywhere else. Mom looks happy for me, and I don't have the heart to tell her, nobody likes me. Whenever I'm around other people, they all wish I wasn't.

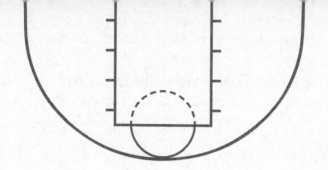

SIXTEEN

IN TEXAS IN JANUARY, there are warm days and cold days—wet days and dry days. You never can tell what you're going to get. But it doesn't matter to me. Every lunchtime, I take my brown paper bag to the basketball court behind Sam's hut, sit on the bench, and eat my sandwiches.

Afterward, I like to shoot baskets. The ball is always where I've left it the day before: under the bench. Whenever a shot goes in, I imagine making a check by my name on the clipboard Mr. Tomski gives me during practice. Whenever I miss, I imagine an *X*.

It's a tough place to shoot. Because of that tree branch on one side and the telephone wire on the other, you have to put a lot of arc on the ball. The rim is hard iron, which makes the ball kind of bang around—sometimes it rattles halfway in and rattles out again. But I feel like I'm on an island somewhere, and nobody can reach me or get to me. The only thing that matters is making the next shot, that's what I'm concentrating on. If it goes in, it's like getting an answer to something, and the answer is yes; and if it doesn't, you just have to keep shooting.

Every day after school, I go to basketball practice and set out the cones and collect the balls and take notes on Mr. Tomski's clipboard. I help put everything away at the end of the day and make sure the uniforms are washed and ready before each game. But I never bounce a ball or take a shot on one of the baskets in the gym—I want Mr. Tomski to know that I'm not having fun. I'm just doing something because I have to do it. Because my mom thinks this is best.

The season's been going since November, but my first game is Friday the 15th—against Pflugerville. Almost two weeks since we got back to school. (Mr. Tomski gave me a calendar with all the game dates, and Mom put it up on the fridge.) We meet in the gym after the last bell. I ride the school bus with them and carry their uniforms in a big duffel bag. It's about a half hour journey. I can't tell you how lonely it feels on that bus. None of the kids talks to me—they're all on the team together, about to play a game—and I'm sitting in front with Mr. Tomski and a bag of clothes at my feet. The sun's going down, we're on the highway, there are cars coming and going below us, and I feel like everything I know is a long way away.

Even Mr. Tomski feels bad for me. He tries to start a conversation but eventually gives up—all I give him are yes or no answers. It's all I *can* give, just saying a word is like lifting a heavy sack. You want to put it down again as soon as possible; you want to stop talking because at least that doesn't take any work. You can just stare out the window.

Pflugerville has a pretty good team this year. They've got this one kid, Travis Brown, who's already got some college scouts looking at him—you can see them in the stands, middle-aged guys wearing jackets, writing notes. Before the game starts, Mr. Tomski takes Pete aside—he puts his arm around him and points into the crowd. One of the men waves and stands up; he walks over to the coach, who introduces him to Pete. All the other kids are doing layup lines, but I'm sitting there on the bench. I can hear Mr. Tomski say, "Keep your eye on this kid, Howard."

It's a pretty close game. The gym is packed; you can feel the heat of the overhead lights; and the Pflugerville kids stamp their feet against the bleachers to make noise—it's like being at the bottom of a ship. Travis Brown is almost six foot six, but he handles the ball a lot, too, and guards Pete on the other end. Pete's too short to shoot over him so he has to be tricky. He head fakes and gets Travis in the air; he leans in and forces the ref to blow the whistle. He takes a lot of free throws.

With fifteen seconds left, we're up by two points, and Pete's at the foul line, shooting two. If he makes both, the game is over—there's no way Pflugerville can come back. And I'm sitting on the bench and hoping Pete misses, and feeling miserable and ashamed at the same time. It's mean, and I feel mean, but it doesn't matter what I feel because Pete makes them anyway; and when the game is over, and the kids are all shouting in the locker room, laughing and goofing around, it doesn't matter what I do because nobody notices me.

But this is what I do: I pick up their sweaty jerseys and shorts from the locker room floor. Then I put them back, soaking and stinking, into the bag and drag it to the bus. That's what I sit with on the ride back to school—a duffel bag full of smelly, wet clothes.

*

It's dark now, and we get stuck in traffic coming back into Austin. You can just see the lights of cars coming and going. The countryside around is pretty flat; there are some trees by the side of the road that look yellow in the streetlamps, and gas stations and taco stands and fast-food restaurants. The engine noise, especially at the front, is very loud. If I close my eyes and pretend to sleep, Mr. Tomski won't try to talk to me, he won't try to include me in the conversation. So I close my eyes and even fall asleep for real, so when the bus pulls into the school parking lot, Mr. Tomski has to wake me up.

"Come on, Ben, we're home," he says, shaking my shoulder. "Your mom is waiting for you."

The school looks different at night—the white brick walls are lit up like a prison, and you can see arcs of pale light on the dead grass. The parking lot is almost empty, apart from a few other cars, parents picking up their kids. It's starting to rain a little, but it isn't cold. I can feel the rain as I get off the bus.

Mom is standing there, holding a sweater over her head. "So, how'd we do?" she says, and Mr. Tomski tells her, "We won."

"Yay," she says, and gives me a hug. Then we drive home together, and I have to pretend to be excited about it all.

*

Next Thursday, Mr. Tomski comes to dinner again. He brings flowers again, and it all happens like it did last time, it's kind of awkward and boring and I don't know what to think about him.

He's got big hands, that's one thing I notice. And tough, thick knuckles. He doesn't always know what to do with his hands. He puts them on his lap like he's hiding them away, but then when he talks somehow one of them escapes—he puts his arm out to make a point, then feels embarrassed, and the hand goes back on his lap. But he doesn't talk much. Mostly he listens.

"I'm so pleased," Mom says, "about the basketball. Ben's like a new person—I see kids talking to him in the hallway. They know his name, it's made a real difference."

"Well, he's been working hard," Mr. Tomski says. "I don't know what Ben's getting out of it yet, but it's made a difference to me."

Mom puts her arm around me—she's sitting next to me at the kitchen table. "It takes a while, but we're getting settled in."

It's like she wants to show off how close we are.

Granma brings out a roast chicken and sets it down on the table—the steam from the tray gets in her face, she blows her hair out of her eyes. She says to Mr. Tomski, "Will you do the honors?" and passes him the carving knife. His tie is tucked into his shirt, but he rolls up his sleeves and leans over the chicken—he's good with a knife, very careful, and carves out nice fat pieces of meat.

"It's good to have a man in the house," Mom says.

They talk about school while we eat—Mom does most of the talking. Mr. Tomski likes to ask questions. He asks Granma about her husband, and we have a long conversation about the merchant marine. Mr. Tomski knows a lot of military history—it's one of his hobbies—and Mom says, "Go on, Ben. Why don't you show him Granpa's pocket watch, the one Granma gave you?"

I don't really want to, but I get up anyway and go to my room. Then I sit on the bed for a minute—the lights are out, I'm not really doing anything. I'm just sitting there for as long as I think I can get away with it. The watch is on my bedside table, and I hear Mom calling out, "Ben? Can't you find it?" so I pick up the watch and come out again and show it to Mr. Tomski. I'm kind of standing by his chair and he takes it gently out of my hand with his rough fingers.

"This is a very fine instrument," he says to me, looking me in the eye. "You must be proud to own a timepiece like this."

He gives it back to me, and I feel myself blushing.

For some reason, I turn it over and show him the

writing on the back—*Acta Non Verba*—and he reads it and laughs.

"Always good advice," he tells me.

After dinner, he offers to clear the table and wash the dishes, but Granma shoos him out of the kitchen. "You, too," she says to Mom. "You both have jobs in the morning. I don't do anything all day but sit on my tail end."

"Maybe you'd like to go for a walk, Jenny?" Mr. Tomski asks, and Mom says, "Maybe a short one."

She gets her coat. "Do you want to come, too, Ben?" she asks.

"Can I watch TV if I don't?" and she laughs.

"I'd rather you came," she says, but she's not laughing now—she's looking at me hard.

"I'd rather watch TV."

"All right, Tom," she says, smiling again. "Just once around the block."

They walk out the door and Granma starts clearing the table, while I turn the television on. Then I feel bad and get up to help in the kitchen.

"Thank you," she says. "You're a good kid."

I carry the plates to the counter and put away stuff like ketchup and butter in the fridge. Granma has pulled on a couple of yellow rubber gloves. The sink is filling with hot water.

"Why don't you have a dishwasher, Granma?"

"When we bought this house, the kitchen didn't have one. And I never felt the need."

"Everybody has a dishwasher."

"I like to do things myself. When your mother was younger, I looked after her, but I didn't have a job. And for a long time after your grandfather died, I was on my own. I don't make a lot of mess. Plus, I like doing the dishes. It's a good time to talk."

But saying it puts an end to the conversation for a while. Eventually she says, "What do you think of Mr. Tomski?"

I don't answer at first—I'm wiping the table clean.

"He's a good teacher," I say eventually. "Everybody thinks it's easy to distract him because all you have to do is ask him about his ranch. But even when he's talking about that he's trying to teach us something. He listens, too. Some teachers just talk and never listen, but he's not like that. He treats all the kids the same."

"That's not really what I was asking about," Granma says, but then Mom comes back. Mr. Tomski just leans in the door—he calls out, "Good night, Mrs. Koehner. Thank you again," and then the door closes and it's just the three of us again.

Later, after I get ready for bed, Mom lets me watch a little TV—Granma tells her that I helped out with the dishes. They stay in the kitchen, Mom makes a pot of decaf coffee. A basketball game is on, but it's the commercials, so I turn down the sound, loud enough so it's like a background noise but I can hear them talking in the kitchen, too.

"You have to be careful with Tom," Granma is saying. "You know that, right?"

"Don't worry about me. I'm fine. It's just nice to have a little attention, that's all."

"How do you think Ben feels about it?"

"Ben likes him. He told me so." Mom gets up—the coffee must be ready, and she pours herself a cup and sits down again. "Anyway, there's no *it*. We're just friends."

"That's what I mean," Granma says. "You have to be careful. For Tom's sake."

"Of all the people involved, he's probably the *last* person I'm worried about."

Then the game comes back on, so I turn up the sound again. It's Spurs/Knicks—I can't decide *who* to root for. Austin isn't far from San Antonio: it's like my new home playing against my old one. But San Antonio is also where Mabley's grandparents live. That's one of the things I write in my diary when I go to bed: the final score, which is 111 to 98. Kawhi Leonard had 25 points and 11 rebounds; Tim Duncan blocked four shots. San Antonio won.

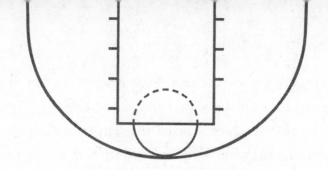

SEVENTEEN

THE NEXT MORNING, Mabley and I sit at the opposite ends of the bus, but somehow we end up in line together on the way into school. "Hey," she says. "What's going on? I haven't seen you in a while."

"Nothing much."

"You're not still mad about anything, are you?" she says. She stops in the hall and puts her hand on my elbow—other kids go past.

"About what?" I can hear my heart beat in my ears; it's pretty loud, and a drop of sweat runs down the side of my ribs.

"I don't know," she says. She's wearing a white shirt, buttoned up all the way: her short yellow hair doesn't reach the collar. I've realized that I'm taller than she is now—she has to look up at me. Her eyes are very pale blue. "Because of the . . . stupid thing at LBJ, and Peter and . . ."

"I thought *you* were mad."

"I'm not mad at you," she says.

Somehow we get pushed into the crowd of kids walking to class. For maybe a minute, we don't say anything—we just walk, navigating the hallways. But our homerooms are in different directions, and Mabley touches me on the shoulder with her hand. "If I don't see you later, I guess I'll see you at the game."

The Hornets are playing at home today. There's a pep rally during lunch; everybody has to go.

I run into Laura on the way to the gym after math.

"I hate sports," she says. Sometimes she makes me laugh—she has all these strong, private feelings. When you look at her, you think she's just a quiet, shy, nerdy type of kid. "Everybody acts like it's such a big deal to be on the basketball team. Why should I have to spend my lunchtime watching them run around like idiots?"

"I don't know. No reason. I hate it, too."

"It's like the only thing that anybody really cares about

is throwing a ball. Music, math, everything else . . ." Then she stops. "Hey, wait. Aren't you on the basketball team?"

"I'm the manager."

"Why are you doing that?"

"My mom makes me do it. She thinks it will help me make friends."

"Who wants to be friends with those kids," she says.

After school, I go to the PE office. Mr. Tomski is there, with the uniforms, and he pulls out a couple of bags of basketballs, which I drag out to the court. The team warms up by running drills, layup lines and shooting drills, and I have to make sure they always have balls to shoot with. It's embarrassing, standing around in normal clothes while the guys on the team run past in their uniforms and everybody else watches from the bleachers.

Other kids have started calling me "Ball Boy," not just Peter. Some of the players, for example . . . not in a mean way, but not in a nice way either. "Thanks, Ball Boy," they say when I pass them a basketball. Then the kids in the crowd (some of them are in my class) pick up on it, too. "Hey, Ball Boy," they call out.

After the game starts, it's my job to sit at the scorer's table and keep the stats. I have to write down every time someone misses a shot or gets a rebound or commits a foul. This keeps me pretty busy, I need to pay attention.

I never listen to what anybody around me is saying. I just watch the game.

When the halftime buzzer sounds, I stand up to stretch my legs. The Hornets are down by three points—against Lamar Middle School, our main rivals. Pete has missed a few open shots, but the truth is, Lamar is double-teaming him, sending two players to guard him at the same time, and Pete keeps trying to force his way past them. He gets called for a few dumb fouls and spends most of the second quarter sitting on the bench. "I hardly broke a sweat," I hear him complain to Mr. Tomski at halftime.

"Keep your hands to yourself," Mr. Tomski says.

Mabley comes down to the court to say hello. I show her the score sheet, and how you have to mark it up. While we're talking, a ball bounces against my legs and rolls away. "Come on," someone shouts. "Get me the ball." It's Pete, still in a bad mood, waiting by the three-point line.

"Don't talk to him like that," Mabley calls over. "Get it yourself."

But I've already chased down the ball and passed it to Pete, who gives Mabley a funny look and turns his back on us.

"I have to go," I say to Mabley.

"You don't have to do what he says," she tells me.

"I sort of do." And I run off to chase down more balls.

At least Mabley got to see what Pete's really like. I have the feeling that she'll like me more if I don't complain about it.

In the second half, Pete plays much better. He starts passing more when they double-team him. We get some easy layups. So the defense has to switch back, and Pete makes a few shots, too. He looks like a different kid. Instead of angry and hunched over, he seems relaxed, almost lazy—the expression on his face has changed, too. He keeps calling out encouragement. When one of his teammates falls down, he helps him up. He pats the kid on the butt.

The Hornets win easily, and after the game Mabley runs down to the court and gives Pete a hug, even though he's sweaty. You can see the sweat patches on her clothes, and she laughs about it. Everybody's in a good mood. Mom comes to pick me up and talks to Mr. Tomski for a few minutes before driving me home.

"I'm proud of you," she says. I'm sitting in the back seat, and she turns to look behind her, before pulling out of the parking space. "You're a part of the team. You won, too."

But that's not what it feels like. "I'm not, not really. You know what they call me, right?"

"What do they call you?" she asks.

"Ball Boy. You want to know why?"

She glances at me in the mirror, and I look away.

I want to say, because of you. Because you called me your basketball boy and Pete overheard you. Because they think I'm a mommy's boy, which isn't even wrong, though they don't know that. Because I'm twelve years old and we still sleep in the same room. Because I haven't seen my dad in six months. But I don't say any of those things, I just say, "All I do is I run around and get the balls. I don't *do* anything."

"That's not true," she says. "That's just not true. You're a part of the team, too." But I can tell even she doesn't really believe it.

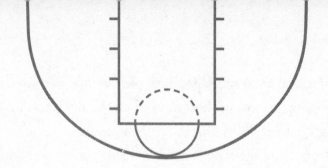

EIGHTEEN

SOMETIMES I IMAGINE that I'm playing in one of the games—taking the shots that Pete makes, and making them, too.

Or time is running out on the clock and the Hornets are down by one, when Pete passes me the ball. "Come on, Ben!" he says. "Just shoot it!"

Then I dribble up to the basket and shoot. If the ball goes in, I can hear a thousand kids cheering. If I miss— well, if I miss, I have to shoot again until the kids start cheering in my head.

One day, after lunch, I'm shooting around by myself. A

big cloud overhead sags above the treetops. It's not warm or cold, just one of those days when the sky seems to send back echoes. I can hear the ball twice at every dribble: the bounce and the echo. There's nothing really on my mind.

"Mind if I join you?"

I turn around, startled. Sam steps out from behind the tree. He's wearing work boots and big blue overalls, and he walks a little the way my dad used to walk after going jogging—as if his hips hurt.

"Pardon?" This is what Granma has taught me to say.

"Here, let me see that ball."

He takes a shot, which bounces off the rim and rolls into the grass. I walk over to pick the ball up and throw it to him; he kind of leans back, shoots, and holds his hand out afterward—his shot has a long high arc. For a few minutes, I chase down the ball and keep passing it back to him, and after a while, he says, "All right, kid. I'm all warmed up now. Let's see what you got."

I start dribbling, and he crouches down low and slaps the ground. When I shoot, he blocks it, and I scramble for the ball and get there first. His boots are really too heavy to play in, and I guess he's not trying anyway, because the next time, he lets me drive past him and I lay the ball in.

"Point to you," he says, and passes the ball back to me. "You make it, you take it."

The next time I shoot, the tree branch gets in the way,

a few leaves flutter down, and Sam ends up with the ball under the basket. He jumps and slaps the backboard and lays it in.

"Home court advantage," he calls it.

We play like this for a while; nobody keeps score. Sometimes he lets me shoot and sometimes he doesn't—all he has to do is stick out an arm to block my shot. But I'm quicker than he is and "keep getting under his feet," that's what he says. He tries to push me off with his elbow, but I sneak under that, too. When the bell rings, he's sweating and breathing heavily; he wipes his forehead with the end of his shirt.

"I've got to go," I say. "That was the bell."

"Pass me the rock then," he tells me, and I throw him the ball. He shoots a jump shot and watches it go in—the net is ragged, but it flicks like a tail when the ball slips through. "You made an old man happy," he says.

As I walk back to class across the field, I turn around—he's still out there, shooting by himself, and when he misses, running in his sore-hipped way to get the ball and shoot again.

It's getting warmer every day. Over the weekend, I start playing out in the garden again—sitting in my den in the bamboo hedge. Granma's house is small; the hedge is the only place I can be alone.

I keep hoping Mabley will come out to use the trampoline. I think, if she comes, I'll ask her if she wants to hang out. I guess I could just go around and ring her doorbell, but if she wants to see me, she knows where I live. I don't want to bother her. That's what it was like with Jake—he never came up to my apartment unless I called him or something. It was always *me* who took the elevator down, to knock on his door. I don't know why, that's just how it worked. But I didn't mind with Jake, because I knew he liked me.

For a while, it's sunny, then it's not. I get cold, sitting between the bamboo stalks, reading a book; the leaves are still damp. Around four o'clock, Mom brings out a bowl of trail mix and a mug of hot chocolate. I've made a little table out of a plank of wood. But Mabley doesn't come, and eventually it gets too dark for me to read.

On Monday morning, though, on the ride to school, she makes a point of sitting next to me. "Where do you go for lunch every day?" she says.

"I don't know. I just wander around. There's a bench out by the football field where I sometimes sit."

"Why don't you eat with us anymore?"

I look at her—she's got what my granma calls "a good face," but the last time I complained to her about Pete she got mad at me, and we stopped talking for a while.

Instead, I tell her, "I kind of feel like, what's the point. I'm not sure how much longer I'm gonna go to this school anyway."

"What do you mean? Are you going back to New York?"

"I want to go to London. That's where my dad is."

I don't know why I tell her this—it just comes out.

"Don't you like it here?" she says. She's sitting right next to me, just a few inches away, but I can't meet her eyes and look out the window instead. We've passed under the highway; there are houses to look at, a lot of construction going on, a woman on a stepladder painting a screen door, two guys in overalls blowing leaves around.

"It's not that, it's just . . ."

"Is your mom going, too?" She sounds almost hurt, or puzzled and upset.

"I don't always know what's going on with them." Somehow this sounds like a grown-up thing to say.

"Do they talk on the phone a lot?"

"He calls me sometimes. And then afterward he says, *Put your mother on the phone.* They don't usually talk for very long."

But then the bus pulls in and the engine rattles off. Everybody gets out. "Do you want to have lunch with me today?" I ask her. There's always a squeeze as you try to get out the door—kids carrying bags, sliding off the bench seats, pushing and stumbling as they get off the bus. It's like everybody just woke up.

"Sure," she says. "See you in the cafeteria."

"I'd rather go outside. I can show you where I eat."

"Okay."

That's all—we drift apart in the different streams of kids.

We meet up a few hours later in the cafeteria lunch line. I buy my carton of chocolate milk, and Mabley pays for a plate of chicken, sweet corn, and mashed potatoes. She carries it all out on a plastic tray.

It's a bright warm day. The trees are starting to grow new leaves; the light when you walk underneath them feels green. We pass the picnic tables, and Mabley asks, "Where are we going?"

"Just wait," I say.

Mabley makes me nervous. I don't always know what to say to her. Sometimes, when I'm alone, I imagine talking to her in my head, asking her interesting questions, like, do you ever think about living on your grandparents' ranch in San Antonio, and answering the interesting questions she asks me. But somehow when I see her again, we never have these conversations.

I lead her past the old bike rack and behind the tree and put my lunch bag down on the bench by the side of the court. "This is where I come."

She sees the basketball underneath the bench and picks it up. "I never knew about this place," she says, and starts bouncing the ball. Then she walks slowly up to the basket and takes a shot, pushing the ball with two hands. It hits the front of the rim and rolls away.

"Not like that . . ." I start to say.

"It doesn't matter," she tells me. "I'm hungry."

I get my lunch bag from my satchel and sit next to her on the bench. She has the tray on her lap; it wobbles a little on her knees when she cuts her food.

"How do you know Pete?" I ask.

She doesn't answer for a minute; she's busy eating, and I can see her jaw move under her cheek as she chews. Eventually she says, "I guess I've always known him. Our moms are friends. They used to . . . when we were babies, they used to put us in the bath together—that's the kind of story they like to tell, to embarrass us. But I don't care. He's like a brother."

When I don't say anything, she says, "Is Pete the reason you don't come to lunch with us anymore?"

"I don't think he likes me."

"Pete's just . . . His dad is one of those real yes-sir, no-sir types of dads. When I'm at his house, Pete has to, like, open the door for me, that kind of thing. I guess he feels like, at school . . ." But then she looks away. "He says to me sometimes, *You're always nice to everybody*. It drives him crazy. He gets a little jealous."

The sun comes through the trees and makes little patches on the bench. I've stopped eating my sandwich, but I take a drink of milk from the carton. It sounds like the milk in my throat must make a noise like a bowling ball going down, but really all we can hear is Sam's lawn mower, the John Deere tractor, driving across the football field about a hundred feet away, and some birds in the trees.

"Come on," Mabley says. "Let's shoot around. This chicken's disgusting."

"All right," I tell her, putting my sandwich away. She passes me the ball and I take a shot from the free throw line. It rattles in, and she catches the ball and tries to throw it at the hoop. She sort of throws it like a football, and the ball bounces right back at her off the bottom of the rim.

"You have to give me my change," I say.

"What?"

"That's what the kids on the team say during warm-ups. My change—if somebody makes a shot, you have to pass it back to them."

"Why?"

She stands under the basket, holding the ball like a sack of groceries, and blowing the hair out of her face.

"That's just how it works. I get to keep shooting until I miss."

"Whatever," she says but passes me the ball, and I shuffle across the lane and shoot again. Again it goes in, and she passes it back to me, and I bend my legs again and shoot.

"But you never miss," she says.

There's sweat in my eyes, but I feel like if I look down, or think about what I'm doing, I'm going to fall. Move and shoot, move and shoot, that's what Sam says. Finally, one of my shots hits the back of the rim and caroms into the grass under the trees.

"What am I doing wrong?" she asks.

So I pick up the ball and show her how to hold it—with your hand held back, resting on the palm. "You use the other hand to guide it, like this."

That's how Sam showed me. She tries again but misses anyway.

I chase down the ball and give it to her again. This time I pull her hand back myself, so the ball rests on the middle of her palm. Then I take her other hand (it's a little sweaty; she's got very small fingers) and lay it against the side of the ball, to keep it in place. "You want to follow through like this," I tell her, letting my wrist roll over as my arm straightens. "Just keep it as simple as possible—it's mostly in the wrist."

She tries again, and the ball floats up and barely touches the rim. It sort of rests on the edge for a second, then trickles in. "Hey, whaddya know?" she says, clapping her hands. Then the bell rings; lunch is over and she grabs her backpack and tray from the bench.

"You coming, Ben?" she asks me. We walk back across the football field together—Sam has finished mowing, the lawn mower is sitting quietly in the end zone. Cut grass lies loosely on top of old yard markings. "When are you moving to London?" Mabley asks. "I don't want you to go."

"I don't know. My dad . . . it's just something I talk about with him. He has to get settled in first. They're . . . his company, he has to work pretty hard."

"So what's the point of moving there?"

"It's not really up to me. My parents just . . . do what they want."

I feel bad about lying to her, even if it maybe isn't lying. Maybe I *will* go to London, and all this, this whole place, and people like Pete, and the school, will just be somewhere else I left behind. But then I'd have to leave Mabley behind, too.

She takes her tray to the cafeteria, and I follow her inside and wait by the door. But after that she has to stop by her locker—she's got math in the afternoon, and I say goodbye and shoulder my bags again and head over toward French.

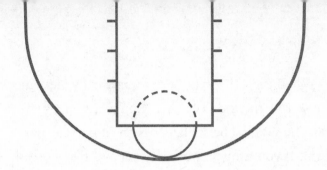

NINETEEN

ON FRIDAYS, when they have a game, all the players wear jackets and ties to class. It's a kind of uniform that shows they're on the team. You can tell how proud they feel, just walking down the hallway or sitting at lunch. The worst player on the whole team is this kid called Blake in my social studies class. He's tall and pimply and really skinny and everybody pushes him around—he falls down a lot. But none of this makes him a nice kid. He spends so much time staring at his reflection in the window that Mr. Tomski finally tells him "to quit messing around with your tie."

When the bell rings, Mr. Tomski calls me aside while the rest of the kids file out. "You're a part of this team, too," he says. "The manager is an important part of the team. If you want to wear a jacket and tie, you can."

But the other players will just make fun of me, especially Pete. I can't say that, so I just say, "That's all right. I don't mind."

"Well," Mr. Tomski says. "It's something you can think about. I'm not going to make you, Ben, but I'd rather you did. I'll leave it at that."

Maybe he said something to my mom, or maybe she noticed anyway, because next week, as she walks me to the bus stop, Mom asks, "How come some of the kids wear a jacket and tie to school on Fridays?"

"Because there's a basketball game."

"How come you don't wear a jacket and tie?"

"Because I'm not on the team."

"You are, too."

"Mom, I'm not. I'm just the manager." She looks at me and then I say, "I'm just the ball boy."

"Who says that? Who calls you that?"

"Everybody does. It doesn't matter. It's what I am."

But Mom pulls me by the arm and stops me on the sidewalk. "Now I want you to listen to me." I keep hoping none of the other kids walk past. "There's one thing I learned from your father," she says. "You don't have to let anybody push you around. You hear me?"

I don't answer, and she pulls at my arm again. "You hear me, Ben?"

"I hear you."

"Next Friday, I want to see you in a jacket and tie like the rest of them. Is that understood?"

"Yes," I say. She lets go.

As the weather warms up, Mabley starts playing outside again, after school and on the weekends, just jumping on the trampoline. On Saturday she sees me in the bamboo bushes and tells me to come over. So I wriggle through the hedge and into her backyard, a little scratched up and covered in leaves.

"There's been—something—bothering me," she says, still bouncing up and down.

"Can I come on?" I sit down to take off my shoes.

"Wait a second. I want to show you something."

First, she starts jumping higher and higher. "To get some momentum going," she says. I don't know how high she gets, but she can see over the bamboo hedge into Granma's yard. She tells me what she sees: my mom's beach towel with a book lying on it, and a soccer ball in the grass. Her next trick is to touch her toes in the air, with straight legs. Mabley does that a couple of times and then sort of gathers herself again. She looks like she's concentrating hard. Suddenly she pushes off just as her feet touch the trampoline, and shoots into the air. Her legs swing out in front of her, and for a second she seems to be hanging upside down. Her head points at the ground. But then she somersaults over and lands on her feet.

"I'm not supposed to do that. But I wanted to show you."

I don't know what to say, except "That was cool."

"I'm a trampolinist. It's a bit like being a gymnast, except you do it on a trampoline."

"I didn't know that was something you could be."

"Well, it is. I just didn't want you to think that only boys get stupid about practicing stuff. I practice all the time."

"Okay," I say. "Can I come on now? It looks like fun."

"Haven't you ever been on a trampoline before?"

"I used to live in New York. Nobody has a backyard. At least I didn't know anybody with a backyard . . . or a trampoline."

She waves her hand and I climb on. The surface trembles under my hands and knees; it's hard to stand up. Mabley keeps jumping and shaking the whole thing. The first time I jump, I have to hold out my arms to stay balanced. Mabley makes it look easy. Also, she can bounce in a way that knocks me over, which makes her laugh. But it's easy to talk on the trampoline, because we're both just busy going up and down. I don't feel shy at all.

Mabley seems different, too. Most of the time she thinks about everything she says before she says it. But not now.

"Your mom is really pretty," she tells me. "You know that, right?"

"Everybody thinks their mom is pretty."

"Well, yours is." And then, for no reason: "Mr. Tomski is one of my favorite teachers. My dad says he's the best teacher in the school."

"Why are you telling me this?" I ask her.

"I just feel, like, kids say stuff all the time, just because they think it's funny. They don't even care what they say." She stops jumping. "I guess I'm not making any sense."

"I don't know." I stop, too. "Are people talking about my mom?"

"Everybody talks about their teachers."

"What are they saying?" I can still feel the surface of the trampoline under my feet. It makes a weird sound, and you have to keep shifting your weight.

"Like, your mom is Mr. Tomski's girlfriend."

She looks at me. I don't know what kind of reaction she wants. Maybe she doesn't want any reaction, because she keeps talking. "I said, Who cares anyway? This is none of our business. And anyway, if they are going out, great, because I really like both of them."

"Well, they're not."

"Okay."

"They're not going out."

"Okay," she says again. "It's none of my business anyway. I just wanted to say something . . . because I hate it when people talk about you behind your back. So if people are saying something, I wanted to let you know. But now I feel bad."

"You don't have to feel bad; it's just not true." But to be honest, I don't know if it's true or not.

"Kids really like your mom," she says after a minute. She's starting to jump again, her short hair is flopping up and down. "They just say this stuff because they think it's funny."

"I don't care what they say. But it isn't true."

"Fine, then. That's fine. Then you don't have to worry about it. Forget I . . . said anything." And she does this funny thing with her hand, like she's wiping something with a cloth, making a squeaky noise, like it's a whiteboard or something, which kids have started to do, which means, like, wiping it clean. "I have to go. I'll see you at school."

I crawl back through the hedge again. Mom calls me in for supper. I guess she really is pretty—I watch her moving around the kitchen. Her hair has gone yellow, her skin tanned. All that Texas sun, Granma says. Mom has started swimming again and you can see the muscles in her arms. She looks happier than she used to look in New York.

Mom finishes eating early, because she wants to go out. She's going to see a movie with a friend of hers and just spends a minute in the bathroom to brush her teeth and put on a little lipstick. I wonder if she's going with Mr. Tomski. After she leaves, Granma and I clear up together.

Granma's very quick at everything. She rinses the plates and stacks them, she rinses out the glasses and lays them in the drying rack. She puts the pots in the sink to soak. I watch her swollen hand in the dishwater and feel sorry for her.

"Do you mind having us stay with you?" I ask. I don't know why—nobody has said anything in about five minutes.

"Do I mind? Who says mind? Of course, I don't *mind*. What put that idea into your head?"

"I don't know. It's something Dad used to say. Do you mind. Mom doesn't like it either. She says it sounds stuffy."

"It's a little stuffy," Granma says. "But people can't always help what they sound like."

She's drying one of the pots with a cloth and afterward gives me the pot so I can put it away. It lives in a cupboard under the kitchen counter. "Bending down," as Granma says, "isn't something I'm good at anymore."

"Do I sound like Dad?" I ask her.

"Hard to say, since you never talk."

"Okay, if you want me to talk, I've got a question." I give her the salad bowl and she reaches up to put it on a shelf. "Is Mom going out with Mr. Tomski?"

"Boy, you don't mess around," she says, but not really in a kidding voice. "Did she mention something to you?"

"No."

"Then you should ask her."

"Does Dad know?"

"I *said*, young man, that you should talk to your mother." But she's only pretending to be annoyed. Her dishcloth is wet, so she hangs it over the back of one of the kitchen chairs to dry. "Okay," she says, "if you've finished your homework, you can watch a little TV."

But I don't want to watch TV, at least not yet. There's something bugging me. "Granma," I say, and she says, "What?"

"Am I creepy?"

She turns to look at me, with her hands on her hips. "What are you talking about? Who said that?"

"Some boy in my class."

"What boy?"

"It doesn't matter."

"I said, *what boy*?"

"It doesn't matter! Just forget about it." For some reason I'm shouting.

"Now you listen to me," Granma says, and she still sounds angry. It's the voice she uses if she wants you to do something, and there's no point contradicting her. But there are tears in her eyes as well. "You are my beautiful boy. And anybody says anything different will have to deal with me."

"But they don't have to."

"What?"

"They don't have to deal with you. You're not even around when they say it. Anyway, I know you love me, that's not what I mean. I mean like, if you didn't know me, if you met me, would you think, He never says anything, he just kind of hangs around all the time, carrying those bags?"

She's just staring at me now. Her wispy gray hair has slipped out of the bun. It's the end of the day and she looks old and tired.

"Is that what you'd think?" I ask again.

"That is *not* what I would think," she says.

"But how do you know?"

"Because I *do* know you, and I know that you're the gentlest, most *honest*—"

"But that's not what I'm asking. Forget about it. It doesn't matter."

"Who called you creepy?"

"It doesn't matter."

"It matters to *me*. That is not a thing you're allowed to call another kid."

"Kids call each other stuff like that all the time," I say. "Anyway, I don't want to discuss this anymore. I just want to watch TV."

She kisses me on the head. "You are my beautiful boy," she says again. "It wouldn't kill you to get a locker, though. And stop carrying around those bags."

Mom still isn't back by the time I go to bed. Granma lets me write in my diary for a few minutes, but then she comes in to turn the lights off. She sits on my bed afterward, and I shift a little to give her some room.

"Are you okay?" she says.

"I'm fine. Dad says there's a school in London just for Americans."

"I'm sure there is. Is that what you want to do? Do you want to move to London?"

"I don't know, Granma. It's like—I've told a couple people about it, like, This isn't my life, I have this other life. So they don't feel sorry for me."

"And you miss your dad," Granma says.

"Mom sometimes tells me, You're just like your father. Not even when she's mad at me—sometimes I think she likes it. But then if she likes him, why are we even here?

And if she doesn't like him, what about me? Why does she like me? I don't understand."

After a moment, she asks, "Don't you like it here?"

"Of course I like it."

"You say that like you have to say it," Granma says.

"If I were staying with Dad in London, I'd probably talk about Austin. It's like, everywhere I go there's somebody missing."

She puts her hands on my cheeks and kisses me on the forehead. "There's a joke people make about marriage. They say the first twenty years are the hardest. Well, you could say the same about childhood. What they mean is, it gets better."

"Great. That's very reassuring."

When she gets up to leave, I ask, "Is Mom going out with Mr. Tomski?"

"Not that I know of," she says. "But you really should talk to her."

After she closes the door, I just lie there, watching the ceiling fan turn slowly in the dark. Every time a car goes past I wonder if it's going to park, then wait to hear if the front door opens. But I guess I fall asleep before Mom gets in.

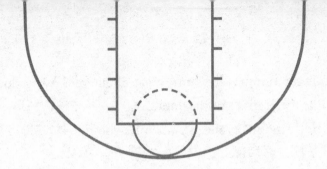

TWENTY

AS THE WEATHER GETS WARMER, Sam comes out to join me more often. He puts on high-top sneakers and jumps around in his green gardening shorts to get loose. "Old knees," he says.

The branch over the basketball court has started to sprout new leaves and twigs—it keeps getting in the way.

"How come you don't cut it down?" I ask Sam. "You're the groundskeeper; you've got all the stuff. Ladders, saws."

"It's a living thing. Plus, it's nice to have a little shade. You just have to shoot higher."

"I'm not strong enough."

"Yes, you are. I used to play basketball on the deck of a nine-thousand-ton cruiser in the South Pacific. I'm talking about twenty-foot seas—big gusts of wind. Don't let a tree branch block your shot."

For a few minutes, I don't say anything—we just shoot and pass and track down the ball. Then I say, "Is that why you have that anchor tattoo?" For some reason, it seems like a personal question, even though he never seems to hide it.

"Twenty-five years in the navy."

"My grandfather was in the merchant marine."

"Where did he serve?"

Sam misses, and I follow the ball into the grass. "I don't really know," I tell him as I pass it back.

"Why don't you ask him?" He holds the ball in his hands for a second.

"He's dead," I say. "I never met him."

"That's a good reason," Sam says, and turns to shoot again. Later he says, "Twenty-five years was enough for me. I missed green things."

He talks about Austin, too. This is where he went to college, but he barely recognizes it now. "You got all this tech money, people moving in from Brooklyn and places like that, California, people with no connection to Austin—they don't even know what Austin is, or used to be. I mean, look at this neighborhood," he says. "It used to be, people like me could afford to live here. But not anymore. My son lives in one of these housing developments off two ninety—it takes him an hour to drive in. Look at this school. The building they tore down was a beautiful building; it had some kind of history. But this looks like a supermarket." He waves vaguely across the football field toward the school. "The only thing left is this basketball court."

This is the kind of stuff he talks about. I don't really know what to say, I just listen. And catch the ball and shoot and track it down again; pass and shoot and move and shoot again.

In social studies, we're learning about the siege of the Alamo, one of the battles of the Texas Revolution. "It all happened a long time ago," Mr. Tomski says. "And after it happened, everybody started telling stories about it, so it got to be pretty hard to tell what happened and what didn't."

Mr. Tomski has brought an old musket to school, a brown Bess, he calls it, which is what many of the soldiers used. He passes it around the room—I get a good look at it.

"This is a flintlock gun," Mr. Tomski says when the gun comes back to him. He walks around the room, pointing out the different parts. "You got your hammer.

You got the jaws of the hammer. And what they're holding is a piece of flint, which comes down against something they call the frizzen—a piece of steel. The idea is, the flint hits the frizzen and makes a spark, and the hammer pushes the frizzen out of the way. Because underneath the frizzen, you got the pan. That's where the gunpowder is. One spark and bang! You can see the pan right here." He holds up the gun and points it at the blackboard and presses the trigger. There's a click but nothing else.

"Now this may look like an old stick," Mr. Tomski says. "The flint is dull and there isn't any powder in the pan or bullet in the muzzle. But this is still a very dangerous instrument in the wrong hands—accurate to about seventy yards. Does anybody know how far seventy yards is?"

"A little shorter than a football field," somebody says.

"That's right. And that's where we're going right now."

It's the middle of March, nice and sunny, and the whole class troops through the hallways and out the double doors into the picnic area. Then we straggle over to the football field, about thirty kids walking and talking in little groups of friends. I'm on my own, but I don't mind. It feels good to be outside.

Mr. Tomski gathers us all together in one of the end zones, and then he marches by himself seventy yards down the field and turns around. I can see him looking at us, shading his eyes with his hand. "All right, class," he calls out, sounding small and far away. "I want you to run to me. All of you. As fast as you can. Starting . . . now!" And he claps his hands; they make a noise like a gunshot.

Some of the kids run hard, but most of them just kind of giggle and jog at the same time. I try to end up in the middle of the pack—I don't want to come last, but I don't want to be first either. And it's warm enough to make me sweat. The field is muddy, with patchy grass left over from the winter. Lots of little green seeds have been scattered over the dirt. It's easy to slip.

Mr. Tomski holds his hand up and checks the time on his wristwatch. When the last kid comes puffing up, he says, "All right, folks. That was just about twenty-two seconds, from start to finish. Now if I were standing guard at the north wall of the Alamo, you would have been in the range of my brown Bess for about twenty-two seconds."

He counts out the seconds again on his wristwatch—using his fingers: one, two, three, four, five; one, two, three, four, five, again and again. Everybody's gone quiet. "You think maybe next time you'd like to run a little faster?" he asks.

Nobody answers. Mr. Tomski waits. "Except you wouldn't have had to," he says at last. "Because on that night, on the fifth of March 1836, almost exactly a

hundred and eighty years ago today, the three men guard-
ing the walls had fallen asleep."

"Excuse me!" A loud angry voice suddenly breaks in.
Sam is striding across the field toward us, in big brown
boots and green shorts. His heavy key chain clatters
against his belt. "You can't be here," he says. "This is the
football field."

"I'm teaching a class," Mr. Tomski says.

"I don't care what you're teaching—this is my football
field. You are not authorized to be messing around on my
football field."

Mr. Tomski raises his voice. "I am a teacher at this
school. I am teaching a class. You will not talk to me in
this way in front of my students."

"I'll talk to you any way I want to talk to you," Sam
says. He looks at the kids. "Now get off my field. All of
you."

I don't know what to do. I don't know whose side to
take. Mr. Tomski is shaking his head. "What is it about
football in this school that makes everybody crazy?" he
mutters under his breath.

But Sam hears him. "You know how long it takes me
to get this field ready for the season? A field of *grass*, in
Texas?"

"The season doesn't start until August."

"Yeah, but the grass grows *now*. Don't make me say it

again. Get off my field."

"I'm teaching a class," Mr. Tomski says as calmly as he can, which only makes him sound angrier. "I am a teacher at this school." He has started to repeat himself. "I'll get off your field when the class is over."

Sam stares at Mr. Tomski. Then he sees me. I'm standing at the edge of a big group of kids, hoping he doesn't notice me. But he does, and we look at each other, until I suddenly look down at my feet.

When I look up again, Sam is walking away from us across the field. His keys swing back and forth at every step. I watch him go, and count out the seconds in my head, the way Mr. Tomski counted them before. One, two, three, four, five; one, two, three, four, five. I get to thirty-seven before Sam disappears inside his hut.

Mr. Tomski has watched him go, too. Eventually he turns to our class and says, "Let's go back in."

That afternoon, for the first time all year, I don't eat my lunch by the basketball court. I sit with Mabley and Pete and a few other kids in the school cafeteria. Everybody has heard about Mr. Tomski's argument with Sam—they're all laughing about it. Mabley laughs, too.

When she gets up to bus her tray, I go with her. "It wasn't funny," I say.

"What wasn't?" She takes her knife out and scrapes the

leftover food into the trash, then puts her cutlery in the tub and slides her tray into the rack. I've just got a milk carton and sandwich bag to throw away.

"What happened with Mr. Tomski. I was there, and it wasn't funny. He didn't think it was funny either."

"You're right," she says, after a moment. "I shouldn't have laughed. Sometimes I laugh just because everybody else is. It's stupid. But why didn't you say something?"

"I *am* saying something."

"I mean to the others, at lunch, if you didn't like what they were saying."

But the bell rings, and people are pushing past us—we have to get to class. "We can talk about it later, if you want to," she says, drifting away, but I don't really want to talk about it, because she's right. When Sam looked at me on the football field, I looked away. When Pete makes fun of me, I don't do anything. I just sit there and take it, and then complain about it afterward or avoid him. That's how it used to be with Jake, too. That's what my dad wanted me to see—you have to stand up for yourself, otherwise everyone pushes you around. But he isn't here anymore to tell me.

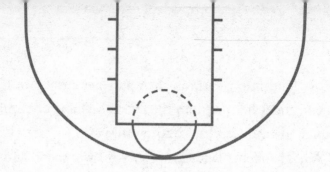

TWENTY-ONE

WHEN I GET HOME FROM SCHOOL, I ask Granma, "Can I call my dad?"

It's six o'clock, and Mom has gone out. She dropped me off after basketball practice and drove away again. It's "girls' night." Once a month she goes to the movies with some of the teachers, including Ms. Fontenot, our school principal. (Mom calls her Bernie, short for Bernadette. "A lot of people wouldn't have given me a job, after fifteen years out of education," Mom says. "But she's divorced, too. She knows what it's like.") Anyway, it's just Granma and me tonight, which is why I'm asking her.

"It's pretty late, Ben," she says.

"I finished my homework in practice today. At least, most of it."

"No. I mean it's later in London than it is here. Your father is probably asleep."

"I thought he was always working. I thought that's what the problem was."

Granma's making spaghetti—I can smell the hot water in the kitchen. "Is that what your mom says?" Sometimes she finds it easier to talk when she's doing something else.

"Sometimes. But I mean, before, when we were still in New York—that's what she used to complain about."

"Well, there are people who live to work, and people who work to live. Your father is the first kind of person. That doesn't mean he doesn't love you."

"But the first thing Mom did when she got here was get a job."

"Yes, but that's only . . ."

"And Dad is always complaining about how hard he has to work."

"What do you want me to say? These things are complicated."

"Do you think they— Did they break up because of me?"

Granma looks at me. "I think for a long time you were the only thing keeping them together."

But I don't know if that's true. Sometimes I remember . . . I remember them laughing when they didn't think I was paying attention. Saying things to each other quietly, so I couldn't hear. Sometimes when I lay in bed I used to listen to them watching TV. Talking while they watched. Their voices sounded different when I wasn't around. Sometimes for no reason they would turn down the sound.

"All right." Granma takes the pot off the burner—she pours the pasta into a colander, and the window over the sink starts to steam up. "If you wake him up, it's no more than he deserves. But don't take too long. Dinner is almost ready."

There's a telephone in the front hall, standing on an old-fashioned wooden desk with a built-in seat. Granma calls it "the telephone chair," but it's also where the mail ends up and she keeps her checkbook. I sit down and dial Dad's number. Mom has written it on a Post-it note and stuck it to the wall. There are a lot of numbers.

I have to wait for a while before the phone stops clicking, and then the ringing tone comes in, beep and then beep and then beep. And then I hear my father breathing in my ear, as close as anything.

"Yes," he says. It doesn't sound like a question.

"Hi, Dad. Did I wake you up?"

"Ben?" There's a pause at the other end. I hear a rustling

noise, as if he's sitting up in bed. "That's okay. What's on your mind?"

"I just wanted to talk to you."

"So talk." After a moment, he adds, "I'm sorry, Son. It's been a long day. I've been working very hard. I was fast asleep."

I don't know what to talk to him about. I want to tell him about Mr. Tomski, but I can't. I want to say, You have to get over here now, there's something going on. But maybe nothing is going on, I don't really know. I just have a feeling that . . . something is happening, which . . . it's going to be hard to take back. Like, when Jake and I were horsing around in the kitchen, and then the mug broke. Even before it broke, you kind of knew, this is stupid, something is going to happen. "Two of my teachers had an argument today," I tell him, just to say something.

"What do you mean they had an argument? In front of the kids?"

"They were shouting at each other on the football field."

"What were they shouting about?"

"One of them wanted to kick us off the field." In my mind, I can see Sam standing there in his shorts and boots, with the big bunch of keys swinging from his belt. "I guess he isn't really a teacher. He's the—he's, like, the groundskeeper. He takes care of all the outside stuff."

"Well, what did *you* think?" my dad asks. "Who was right?"

I can hear Granma in the kitchen, setting the table—she always makes a lot of noise when she moves around. For some reason, I want to keep my voice down. I feel like I'm having a secret conversation. "Nobody was right," I say. "Everybody was wrong."

"Well, that's what it's like sometimes."

"It's weird because I kind of know both of them pretty well."

"What do you mean?"

"The caretaker guy, he's called Sam. There's this old basketball court behind the football field, and he lets me play there at lunch. Sometimes he even shoots around with me. And the teacher, Mr. Tomski—"

"What about him?" Dad says.

"Well . . . he's my teacher. He's also the basketball coach. So I see him at practice every day. You know, I'm the manager."

"I know," he says. "Your mother mentioned that. I would rather you played."

"Dad, that's not what I want to talk about right now."

"Okay," he says. "Okay. So what happened? What did you do?"

"Nothing really. Sam walked away, and then Mr. Tomski kind of gave up, too. We went back inside. I didn't do anything. I just felt . . . bad. I felt like I let him down."

"Who?"

At first I don't answer. "Sam. He looked at me and I kind of looked away."

"Well, it doesn't sound to me like you were the problem, Ben. It's not always your fault. And it's not always your responsibility to fix a situation."

We don't say anything for a while—I'm just kind of staring at the shoes in the front hall. Eventually my dad breaks the silence. "One day I'd like to tell you my side of the story. But maybe that's the last thing you need to hear."

A car drives past the house, with the lights on. The front door has glass panels on either side, and the lights flash against them and then flash away. For a second, I think that Mom is coming home early.

"When am I going to see you again?" My heart's beating very quickly, like it does when you're doing something that could get you into trouble.

"Soon. As soon as I can. I thought it might be easier for both of you if I stayed away for a while."

"Maybe it is easier. For Mom."

I can hear him shifting around in bed, adjusting the pillows or something. There's a kind of sound the phone makes, as if it's brushing against his face, and he hasn't shaved. A crackling sound. But maybe that's just the telephone connection.

"Is she there?" he asks me. "Does she want to talk to me?"

"No. She usually goes out on a Wednesday night."

"Who with?" he asks.

"I don't know, it's girls' night. That's what she calls it. They normally go to the movies."

But I'm thinking of Mr. Tomski, and I wonder if I should say anything. Instead I ask him a question. "Dad, if I wanted to move to London . . . with you. I mean, if that's what I wanted to do . . ."

"Yes?"

"I mean, what would I have to do? Is there . . . like, I mean, would you just come and get me?"

"Is that what you want me to do?"

"I don't know." And it feels like, almost for the first time in my life, what I say is going to . . . I mean, it's important for me to be honest, to say what I mean, because what I say matters, and I have to get it right. "I like . . . I guess I like knowing that it's an option."

"It's an option," he says. "And if this is something you want to do, this is something we can talk about. This is something we all need to talk about. I mean, your mother, too."

"Yes."

"Have you told your mother how you feel?"

"No. I don't know. Not really."

"Why not?" my father says.

"She's kind of . . . she's got a lot . . . going on. And right now, we still share a bedroom, and it's like . . ." But it feels like I'm discussing Mom behind her back. "Anyway, I don't always want to talk to her about everything."

"I understand." Then he says, "Do you want me to start the conversation?"

I think about this for a minute. "Not yet."

And that's that. We say good night and hang up. "Okay, kid," he says, and I say, "Sleep tight."

Then Granma calls me in to dinner, and I sit down to a plate of spaghetti. The windows are still steaming in the kitchen. "How was your father?" she asks. "Did you wake him up?"

"Fine," I tell her. "Yes, I woke him up."

She looks at me while I eat. "I wish I had a nickel for every time you said *fine*. I'd be a rich woman."

But I'm lying in bed now and thinking about that call—going over everything we said and remembering the way my heart suddenly started racing. Just thinking about it makes my heart beat faster again. But I don't feel sad. For some reason, I feel excited—about *what*, I can't figure out.

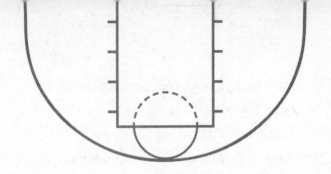

TWENTY-TWO

THE NEXT DAY, I take my lunch out to the basketball court again. But first I stop at Sam's hut and knock on his door.

There's a television sound coming from inside, like the noise of a baseball game. I wait and listen, feeling the sunshine on the back of my neck. Bugs are flying around; I can hear them, too. Eventually Sam comes to the door, with a sandwich in his hand.

I've spent all morning working out what to say, but for a second I forget and can't even remember why I wanted to talk to him. Then it comes back to me. "I'm sorry I didn't do anything. When Mr. Tomski took us out on your field."

"What could you do?" Sam takes another bite of his sandwich.

"I'm sorry I didn't say anything."

"What could you say?"

"I don't know. But I'm sorry anyway."

Sam has a way of looking angry and like he's kidding at the same time. After a minute, he says, "It's all right. Mr. Tomski came over yesterday to apologize himself."

"What did he say?"

"He said what he needed to say." Sam laughs. "Come on, big man," he says. "Let's shoot some hoops." He finishes his sandwich and steps inside to get the basketball.

It's a short walk to the court, just a few steps. On the way, Sam asks me, "Are you getting skinny on me, kid?"

"My mom says I eat too much. I eat all the time."

He looks me over again. By this point, I'm standing under the basket.

"Reach up your hands." So I stand up straight and lift my arms in the air—then jump up and touch the bottom of the net.

"Big man is getting bigger," Sam says.

Usually, we take turns to shoot, but today Sam keeps feeding me the ball. "Move and shoot," he tells me. "Move and shoot." I run to a spot on the court, and he passes it to me. Then I shoot and he passes it to me again. I'm not really thinking about anything, but sometimes I catch a glimpse of the ball in the air—trees in the background, the telephone wire, a few clouds, something falling out of the sky toward the rusty brown rim with a ragged old net like a bucket at the end of a rainbow. Then I run to another spot and Sam passes me the ball.

Afterward, when the bell rings, Sam says, "I told him about you."

"Who?" I'm still sweating a little and have to get my stuff together. I didn't even have time to eat lunch—it's still in the bag.

"Mr. Tomski. I said, look out for Ben. The kid can shoot."

Walking back to school, across the football field, I eat my peanut butter sandwich and throw the rest away in one of the metal trash cans by the back doors. I can't work out if I'm glad Sam said what he said, or not—if I want Mr. Tomski to know.

The regular season is almost over. On Friday Mom takes home the school newspaper to show Granma. It has a story about the basketball team, with the names of all the players: Pete Miller, Adam Hancock, Daniel Krasnick, Gabe Hunterton, Breon Joyner, Cory Caldwell, Dai Menudo, Blake Snyder, Steve Chou, Amir Brown. Coach:

Harlan Tomski. Manager: Ben Michaels. Granma says, "Look at you. Your name in lights."

"I'm just the manager, Granma. I'm basically the guy who does the laundry."

"Let me be proud of you if I want to be," she says.

We have a week to prepare for the first round of the playoffs. From that point on, if we lose, that's it—we can all go home. No more practice after school. No more games on Friday night. But if we win the next game, we have to play another; and if we win that game, too, we have to play another game after that. Five straight wins will make us the state champions.

For the first time all year, Mr. Tomski makes us show up for practice on Saturday—we've got the gym all day. It feels weird coming to school with nobody there. The parking lot is empty, the corridors echo. Even the gym feels different. The light coming in the big windows behind the basket is weekend light—you can feel the whole afternoon slipping by outside, while we're stuck in here. But it's not a bad feeling, everybody has a job to do, and nothing else matters.

Mr. Tomski decides that we need to get in better shape. We have one star player, Pete Miller, and a lot of average players. But even average players, if they run hard, can cause trouble for a short amount of time. Mr. Tomski plans to use plenty of substitutions. There are kids like

Blake and Steve who have hardly played all year, but Mr. Tomski warns them, you better be ready. "A basketball game is two hundred minutes long—that's how I think about it. You need to put five kids on the court for forty minutes of game time. I need minutes from everybody. That means *everybody*. Run your hearts out."

We're standing at half court. Dust rises in a shaft of sunshine over our heads; everything looks faded, like a black-and-white movie. I've got the balls ready, and kids are waiting to hit the layup lines, but Mr. Tomski keeps talking. His voice sounds different in the empty gym, it bounces off the hardwood floors. "Every team we play from here on in is going to be bigger and better and stronger than us. What we have to do is try harder. But don't worry, we've also got a secret weapon. The best player in the city. Maybe the best player I have ever coached."

I notice that whenever Mr. Tomski says things like this, Pete smiles but also ducks his head and looks away. Like he doesn't want to think about it.

We have lunch outside on the picnic benches—everybody eats their sandwiches, but Pete sits in a corner and doesn't talk much. People leave him alone. Around three o'clock, Mr. Tomski lets us out, and we wait in the parking lot for our parents to pick us up. Pete's mom comes before mine, and I see her get out of the car—she's wearing heels and wobbles a little when she walks. She calls him *honey*. "I'm not going to touch you, honey," she says. "You're kind of gross right now."

On Monday, everybody comes to practice early and leaves late. Nobody goofs around. They even stop calling me Ball Boy. For one thing, everybody's too tired—Mr. Tomski is "licking us into shape." That's what he calls it. He makes the players run "ladders" over and over again—sprinting from one side of the court to the other as fast as they can. Afterward, everybody has to take a couple of free throws, and if anybody misses both shots, the whole team has to run more ladders.

I start to feel bad, standing on the sideline, watching them run. Mr. Tomski can be short with me, too. He complains about the way I set up the cones or fill the water bottles or collect the balls. "Hustle up," he says. "You see how hard everybody's working." Another time he makes me run ladders with the rest of the team. "Just so you get a taste of it."

It's almost a relief, but I feel like throwing up afterward. My school shoes have big rubber soles. It's like running with weights on your feet. One of my toes gets a blister, and I have to wear a Band-Aid under my sock for the rest of the week.

Even Pete looks worn-out by the end of practice. Every time there's any kind of race, he forces himself to win it.

Afterward, in the showers, he stands with his eyes closed and lets the water fall over his face. Only two showers work—the hot water on the other wall is broken, and since Pete isn't moving, kids have to take it in turns to wait for the second one. By the time he comes out, everybody else is already getting dressed.

Two days before the big game, Mr. Tomski takes us all aside at the beginning of practice. "No more running," he says.

He's dressed in plain brown pants and white sneakers and the kind of shirt camp counselors wear—short sleeved with a collar. He has a whistle around his neck. You can see where he stopped shaving that morning.

"Now I know y'all are a little mad at me right now." Even when he loses his temper, he doesn't speak loudly—you have to lean in to listen. But he isn't angry now, and his voice gives you a kind of slow-burn feeling. "And you *should* be mad," he says. "I've been working your tails off. But now's the time to get mad at somebody else. Get mad at Murchison. That's who you should get mad at."

Murchison Middle School is who we have to play against on Friday night. The Murchison Matadors—they wear gray uniforms and come from the other side of town, across Route 1. Nobody likes Murchison.

For the first hour of practice, the team just

scrimmages—they play games. Everybody has a good time. But then Mr. Tomski tells the kids to cool off, take a water break. Afterward, they walk through some of their sets on offense and defense. He shows people where they need to stand on the court, and what they need to do, depending on the situation.

"Everybody should know these things by now. Still, it can't hurt to be reminded."

But somehow the players keep making mistakes. Mr. Tomski loses his temper. Eventually, he calls over to me—I've been sitting on one of the bleachers by the side of the court, just watching.

"Get on out here, Ben. Do you know the plays?"

"Yes, sir. I think I do."

"Thinking's got nothing to do with it. You know or you don't. Okay, now, show these people where they need to be."

And for the next half hour, I run through the plays with Pete and everybody else. Almost like I'm part of the team. Nobody bounces the basketball or takes a shot, but we pass it to each other, back and forth, and move around the court as Mr. Tomski tells us to.

I'm wearing long trousers and my heavy school shoes. Usually I don't need to get changed after practice, but by the time we finish I'm in a real sweat.

Mom drives me home afterward. It's still light enough

that she lets me play in the backyard for a few minutes before dinner. I can hear Mabley jumping on the trampoline next door. It makes a kind of thump and twanging sound when she's out there. So I walk over to the bamboo hedge and crawl into my little hiding place between the leaves.

I can watch Mabley flying through the air, twisting and spinning and turning somersaults. She isn't smiling—she has to concentrate too hard for that—but somehow she looks happy anyway. She looks like she's showing off.

Then she slows down, bouncing more and more gently each time, and somebody else climbs on to the trampoline. It's Pete Miller. I hear him say, "You're going to get yourself killed, jumping like that," and then they both start trampolining together. Pete isn't bad, but Mabley can make him fall over whenever she wants, which makes her laugh. He doesn't seem to mind.

For a while I just sit there, hoping that Mabley will notice me and ask me to come over. And then I hope that she won't, and that Pete won't either, that nobody will see me. The sun is going down, it's a warm evening, and everything glows a little and looks strange, and I feel like, I don't belong here, this isn't my place, nobody really wants me around. I watch them until Granma calls me in to supper. Mom has gone out with "the girls" again—it's just another Wednesday night.

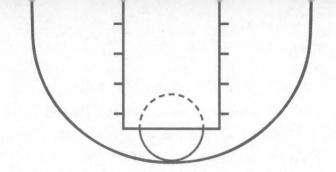

TWENTY-THREE

ON FRIDAY MORNING, Mom takes my arm on the way to the bus stop, like she's an old lady and I'm helping her along. "Now, I don't want you to get excited. But your father has a conference in Houston—he flew in last night. I told him about your game."

"Wait, what? Dad's here? But it's not my game. I'm not playing."

"I told him about your game," she goes on, ignoring me, "but I don't know if he can make it, I don't know what his schedule is. Anyway, you'll see him sometime this weekend."

"Why are you telling me now? Why didn't you tell me before?" For some reason it sounds like I'm freaking out, but I'm really not—I just want to know. My voice isn't totally under my control.

"I got an email this morning. You know your dad. That's how he always does things. He pays attention to things when he has time to pay attention to them—when they're the next thing on his list." She pauses. "Your father is a very busy and important person." And I remember what it was like in New York.

It's about five blocks from Granma's house to the bus stop, and eventually she lets go of my arm. Some of the sidewalks have trees leaning over them or agave plants spreading across the pavement. They look kind of like ordinary spider plants except the leaves are stiffer and have little spikes, or teeth, running along the edges—I never saw one in New York, but in Austin you see them a lot. But the roads are big and quiet enough that we sometimes walk in the middle of them; there isn't much traffic. Nobody says anything for a few minutes, which is totally normal—I mean, it's pretty early in the morning, but for some reason it feels weird to me. I mean, I feel like Mom is holding something back, or waiting to say something, and eventually she says it.

"There's something else he said in his email." This is how she begins. Because it's a school day, she's kind of already in teacher mode—she's wearing slacks and a little jacket, and her shoes that go clip-clop on the street. "I don't want you to think I'm mad, Ben, because I'm not. But I just wished you felt like you could talk to me about it, too."

"What?" I say. "I don't know what you mean."

"He wrote that you talked to him about moving to London. He said that's what you wanted to do."

I don't say anything, and she says, "Is that true?"

"I guess I talked to him. I mean, we just talked. He's my dad and he's in London—so it just seems like—it's something we talked about."

"Is that what you want to do?" She sort of stops in the road to look at me.

"Do *you* want to—I mean, would you come to London, too?"

She sighs. "I'm happy here, Ben. It means a lot to your grandmother—she was lonely before, and I used to worry about her. It's not easy being the only child, I guess you know that. But we have a good life here. I'm working again, I have friends. I like it here. I thought you did, too."

"No, you didn't."

We're standing in the middle of the road now, facing each other.

"What do you mean?"

"I mean, if that's . . . You don't listen to me. It's like you're not even listening to yourself. I don't have any friends."

"What about the basketball team? You're friends with those boys."

"I'm not on the basketball team. That's just something you make me do. The kids there . . . they make fun of me."

A car comes by, and we have to move to the sidewalk.

"What do you mean? Who makes fun of you?"

"I don't know. Pete Miller. Everybody else on the team."

"That's not true. Tom said . . ." But she can't remember what he said, and sighs again. "Ben, it's still . . . it's early days. Give it a chance."

"Mom, it's been almost a year."

"The first year is always the hardest. It was hard for me when I first moved to New York."

"Granma says it's the first *twenty* years." Mom sort of shakes her head, exasperated. "How long did you live in New York before we left?" I say, and she looks at me but doesn't answer. "Did it get better after that first year?" I ask.

She starts walking again. "We can talk about it this weekend."

"Is he coming to Granma's house?"

"We thought it might be easier for everybody if I dropped you off at his hotel. But we can talk there, too. We can all talk."

We get to the bus stop early. Only a couple of other kids are waiting; more cars go by. It rained in the night (it woke me up, clattering on the roof), and the roads are still wet. You can hear the tires squeak on the asphalt, but the sky looks clean and blue. A woman from the house on the corner walks outside barefoot to pick up her newspaper from the grass.

Mom says, "Apparently, they've got an all-you-can-eat breakfast. At the hotel. Apparently, it's famous. You'll have a good time." Then she says, "Don't worry about it, Ben. We'll sort everything out." But she doesn't sound like she believes it.

Then the bus comes and I have to get on it with everybody else.

For the first few classes, all I can think about is my dad. He's coming to see me. This makes it hard for me to pay attention to the teacher. One of them, Ms. Kaminski, says to me, "I know you've got a big game today, Ben. But right now, we're talking about triangles. That's what you need to be paying attention to."

I stare at her.

"Triangles," Ms. Kaminski says again, pointing to a

picture on the blackboard. "Not basketballs."

"I'm not on the team," I tell her.

"I thought you . . ." she begins to say, looking puzzled. Mom has made me dress in a jacket and tie that morning, so I look like all the other players. "I thought you were."

"Well, I'm not."

After lunch, the whole school gathers in the main gym for a pep rally. Mr. Tomski and the rest of us wait in the second gym, next door. All the boys apart from me are wearing basketball uniforms, long shorts and tank tops that look shiny under the lights. I'm still wearing my jacket and tie and big-soled school shoes.

There are double doors between the two gyms, and Mr. Tomski opens one of them a crack to see what's going on. The bleachers are full of kids. I can hear the noise they're making, it sounds like a train passing by—a train that keeps going and going. I remember taking the subway to Coney Island with my dad and holding my ears against the screech of the wheels against the metal tracks. Suddenly, my heart starts racing again, I don't know why.

After a minute, somebody gives the signal to Mr. Tomski, and he swings both doors open. The players in their uniforms run into the main gym through a kind of human tunnel: two lines of kids holding their arms overhead, touching hands and making a long arch. The cheering gets even louder. The school band plays a march-ing song, and the principal stands in the middle of the court with a microphone in her hand.

Pete Miller's the last player to come out, and he walks instead of runs. I don't think the noise can get any louder, but it does. I feel something on my shoulder, and Mr. Tomski leans down to shout in my ear.

"They're playing our song," he says.

"What?" I can hear him, but I don't understand.

"It's our turn. To walk out there."

"But—I'm not on the team. I don't have a uniform on," I say.

"Neither do I. Come on, son. This isn't a choice."

He puts his hand on my shoulder again. He has a heavy hand, and together we walk out into the bright lights of the main gym. It's so loud it's almost like you can't see—and not just loud but warm. The air is thick with all the kids crowding on the bleachers and stamping their feet and cheering.

When we reach the middle of the court, Mr. Tomski lets go of me, and I walk over to the players lined up next to the principal, Ms. Fontenot, in two rows. I sneak in behind them because I feel stupid standing there in my jacket and tie, the only boy not wearing a uniform.

Ms. Fontenot makes a short speech, after raising her hands until everyone quiets down. "This just shows what you can do if you put your minds to something." Her voice is real Texan, or southern anyway—sweet and slow. "All of these boys have sacrificed two hours after school every day to get here. They've put in the time and they've done the hard miles—I know Coach Tomski likes to make them run." She smiles, but it's hard to be funny if you're the principal. Everybody knows you have to say all the stuff you have to say. My mom likes her, though. Ms. Fontenot doesn't take any baloney from anyone, Mom says. She's got gray streaks in her hair, which she doesn't bother dyeing, and likes to wear cowboy boots—you can hear them click as she strides around the hallways. I can see them now, under her bright red dress. "The work you put in, you get that out in the end. This is what we call a teachable moment, where all of you sitting out there can think, *I* want to be on that court, with these kids . . . fighting for something together."

I'm standing with all the other players, but it's like, I don't know if she's talking about me, too. I feel like a big phony. The band plays the school song, everybody cheers, but then it's suddenly like an ordinary lunchtime afternoon, kids talking and filing out, shuffling along the bleachers, waiting at the doors. Going back to class.

The band is the last to leave. It takes them a while to pack up their instruments; Mabley looks at me as she gathers her music up and puts her sax away. She gives me a little wave. Then one of the janitors gets out a big double broom and sweeps the floor—going up and down in rows. After the court is clear again, Mr. Tomski starts to lead the team through a light practice. Ms. Fontenot has let them skip class for the rest of the school day to get ready for the big game. I'm walking away when the coach calls out to me.

"Where are you going?"

"I've got French," I say.

"Come here," Mr. Tomski tells me.

The rest of the team are practicing free throws, lining up and taking turns. I don't move, I just stand there. Mr. Tomski jogs over to me by the doors to the hallway that lead back to the rest of the school.

"What's up?" Mr. Tomski says. When I don't answer, he goes on: "Come on, son. I'm not just your teacher here. I'm your friend. What's on your mind?"

For a minute, I just stare at my shoes, the ones that give me blisters when I run. Then I look up at Mr. Tomski. "Mom said my dad might come to the game."

He doesn't say anything, and finally I ask, "Did you know he was coming?"

Mr. Tomski has brown eyes and wrinkles around his eyes, but they don't look like smiling wrinkles. He spends a lot of time at his ranch, out in the wind and sun. Eventually he says, "She said something to me this morning.

I'm glad he can make it to the game."

"Well, he might come. Or he might not. Mom wasn't sure."

I can hear the sound of basketballs bouncing against the wooden floor and echoing against the high ceiling of the gym. It's a nice lazy sort of sound but loud enough that I feel like I can say whatever I want to say to Mr. Tomski, and nobody else will hear us.

"Do you want him to come?" Mr. Tomski asks. He has a way of sticking his tongue into the pocket of his cheek, as if he's got a big piece of chewing gum in his mouth.

I think about this and look down at my shoes again. "I don't want him to see me . . . like this."

"Like what?" Mr. Tomski starts to say but then stops himself. "I tell you what. I'm pretty sure we got a spare uniform somewhere in the office. How about you put that on?"

He has to repeat himself before I nod.

"But I'm warning you," Mr. Tomski says. "If you put on that uniform, I might just have to play you. There's a rumor on the grapevine that you can shoot."

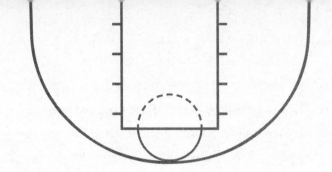

TWENTY-FOUR

FOR THE REST OF THE AFTERNOON, all I can think about is the game. After practice, the players shower and throw their shorts and shirts on the locker room floor, and I go around with a laundry bag, picking up the wet clothes. These are just the practice uniforms. We have a different set for games.

It's my job to make sure the real uniforms are clean, to carry them on the bus for road games, and to hand them out to all the players before tip-off. (There's a big Whirlpool washing machine in the office, with a Maytag dryer stacked on top of it, next to the restroom door.) Mr.

Tomski has found a spare uniform for me, but I'm still wearing my school shoes. That's what worries me most, but I tell myself it doesn't matter, that I'm not going to play anyway. And if Dad sees me sitting on the bench, he probably won't notice.

After the final school bell, the boys head for the showers and get changed. Everybody comes out looking sharp, in jackets and ties. Pete Miller's tie has a picture of Michael Jordan on it. I'm wearing an old green tie that used to belong to my dad. I've also got a checklist of things to remember—Mr. Tomski's clipboard; the medical kit; and, most important of all, the big duffel bag of fresh uniforms. I sling it over my shoulder on the way to the bus.

It's only about a twenty-minute drive to Murchison Middle School. I know the first part of the way pretty well—it's the same road the school bus takes driving me home. The neighborhood seems to be changing, like Sam says. There are fancy new houses, made of metal and glass, some of them still under construction, and a few run-down-looking houses, with sagging roofs, and leaves still on the roofs, and wooden porches. One of the front yards has an old car propped up on the grass—it's missing a few wheels. There are cement blocks holding it up.

Staring out the window, I remember something Mabley

told me once. It was early in the morning, and she had squeezed in next to me on the bus. I said to her, just for something to say: "I guess the people around here like to hang on to their cars."

"They don't have much money." There was something in her tone of voice that made me blush.

"When I lived in New York, we didn't have a car," I said.

"That's different."

"Why is it different?"

She looked me over. I didn't know if she was teasing me. "I could tell when I met you that you were one of those kids."

"One of what kids?"

"That you weren't used to thinking about certain kinds of stuff," she said.

It makes me a little angry, going over this conversation in my head. For some reason I want to say to Mabley, "*You* were the one who laughed when Sam and Mr. Tomski argued about the football field." But I also remember telling my dad, when I left the apple core on the sofa: Maria can clean it up. That seems like a long time ago, like something that happened in a different world. I want to explain myself to Mabley. I want to say, "Maybe I've changed."

Eventually the bus rumbles onto the highway, and all I

can see is the other cars and sometimes a strip of shops by the side of the road. Then we come off the highway and drive through quiet, hilly streets with big new houses on them. Their front yards have fences along the sidewalk so you can't see in. But Murchison itself, when we pull into the parking lot outside the gym, looks pretty much like our school. It has brick walls and pillars by the entrance.

The parking lot's already full, and when we walk in the side door, I can see that the gym is filling up, too. It's starting to get that hot, loud feeling I remember from the pep rally. My heart beats quicker again, and I can feel my hands sweat.

In the locker room, I give out the uniforms. Afterward, there's still one left over at the bottom of the bag: number 22. Mr. Tomski says, "Folks, we got a new teammate. Somebody y'all know pretty well." Everybody stares at me; nobody says anything. "Against these guys," Mr. Tomski goes on, "we can use all the help we can get."

On the way out to the court, Blake Snyder notices my shoes. He can't think of anything funny to say, so he just says, "Look at his shoes!"

A few people laugh, but not Pete. "Don't worry," he says, putting his hand on my shoulder. "I don't think we'll need you today." He's sort of kidding and sort of not.

The gym has big windows on either side, like a church. It's five o'clock and sunlight fills them—the baskets come down from the ceiling on poles and cast long shadows onto the court. The overhead lights make shiny patches on the wooden floor. I see sparkles everywhere. It's hard to focus, and suddenly I remember that my dad might be in the crowd.

But I don't get a chance to look for him because Mr. Tomski tells all the players to get into layup lines. We have a couple of balls and take it in turns to dribble up to the hoop and shoot. Then somebody else comes from the other side and picks up the ball and passes it to the next person in line.

I've watched this drill a hundred times but have never gone through it myself. The ball keeps slipping out of my hands; my palms are too sweaty. And I feel clumsy in my heavy school shoes. The first time I try to lay the ball in, it clangs off the bottom of the rim and bounces away.

There's a big scoreboard fixed high up against the white brick wall of the gym. The digital clock shows minutes and seconds and tenths of seconds. The last number in the row changes so fast you can hardly read it, the next number moves more slowly, and so on. It's like a funny kind of domino chain. Just watching it seems to make your heart go faster.

When the number in the first box goes from 8 to 7, I realize the clock is counting down to the start of the game: seven minutes to go. The bleachers are almost full, though people seem to keep coming in, parents and other kids. A couple of girls sit by a table near the entrance, taking tickets. The referee, in his striped shirt, stands in the middle of the court, testing a bag of balls. But I can't see my dad in the crowd. Or my mom.

I see Sam, though. He's sitting at the end of the first row of bleachers, as if he might want to sneak away later. I try to catch his eye, but he's sort of hunched over and keeps staring at the entrance. With five minutes left on the clock, Mr. Tomski calls us in to practice free throws. We make a circle around the foul line and take it in turns to shoot. Everyone claps together after each shot—two claps if the shot goes in, and one if it misses. Everybody gets two shots.

Pete goes first and makes both of his free throws. I'm last, and even before anyone passes me the ball, sweat has started running off my forehead and into my eyes. I try to wipe them dry, but my uniform is made of this cool, shiny material that doesn't soak up anything. The salt in my sweat stings when I blink it away.

Standing at the line, I remember what Sam always tells me: *Point your elbow at the rim and bend your legs. Follow through.* I'm just about to shoot when a big horn sounds, so loud I almost drop the ball. The game's about to start.

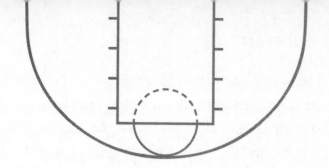

TWENTY-FIVE

AFTER THE WARM-UP, I gather all the balls and put them in a couple of bags, then drag them over to the sideline and sit down on the team bench. Usually I sit at the scorer's table, but there's an official scorer for playoff games. So now I'm with all the other players, just another kid in uniform. For a few minutes, I look for my dad in the crowd. But instead I see Mom, three rows up on the other side of the court. She smiles at me, the kind of smile you make so someone can see it a long way off. Granma's there, too, wearing a bright orange sweatshirt with a picture of a hornet on it—the school mascot.

The horn sounds again, and the ref throws the ball up in the center circle. Breon's our best jumper, but he's going against the tallest kid I've ever seen. Big number 7 looks red in the face already; his mouth guard makes his lips swell out. His feet hardly leave the ground, but it doesn't matter: he swats the ball back, and one of the Murchison players dribbles up court. The game has started. Kids are shouting, and I look over and see Mabley standing on one of the bleachers in a row of Hornets fans—she's painted her face orange and black. Her mouth is a big O, but her voice is just the voice of everybody screaming at once.

After that I try to concentrate on the game. Murchison has some good players, but nobody as quick as Pete, and they have trouble keeping up with him. Number 7 is a problem, though. It's hard to shoot over him; and every time one of his teammates misses, he just seems to reach over and tap the ball in.

Mr. Tomski keeps doing what he said he was going to do—and substitutes players. Everybody except for Pete. When he sends a new kid onto the court, Mr. Tomski puts an arm around his shoulder and says, "The only thing I expect is that you play hard. Don't save anything for later. There is no later. Later is now." Then he shoves him out there with a pat on the back.

I'm so nervous that I sit on my hands just to warm them up, they feel so cold. At least Mr. Tomski won't put me in the game, that's what I tell myself.

At one point, Pete drives hard to the basket. Big number 7 is standing under the rim and jumps up to block Pete's shot. Maybe if you know him he's a nice boy, but on the basketball court number 7 looks like a grown-up playing with kids; he looks like a bully. And after blocking the shot, he seems to lean forward a little—and lands on Pete's shoulder. It looks like he pushes him to the ground.

Anyway, Pete falls in a funny kind of way, twisting as he falls. The referee blows his whistle, and Mr. Tomski rushes out of his chair and starts to shout. Everybody's shouting, even Granma. I can see her standing up in her seat.

For a few seconds, Pete just lies there. Then Breon helps him up and Pete limps over to the free throw line. The ref gives him the ball, and Pete takes a deep breath and turns the ball around in his hands.

He misses the first free throw. Then he misses the second one. There's a scramble for the ball, and somebody knocks it out of bounds. Mr. Tomski steps on to the court and calls time-out.

All the players gather around him in a circle. I stand up, too, and try to push my way in. I can hear Mr. Tomski saying to Pete, "You all right, son?" and I can hear Pete saying, "I'm fine. I just missed a couple of shots. It happens."

"Take a seat for a minute," Mr. Tomski says. "Catch your breath."

"I'm fine!"

"No point playing the hero now. We got a long way to go." He turns and looks at the players standing in a circle around him. Then he looks at me. "Ben! Check in for Pete," he says.

I don't have time to think. The horn sounds, and I wander onto the court, trying to dry my hands against my jersey. "Wait a minute," Mr. Tomski calls out. "You have to check in."

"What?"

"You have to check in."

"What?"

It's too loud in the gym; everybody seems to be talking. The words don't make any sense.

Mr. Tomski looks at me calmly. "Go to the scorer's table and tell them that you're coming on for Pete Miller. Then get your butt out there."

The whole thing lasts about a minute—I hardly have time to breathe. The ref blows his whistle and suddenly I'm running, but I don't know where. One of the Murchison players seems to be standing alone under the basket. I can hear Pete shouting, "That's your man." He sounds like he's shouting from the other end of a long tunnel, and then the kid has the ball and lays it in. Everybody starts running again.

Mr. Tomski calls something out, but I can't understand him. I feel like I have weights on my feet and can hear my own footsteps—clump, clump, clump—in spite of the noise of the crowd. Or maybe it's just the beating of my heart, very loud, in my ears.

For some reason I find myself standing in a corner, alone. And then the ball comes to me. I think, At least I caught it. That's something. A Murchison player runs at me, waving his arms. I try to dribble but get stuck after one bounce.

Now there are two Murchison kids trying to take the ball away from me. I hold it like a football and swing my elbows around. Everybody seems to be calling my name or shouting. I can hear them, but I can't see them; there are too many arms and legs. I throw the ball as hard as I can in the direction of one of the voices, and somehow Daniel Krasnick picks it up and shoots it. The shot goes in. A whistle blows. Somebody taps me on the shoulder. It's Pete; he gives me a look, twisting his mouth to the side, like, I'm not saying anything. I can sit down again.

At halftime, I check the stands for my mother, but only Granma's there in her orange sweatshirt. I want to see

Mom, but before I can find her, Mr. Tomski calls everyone into the locker room.

On the way over, he puts a hand on my arm. "Keep your head next time," he says.

"Pardon me?"

"The game is as slow as you make it."

As the manager, it's my job to make sure everybody has water to drink. But I've been worrying about the game and have forgotten to refill the bottles. "Come on," Pete says, kicking an empty bag.

"I was playing, too."

Pete just stares at me.

I walk to the sink and run the tap, testing the water to make sure it's cold. Then I pick up all the bottles and fill them. The first person I give a bottle to is Pete.

While this is going on, Mr. Tomski checks his clipboard—he has the notes from the scorer's table clipped under the metal bar and starts reading out the numbers. Pete has twenty points. Everybody else on the team, put together, has eight.

"You have to start helping him out," Mr. Tomski says. He's standing by one of the locker room showers in a puddle of water. His trousers are too long, the bottoms have gotten wet. But he doesn't seem to care. He's thinking about what to say next.

"You know what they're trying to do, don't you.

They're trying to bully you out there. But let me tell you something, I don't care how big they are. They can only bully you if you let them bully you."

He calls us into a huddle, and we put our hands together over our heads. "Hornets on three," he says. "One. Two . . ." and we all shout "Hornets" together on the third count. Even me, though I feel a little silly—I feel like I'm pretending. Then we run on court again and get into layup lines. While I'm waiting for a rebound, someone pulls me aside. It's my mom, with a plastic bag in her hand.

"I brought your shoes," she says. "Your sneakers."

I sit down by the side of the court and take off my heavy school shoes. There's a little blood on one of my socks, but I can't feel anything. Mom bends down to help me put on the sneakers.

"I can do it myself!" But my fingers are cold and clumsy; it takes me a while to tie the laces.

"I'm so proud of you," she says quietly.

"Well, you shouldn't be. I suck."

"Who says?"

"Your boyfriend," I tell her, standing up, and run off to join the others.

They're practicing free throws now, standing around the key and taking it in turns to shoot. Clapping once for a miss and twice for a make. I squeeze into the line—last again.

Pete makes his free throws, most of the other kids miss one. For some reason, when my turn comes, I don't care anymore, I'm not nervous. Both of my shots go in, everyone claps twice.

When the horn sounds for the second half to start, I turn around to look for Mr. Tomski. But he's standing with his back to us, talking to the referee. So he didn't see me. My heart sinks, and I walk with my head down back to the bench, with all the other bench players. We don't have to worry about playing. At least, not yet. We can sit and relax and watch the game.

On the way, I hear someone calling out to me. "Big man, hey, big man." Sam walks toward me, a little stiffly, as if his knees hurt. He's wearing a pair of dark jeans and a button-up shirt. A soft cap covers his shaved head. He looks different—it's like he's dressed up for the occasion.

"You know what to do when someone passes you the ball, right?" Sam says.

"What?"

"Just shoot it."

For a second, I don't say anything, and he asks, "Why are you looking at me like that?"

Because everybody keeps telling me what to do, I feel like saying. But that's not really Sam's fault. "It's scary out there," I tell him eventually. It feels like a confession.

"Everything happens so fast."

"Let it happen."

"What if I miss?"

"There are worse things," Sam says. Then he slaps me on the back and shoves me lightly away—toward the court.

The second half starts, and Murchison keeps trying to push Pete around. That's their plan. Every time he goes anywhere, someone throws an elbow at him or sticks out a knee. I don't like Pete, but I can't help admiring him. No matter what Murchison does, he gets back on his feet and finds ways to score.

Also, I suddenly want to win—I want the Hornets to win.

About a hundred kids from our school have made the trip over to Murchison. They're sitting behind one of the baskets; they have a section to themselves. For the whole second half, all of them stay on their feet; nobody sits down.

Mabley is there, too. The paint on her face has started to streak, as if she's been crying—but it's only sweat. The orange and black have mixed together, she looks like a crazy person. And whenever I look at her, she seems to be screaming. Her mouth is always open. The score goes

301

back and forth; it's a close game. Murchison gets all the rebounds. It doesn't matter if they make their shots or not, big number 7 cleans up the glass.

At the end of the third quarter, Mr. Tomski sends me into the game again, just for a minute. This time when I get the ball, I shoot. Adam Hancock passes it to me out of the low post, and without even thinking I bend my legs and follow through. The ball rattles in. My head feels clear, I can breathe normally. And I want to keep playing when Mr. Tomski pulls me to the side at the next whistle.

"Come on! I made my shot."

"You did okay," Mr. Tomski says. "Sit down."

The fourth quarter starts. Everybody's standing now, including the Murchison fans. The gym feels as hot as the laundry room in Granma's house when both the machines are running. Even Mr. Tomski looks red in the face. The noise hurts my ears. Kids stamp their feet on the bleachers, banging them like drums.

The sun is setting and colors the big church-like windows with an orange glow. Sometimes it's hard to see against the light—there's a lot of dust in the air. I feel like I've been there for days, stuck in that gym. It's hard to imagine a world outside, where people go about their business, driving around and picking up groceries. Mowing the lawn.

With a few minutes left, Breon steals a pass and starts

racing down court. I think, maybe he's going to try to dunk. One of the Murchison kids comes flying in and tries to block his shot. But he misses the ball and ends up falling into Breon, who lands in a weird way—his foot twists, and then his knee buckles, and you can hear him scream. Even over all that noise.

For a long time, he just lies there. A doctor comes out to look at him—Mr. Tomski has to pull all the players away. "Give us some room," he says. "Come on, give us some room!" His voice sounds hoarse; his face is shiny with sweat. Patches of black hair are plastered damply against his forehead; the rest are sticking out. But he doesn't care; he kneels on the floor, listening to the doctor. It's too loud to hear.

After a while a couple of men walk out with a stretcher. They pick Breon up and lay him on the stretcher and carry him out. Everybody in the crowd stands up to cheer him—the Murchison fans, too.

Mr. Tomski follows them part of the way. He says something to Breon, who turns his head and glances back at us. He looks like he's concentrating hard, like he's holding something heavy and trying not to let it spill.

Breon can't take the free throws, so Mr. Tomski has to send someone else in his place. He puts his hand on my shoulder and says, "Well, kid. Here's your chance." I remember to check in at the scorer's table, and the next thing I know, I'm wandering onto the court. It's like climbing onto the stage in the middle of a play. The ref hands me the ball; there are kids lined up along either side of the key.

Sweat keeps running into my eyes. I try to wipe it away, but my hands are sweaty, too, so I bend down and dry my fingers against my socks, which are made out of cotton and not slick nylon like the uniform. Well, there's only one thing to do. I step up to the line and shoot.

A little short, maybe, that's how it feels. The ball hits the front of the rim then the backboard and rolls in. I look up to check the scoreboard against the wall—tie game—and see my mom in the crowd. She and Granma are holding hands. Granma is easy to spot, a white-haired old woman in an orange sweatshirt that looks too big for her. Standing next to her, but a little way apart, is a man in a dark gray suit with a bright green tie.

My dad has come.

The first thing I think is: I wish he hadn't. Because my dad will make me nervous, and if I'm nervous, I'll miss.

"Come on, Ben," Pete says. "You got this." He's standing behind me at the three-point line. When he's playing, it's like he's got this electric current going through him that he can't quite control—he keeps shifting his feet and tucking and untucking the uniform inside his shorts. Another thing to make me nervous, and I reach down and dry my hands again against my socks. The ref gives me the ball and I close my eyes and imagine the court behind the football field where I eat my lunch. As if I'm alone and nothing matters anyway. Then I open my eyes and bend my knees and follow through.

I make the second shot, too.

There's still a minute left, and now we're up by one. Murchison comes down court and passes the ball inside to big number 7. He turns around and dunks, pulling himself up on the rim, so that it snaps back into place when he lets go. Murchison fans are going crazy; they're up by one, and keep shouting the same thing over and over again: "Keith, Keith, Keith." When he runs, there's something funny about his arms: it's like he has to pull himself along. You want to get out of his way.

Pete dribbles across half court and takes a jump shot from the top of the key—nothing but net. Hornets by 1. Murchison throws the ball inbounds, but Daniel Krasnick has been hanging back. He manages to stick out a hand and knock it toward half court, where he chases it down. But Murchison traps him against the sideline. I can hear Mr. Tomski calling out behind me, "Time-out, time-out!" Nobody listens. Pete cuts to the basket, and Daniel tries to find him with a pass. But there's no way through, Murchison steals it, and suddenly we're all running the other way. One of their guys has been cherry-picking at the other end, and Keith throws a long pass over our heads. The kid lays it in and Murchison is up by one.

"Time-out!" Mr. Tomski calls again, and the ref finally hears him. He blows his whistle and we all jog over toward the bench.

What happens next happens in a kind of silence. Mr. Tomski is talking but I can't really hear him—he's got his clipboard in hand and is drawing up a play. Everybody else is talking, too, five hundred people in the gym all talking at once, but the noise is like traffic when you're on the highway, it's everywhere and all the time and there's nothing you can do about it, so somehow you close your ears and shut it off, but that means shutting everything else out as well, including Mr. Tomski. There's a whistle and I feel someone hitting my back and then I'm jogging out onto the court again in the middle of all the lights with nine other boys.

There are only seventeen seconds left in the game, but seventeen seconds can take a long time if you count them out slowly. The way Mr. Tomski counted out the seconds on the football field, using his fingers: one, two, three, four, five; one, two, three, four, five, and so on. Pete has the ball and dribbles up court. He's letting the clock run down—he wants to take the last shot. Mr. Tomski calls out, "Fifty-one! Fifty-one!" and Pete puts his fist in the air. I run down to the block to set a pick for Daniel, who sprints hard to the free throw line, but I can't remember what to do after that. Suddenly I notice that Mabley is sitting right there, a few rows up behind the basket, screaming silently it seems with her face a mess of orange and black. My hands feel as cold as ice.

Meanwhile, the clock keeps ticking. Some of the crowd start chanting out the time, counting down to zero. Eight, seven, six. And I run to the corner just to get out of the way and drift along the three-point line. Murchison sends two players at Pete, who splits the defense but ends up at the free throw line with Keith standing right in front of him. Five, four. Pete has picked up his dribble. Three. He sees me on the wing. At least, he sees a kid in a Hornets jersey and passes me the ball. Daniel sets a back screen and Pete cuts to the rim and claps his hands. He wants the ball back, the lane is clear, but I'm too slow so he slides along the baseline into the corner. Two. "Pass," he says. "Pass." Pete's open now, but it's all happening too fast. "One," the kids on the bleachers shout, stamping their feet. Time is running out and instead of passing, I do what Sam told me to do. I shoot.

As soon as the ball leaves my hands, I know it's going in. Sixteen-footer from the wing—it's the same shot Michael Jordan took to win his first championship, as a freshman at North Carolina. (Mom sometimes lets me look at highlights on YouTube.) He gets the pass, he steps into the open space, he shoots. It's like he's not even thinking about it. My legs feel strong, I leave my arm out on the follow-through; the line is true. The horn sounds and at the same time the ball hits the back of the rim and bounces out . . . and rolls harmlessly away on the ground.

I guess I must have had too much adrenaline. The shot was two inches long, and the Murchison kids run on to the court to celebrate. Game over. We've lost.

Pete is still standing in the corner, as if he's waiting for the ball. "Why didn't you pass?" he says to me. "I told you to pass."

"What?"

I feel pretty close to tears and can see Mr. Tomski walking across the court. Daniel Krasnick is sitting down under the basket, too tired to stand.

"I told you to pass," Pete says. His face looks like a little kid's when he doesn't get his way; it's all scrumpled up. Maybe he's crying, too.

"I'm sorry," I tell him, and Pete picks up the ball. I don't know what he's going to do, but suddenly he throws it at me. He's standing about five feet away and the ball hits me in the stomach, knocking the wind out, but I catch it anyway, hugging the ball and doubling over.

"Hey," Mr. Tomski breaks in. "Let's cut that out."

"I told him to pass. We could have won."

Even though everybody's crowding onto the court, it still feels lonely. The Murchison fans have drifted toward the other side of the gym by the exit, where the girls who sold tickets are now selling T-shirts. Most of the kids from our school are heading home, but Mabley finds Pete and gives him a hug from behind. He kind of shrugs and pushes her away.

"We win together, we lose together," Mr. Tomski says.

"You know how to pass?" Pete says again, and without even thinking about it, I throw the ball back at him.

"Like this?"

Pete has his hands down. It hits him in the face, and for a second nothing happens, then he runs at me.

"Hey," Mr. Tomski shouts, and sort of reaches out his arm to get between us, but I've already turned away, and he catches me in the neck. It doesn't hurt exactly, but I can't breathe, it's like breathing in a glass of water, then I cough and the air comes flooding back.

"What's going on here?" My mother has come; she sees me bending over. "Tom," she says. "What's going on?"

Granma is there, too. She bends down with me and I can see her orange shirt; she puts her hand on my shoulder.

"You all right?" she says.

"I'm fine."

But Mom is still mad. "What's going on?" She's starting to repeat herself. Tomski is always a slow talker; he doesn't say anything right away. There are other parents around, picking up their kids. People come and pat him on the back. But Mom keeps at him. She says, "How can you put him under that kind of pressure? When he hasn't played all year." Since she started teaching again, she's gotten better at what she calls her "angry" voice—she doesn't sound like somebody you want to disagree with. And Mr. Tomski isn't good at disagreement anyway.

"Mom," I say, "Mom. It's okay," and Granma says, "Calm down, Jenny."

But she keeps going, she's really lost it. "You don't know what it means to raise a boy on your own, a kid who doesn't talk to anybody, who doesn't have any friends, who doesn't want to be here, who doesn't want to be on the goddamn *basketball* team, where it's like, I always have to be happy enough for two people, just in case a little of it rubs off. . . . It's *your* job to make this stuff easier, it's not your job to throw him to the lions like that, where everybody's watching him, just so they can watch him mess up, which is what everybody wants him to do anyway, because they're all a bunch of . . ."

Finally, Mr. Tomski gets a word in. "He did great, he played great. You should be proud of him."

"Don't tell me what to feel about my son," she says. It's still hot in the gym, and her voice is cracked from screaming—her face looks red and sweaty—but she sounds teary, too, and she keeps brushing the hair out of her eyes. "Of course I'm proud of him," and she reaches out her hands to me. "I'm sorry," she says to me, quietly this time. "I'm sorry about all of it, the whole nine yards," and closes her arms around me.

Then my dad walks up, wearing one of his suits and looking about eight feet tall.

So for now at least everybody's there—Dad, Mom, Granma, me, like a normal family. It feels weird seeing him again, especially since I'm covered in sweat. I don't want to hug him and get stains on his suit. But he waits for Mom to let go of me and then he hugs me, too.

"I'm sorry we lost," I say into his shirt. "It was my fault."

"Nothing's your fault. You played as hard as you could."

Pete has walked away. His dad is this real Texan-looking guy, with super-clean blue jeans and sunglasses on a string around his neck—I think he's a dentist. His mom is there, too. She has the kind of hair where every hair is exactly where she wants it to be, and you feel like, don't touch. Next to them, Pete just looks like a kid. Mabley says hi to his parents, but Pete just wants to leave, and Mabley has no one to talk to—she wanders back to us.

"Who's this?" my dad says, so I say, "This is Mabley; she lives next door," and Mabley says, "I thought Ben played great. You must be proud." She's good at talking to grown-ups; at least, she says the kinds of things they like to hear. But she also looks basically like a crazy person, with her face covered in paint, in orange and black like a hornet; the colors have run together.

Mom has her purse out—she's trying to wipe the mascara off her cheeks. Maybe she also wants to give us a little space. Maybe she also wants to look nice for Dad; at least, less like an emotional wreck. Granma is just kind of standing around, like she doesn't want to get in the way of our reunion. When she's tired, I notice, sometimes she rubs her swollen hand, like it hurts. The game is over, there's really nothing to do. Everybody's waiting for somebody to say, I guess we should go, but then I remember Mr. Tomski. A lot of kids are going home in their uniforms, they're leaving with their parents, but I still have to get everything together—the balls and towels and water bottles, and the practice uniforms and everything else.

So I say to my dad, "I've got to do something," and just . . . I just leave. I walk over to the bench on the other side of the court, by the scorer's table, and start picking stuff up.

Mr. Tomski is there. He's talking to one of the parents, but then he sees me. "I can do that, Ben. It's all right."

"That's okay, it's my job."

He sort of looks at me, and I sort of look at him. I wonder if he's thinking, "That's his dad over there," but I don't want to say anything about it. And I kind of feel sorry for him, too. After my mother shouted at him, in front of all those people. I feel like . . . in a funny way I feel like . . . I'm going to miss him, even though he's right there—as if something has changed, or is going to.

"I'm sorry, coach."

"What are you sorry about?"

"For missing that shot."

Mr. Tomski shakes his head. "You played great, Ben." But I don't think he's really thinking about the game. His tie is loose, and he's unbuttoned the top button of his shirt. The bottom of his shirt has drifted out of his pants. He looks like he's walked about ten miles in the rain.

There's something else going on in my mind, which is just that I like the idea that Mabley is stuck there with Mom and Granma and Dad, standing around and talking. I mean, I'm glad they're all talking to her and getting to know her. But I'm also glad that I'm not there, that I don't have to listen . . . and start picking up our team balls and separating them out from the Murchison balls.

The gym is about half full now. The girls by the entrance who sold tickets are still there, gossiping with some of the other kids—they look older, like they go to high school. And the whole place feels like somewhere that something has happened but it's not happening anymore. There's a little breeze coming in through the open door; it doesn't feel so hot; it's quieter, too, just a lot of different conversations going on in normal voices at the same time. Just normal life.

For some reason, I think of Jake. I really miss Jake. Because he always did all the talking, and I didn't have to decide what I thought or liked or wanted to do. And also because—I didn't choose Jake. I mean, Jake was just my best friend because he lived three floors below me, and our moms used to take us to kindergarten together when we were five years old. It's like we didn't even have any choice. Maybe that's what it's like if you have a brother or sister, I don't know. But it means you don't have to think about it, he's just there. At least he was. But now I feel like . . . Mom and Dad are expecting me to choose something. It's up to me, and I have to figure out for myself what I want.

Mom is right. I can't be miserable anymore. It makes everyone unhappy.

Mabley is still there, listening to my mother. They're standing under one of the baskets—the basket where I missed the last shot. On the other side of the court, I can see Pete's dad talking to some girl; maybe it's his daughter. It's like he's saying, Come on, and Pete is just waiting, like he wants to go home.

It's funny to see Mabley talking to my mom—with my dad hanging around and thinking, Now Ben is friends with girls, the kind of girls who paint their faces in school colors, and I have to find something to say to them, or something like that. He's standing there, not saying anything, which is one of his signature moves. He's just being tall, that's something he does—he looks tall and important so nobody wants to talk to him. But I can't stand around here forever putting balls in a sack.

At some point I'm going to have to go back there and talk to Mom and Dad and everybody else, and have an all-you-can-eat breakfast at his fancy hotel, and say good-bye to him at the airport, and watch him walk through security in his pinstripe suit with his briefcase in hand. When a plane takes off, I'll wonder if it's his—on the way to London, where the Beatles recorded their music and there's a school just for American kids. At some point I'm going to have to decide what I want to do—where I want to live and who I want to live with. If I want to stay here, with Mom and Granma . . . and Mabley and Pete and Sam and Mr. Tomski, and just accept that this is where I am, and make the best of it. Or move to London with my dad and start again. Anything can happen, and somehow it feels like the ball is still in the air.

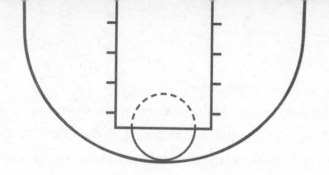

TWENTY-SIX

I COULD HARDLY SLEEP last night. Everything kept going through my head. Making those free throws, missing the last shot, it's almost like, if I imagine it over and over again, I can imagine it different—something will change. Pete throwing the ball at me after the game. Me throwing it back. Mom shouting at Mr. Tomski. Dad coming.

After the game, Dad said, "Listen, Ben. I'm a little bushed right now. I flew into Houston last night. It's a six-hour time difference; this feels like midnight to me. And then from Houston it's a three-hour drive. I haven't even checked in to my hotel here, I drove straight to the gym. I really want to see you, but I need to go to bed. But we've got all day tomorrow—anything you want to do."

I don't say anything for a minute, and eventually he says, "The hotel I'm staying at is famous for its breakfasts. All you can eat. I can pick you up in the morning, any time."

"I think I'd like to go for a bike ride."

He looks at me. "I didn't really . . . I don't have a bike, Ben."

"You can use Mom's."

For a second he stands there, pursing his lips. He's making up his mind. Then he says, "You know what, let's do that. I'll figure something out. We'll go for a ride together, that's a great idea."

We walk to the parking lot, Mom and Granma and Dad and me, and on the way out, I see Sam—he's standing by the table at the entrance. Maybe he's waiting for me, and I say to Dad, "There's somebody I want to introduce you to."

But Sam has already come up. "You look like you used to play a little ball yourself," he says to my dad, checking him over.

"I'm tall enough, but I'm too skinny. People used to push me around."

"I don't believe that," Sam says. He says hello to Mom

and Granma, too, and I say, "This is Sam—he takes care of the school grounds. There's a court near the football field where I have lunch . . . he lets me play on it."

"I just wanted to introduce myself," Sam says. His arms are crossed, like he's angry, but it's really just to keep his hands warm. Sometimes he complains about his circulation, so he tucks his hands in his armpits and sort of leans forward, but it looks like he's restless or uncomfortable.

We stand there for a minute. It's a little awkward—my dad doesn't really know what to say. "Sam taught me how to shoot," I tell him.

"You mean, it's my fault," Sam says, laughing.

But my dad looks at him seriously. "I'm grateful to you. I haven't always been . . . around to do these things."

"Well, I know what that's like."

They shake hands, and on our way out, Sam calls after me. "See you on the court."

All of these things, these little conversations, are things I go over in my head as I lie in bed.

My feet hurt when I finally get up—there's still a little dried blood on one of my toes. I'm thirsty, too, and when I stand in the bathroom, trying to pee, it's like I don't have anything in me. But everything hurts in kind of a good way; it's nice just to walk around barefoot in the house and feel like all of your muscles are doing their job—they're getting stronger.

Around nine o'clock the front doorbell rings. I'm just finishing my second bowl of Great Grains, and Dad calls out, "Hey, anyone home?" Granma never locks the door after picking up the newspaper from the front yard.

When he comes in the kitchen, he's wearing chinos and canvas sneakers; he's got a short-sleeved collared shirt on. "Morning, Dorothy," he says. That's Granma's name, but it's funny to hear him say it—like, he's being polite, but it's a kind of politeness where you can tell people have known each other for a long time. "Hey, Jenny," he says, because Mom just walked in.

She's wearing a faded yellow dress, which she bought secondhand at a Mexican market in town, and leather sandals that go halfway up her ankles. Her hair smells nice—she just got out of the shower, and somehow when she walks in you can smell soap scent all over the kitchen. She looks good. She's still got a summer tan, because the sun never seems to go away in Texas; and her hair's a little longer than it used to be in New York; and she still goes swimming once a week, and you can see the muscles in her arms.

"Morning, Spencer," she says. And there's that same politeness in her voice—people being nice to each other who know each other really well, but maybe haven't always been so polite but are trying now. "What do you boys have planned for today?"

"Did you manage to get a bike, Dad?"

And he looks at me, smiling; there's sweat on his forehead. "That's the thing about staying at ridiculously expensive hotels. You tell them you need something, and they sort it out."

I suddenly feel kind of stupidly happy.

"You ready to go, Son?" he asks. "You don't get mornings like this in London at this time of year."

My shoes are by the door, and while I'm putting them on, Mom says, "When are you going to bring him back?"

Dad says, "I don't know. I don't really have any plans."

"I guess what I'm asking is, should I get something ready for lunch?"

"It's up to Ben," Dad says, and for some reason, Mom loses it.

"Can't you make any decision that involves some commitment to other people?"

"Jenny," Granma calls out from the kitchen. "Just let them go."

It must have rained overnight, because the lawn is wet and the trees that stretch over the road are dripping a little—sometimes a few drops hit you in the face as you bike past. But the sky is totally blue. It's probably sixty-five degrees, just cool enough that you don't mind working up a sweat. First we just bike around the neighborhood; it's very flat and all the roads are empty, because it's Saturday morning. My dad is good at biking without his hands—he's got a real racing bike that makes you lean over for the handles, but he can also lean back in his seat and pedal without holding on. He looks funny—like he's relaxed and concentrating at the same time. He can even turn corners that way.

"You're just showing off," I tell him.

Around ten o'clock he gets hungry again. "That's the thing about jet lag," he says. "I wake up at three in the morning and want coffee and a piece of toast. By nine o'clock I'm ready for lunch."

We stop off at a diner and order a pancake breakfast, with bacon and eggs, the whole works. Dad puts a lot of Tabasco sauce on everything—he really is hungry. They do milkshakes there, too, and I ask him, "Can I have a milkshake?"

"At ten in the morning?" he says, but then changes his mind. "Sure, why not."

When the shake comes, he asks for another straw and sticks it in. "This is what they call a stealth tax," he says. "The government always needs a cut." He sucks in a mouthful (it's chocolate and Oreo), and leaves the rest to me. After that, we get busy eating; all you can hear is the sound of knives and forks on our plates and the background noise of the restaurant—the waiters talking to each other and some of the other diners making conversation. Some guy is on his phone, trying to order a new cartridge for his printer. It turns out to be pretty complicated.

"Coach Tomski seems like a nice guy," Dad says eventually, just to break the silence. Maybe he feels he should talk about my life.

"He's a good teacher." But I feel funny saying it like that, like I'm being disloyal or something, but I can't tell to whom.

"That kid Pete can play." It's like he's just fishing, hoping for a bite.

"He's a bully, I don't like him much. He used to call me Ball Boy. He's the kind of kid who makes up names for people."

"Maybe he's just competitive."

"With me? What's he got to be competitive about?"

"I can think of some things," Dad says. For a second I think he means Mabley, but then he says, "You're not a bad player yourself." The waiter comes, and Dad asks for the check. He takes his wallet out and puts it on the table; he's got all these receipts bursting out of it, and English money and different kinds of coins—it takes him a while to find a twenty-dollar bill.

"Are you serious about coming to London?" he asks.

My plate is sticky with maple syrup; there's a bit of bacon left over, which I drag through the stickiness before eating. So we're finally having the conversation.

"Do you want me to come?" I ask, without looking up.

"Of course I want you. It's been a hard six months for me. A lot of adjustments, too much work. I've missed you." Then he says, "I guess it's been harder for you."

"It's been okay," I say.

Then the waiter returns, and Dad pays him, adding another receipt to all the pieces of paper in his wallet. We unlock our bikes and ride to the park. It's about fifteen blocks away—you can tell, because the streets in this neighborhood are named after numbers and letters. We just have to get to 44th and Avenue G. It's like a simple math problem. Meanwhile the sun has climbed over the treetops, it's almost noon. I can feel the heat on the back of my neck.

"What would Mom do if I came to London?" I say. "Would she come, too?"

"You can ask her." He's pedaling beside me, the roads are still empty, there's just the sound of my chain going around (it got a little rusty in the shed) and sometimes a nut or twig cracking under one of our tires.

"Isn't that something you should talk to her about?"

He slows down for a moment, and I coast next to him.

"You're right, I'm sorry," he says. Then we both drift to a stop. "The truth is, Ben, I don't want you to get your hopes up about anything like that. You're old enough now . . ." but he interrupts himself. "Nobody's ever really old enough for this. I know I'm not. I guess when something like this happens, you realize that your parents are just . . . blundering people, too. But I want you to feel that you have choices to make, that it's not just other people telling you what to do."

"That's not really what it feels like," I tell him.

"I mean, it's fine for you to think, at a certain point, I have to protect my own interests. I have to live my own life. My parents' problems are not my problems anymore. Am I making any sense?"

"I guess."

He waits for a minute and then he asks, "Why aren't you saying anything?"

"Because I'm thinking."

The swimming pool is still drained when we get to the park; the bottom is full of wet leaves. There's a chain-link fence around the whole thing, and the gate is locked. It's all a bit sad, like leftover summer. But a couple of kids are playing basketball on the court next door. They look like high school kids. One of them has a Tony Romo Cowboys jersey on, which is too big for him, even though he's a pretty big kid. The other one is skinnier and dribbles a lot. Dad can't help himself; he watches from the sideline—our bikes are lying on the curb.

"Do you want to play?" he says to me quietly.

"They're just hanging out. They don't want to play with us."

"Well, we can ask them." And he steps forward onto the court. "You guys want to play a little two on two? This is my son here."

"Sure, okay," the Tony Romo kid says.

So that's what we do. My dad looks funny when he plays—he moves like a different person. He has all this crazy pent-up energy and his legs and arms seem twice as long as everybody else's. The skinny kid misses a shot, and Dad gets the rebound and passes the ball to me. "Shoot it," he says. I'm about fifteen feet away, and when I miss, he gets the rebound again and passes it back again. "Shoot it again," he says, and this time the shot goes in. That's what it's like.

"Dad," I say quietly, when we get the ball back. "Give them a chance."

We don't stay very long, we just play to seven. He lets them score a couple of baskets. He's very friendly and asks their names and asks them about school, but it's also kind of weird, and I know they just want us to be gone.

On the final shot, my dad steps back and takes a twenty footer, which touches nothing but net. It's the first shot he's taken all day—the rest of the time, he's just been setting me up.

"How about that?" he says afterward. I can tell he's pleased; this whole thing has put him in a good mood. He takes a handkerchief out of his pocket and wipes his forehead. We get back on our bikes and the two kids just start messing around again like nothing happened—with the skinny kid dribbling around, and the Tony Romo kid trying to catch him. But it's nice to feel the wind in our face again. Dad is shaking his head. "I shouldn't have done that," he says, pedaling beside me. "Sometimes I can't help myself."

It's funny, though. Even though I was embarrassed, I'm glad we won; it feels like something has happened, a story, we were on the same team, and this time the shot went in. I'll probably tell Granma about it later, and turn it into a joke, because those kids must have thought, What the heck? These two guys show up and kick our butts for five minutes, and then ride off again; but I also feel sad, because I think it probably won't happen again.

We're getting pretty close to home now—Dad doesn't know where he is, and it's up to me to lead the way, so I cross over 45th Street (there's a little traffic at the lights), and then take a left toward Granma's house, on one of the quieter back roads. I like showing my dad that I know this place, I like being in charge, but I also worry that maybe when he sees the house again, he'll think, Ben is bored with me, he's had enough. But there's only so long we can bike around. Something has shifted. It's not like I've made up my mind; it's more like certain things are becoming obvious, and what really needs to happen is everybody needs to talk about them. Maybe Mom will have gotten some lunch ready, we can sit down around the kitchen table, like a family for once, though I'm not really hungry anyway.

Dad doesn't say anything when he sees the house.

"When do you have to go back to Houston?" I ask him. He's climbed off the bike and is locking it against one of the streetlamps.

"Not till tomorrow," he says.

"So we've got all day."

"We've got all day."

I wheel my bike across the lawn, toward the shed at the side of the yard. It's funny, I can see him standing in the front yard, hesitating—he doesn't know if he should wait for me or if he should just go in. But then I guess he feels silly, or he makes up his mind, because he walks up the front steps, while I pull at the shed door, which always gets stuck in the grass, and shove my bike inside. Somewhere I hear the doorbell ringing but I also hear, across the fence, the noise of someone jumping on a trampoline—and I stand there listening for a while, to the slap of bare feet on canvas and the jangling of the springs, before I squeeze through the bamboo hedge to tell Mabley I'm staying.